# GINA WILKINS

## The Soldier's Forever Family

HARLEQUIN® SUPERROMANCE®

Recycling programs
for this product may
not exist in your area.


ISBN-13: 978-0-373-64024-9

The Soldier's Forever Family

Copyright © 2017 by Gina Wilkins

**Printed in U.S.A.**

Before she even learned to read, **Gina Wilkins** announced that she wanted to be a writer. That dream never wavered, though she worked briefly in advertising and human resources. Influenced by her mother's love of classic Harlequin romances, she knew she wanted her stories to always have happy endings. She met her husband in her first college English class and they've been married for more than thirty-five years, blessed with two daughters and a son. They have two delightful grandchildren. After more than one hundred books with Harlequin, she will always be a fan of romance and a believer in happy endings.

## Books by Gina Wilkins

### HARLEQUIN SPECIAL EDITION

#### Proposals & Promises

*The Boss's Marriage Plan*
*A Reunion and a Ring*
*The Bachelor's Little Bonus*

#### Bride Mountain

*Healed with a Kiss*
*A Proposal at the Wedding*
*Matched by Moonlight*

*A Match for the Single Dad*
*The Texan's Surprise Baby*
*The Right Twin*

*His Best Friend's Wife*
*Husband for a Weekend*

#### Doctors in the Family

*Doctors in the Wedding*
*A Home for the M.D.*
*The M.D. Next Door*

#### Doctors in Training

*Prognosis: Romance*
*The Doctor's Undoing*
*Private Partners*
*Diagnosis: Daddy*

Visit the Author Profile page at Harlequin.com for more titles.

For John and Kerry, the fiercest dad-daughter air hockey competitors ever. And for the rest of the family who have to bravely avoid flying pucks! I love my nutty family.

# CHAPTER ONE

DAWN WAS ADAM SCOTT'S favorite time of day at the South Carolina coastal resort where he both worked and lived. Suspended between darkness and light, the beach was quiet but for the sound of the waves breaking on the shore and the drumming of his feet on the wet sand. He ran every morning before beginning a long day of work. He passed the occasional beachcomber or fisherman, but they rarely exchanged more than civil nods. Folks out this early weren't looking for conversation.

This was his time to clear his head, to organize his plans for the day. A chance to savor the solitude that was increasingly rare for him as his responsibilities at the resort had increased over the past three years. He didn't always go to bed alone, but he never invited anyone to join him on these morning runs. For this hour every morning, he had at least the illusion of complete freedom, no one making demands on his time or attention, no obvious reason he couldn't just keep running if the mood struck him.

A small form appeared ahead, hunched on the sand, barely visible in the pale light from the pink-streaked purple sky. Adam squinted, trying to make out the shape. Was it a dog? No. A child. A young one, at that. What was the kid doing out alone at this time of day?

Estimating the boy to be four, maybe five, Adam approached slowly. He didn't want to scare him. "Hey, buddy. Whatcha doing out here by yourself?"

Still crouched over a shallow tide pool, the boy looked up. Maybe it was a trick of shadows or the watery light of dawn, but there was something eerily familiar about this kid with his tumbled dark hair and smoky gray eyes. Perhaps Adam had seen him around the resort before? Clouds shifted overhead and the light brightened enough for him to see more clearly. No. He was sure they'd never met. But still there was something about this child...

"I'm not allowed to talk to strangers." The boy didn't look particularly concerned as he shared that rule.

"That's a good policy, but I work for the resort," Adam assured him, keeping his distance for now. "My name is Adam."

The child frowned thoughtfully. "You could still be a bad guy."

Adam was startled into a chuckle by the little guy's logic. "Well, yeah, I guess that's true. But I'm not."

Apparently satisfied, the boy extended one hand. "Do you know what kind of shell this is?"

Glancing at the cylindrical shell on the outstretched palm, Adam nodded. "It's a lettered olive. It belonged to a type of snail."

"It's cool. I want to find a starfish, too."

"You find them here occasionally. So, where are your parents? Do they know you're out by yourself?"

As if in answer, a woman's anxious voice called out. "Simon? Simon! Where are you?"

The boy winced. "That's my mom."

A woman emerged, almost running, from the canopy of tropical trees that marked the edge of the main resort grounds. She wore a tank top and plaid cotton shorts with flip-flops, and her collar-length brown hair was disheveled, as though she'd just climbed out of bed. "Simon! You know better than to wander off like this. You scared me half to death."

The voice was an echo from Adam's past. He took a step back, his startled gaze locked on the woman's anxious face. Her attention was focused on the boy, so she hadn't spared Adam more than a quick glance. Would she recognize him when she looked more closely, or had she forgotten all about the man she'd known so briefly all those years ago?

Joanna looked so much the same that it was hard to believe it had been six years since he'd last seen her. Her hair was a few inches shorter than the style she'd worn before, but was still a glossy chestnut that complemented her green eyes. Her fair skin was smooth, her cheeks flushed with heightened emotion. Seeing her now affected him as strongly as when he'd met her on this very beach. He'd wanted her from the moment their paths had first crossed. Apparently, that physical reaction hadn't changed in the ensuing years, though there was little to no chance the outcome would be the same this time.

He was aware that he'd changed a lot more than she had. When they'd met before, he'd been rail thin, brimming with impatient, brash energy. His dark hair had been cropped in a military cut. He was a healthier weight now, more muscle than sinew, tanned and generally relaxed. His last deployment had left physical traces in the carved lines around his eyes and mouth, in the scars hidden beneath his clothes, and in the strands of premature gray that peppered his hair, long enough now to brush his collar and usually mussed by the ocean breeze. He thought he looked more surfer than soldier these days. He wasn't surprised she hadn't immediately recognized him.

He couldn't believe she was really here. He'd figured she'd long since moved on with her life, finding new places to visit on vacations. Six years was a long time.

"I'm sorry I scared you, Mom. I wanted to find shells before the other people come out. You were asleep."

So she had at least one kid now. No doubt a husband waiting back in their suite. Adam told himself he was happy for her. Then wondered if he'd ever crossed her mind in the years since they'd parted.

Holding her wind-tossed hair out of her face with one hand, Joanna spoke more calmly now that her first surge of panic had subsided. "You should have woken me. Or asked last night and I'd have gotten up early with you. Don't ever come out again without telling me, understand?"

The boy sighed. "Yes, ma'am."

Joanna nodded in satisfaction, and then turned to look up at Adam. He realized he was still gaping at her. Belatedly remembering he was now an employee here, he gave her a professional nod. "Good morning."

He figured he'd leave it up to her to decide whether to acknowledge that they'd met before. Maybe she'd want to pretend that their vacation fling had never happened. Hell, maybe she didn't even remember him. For all he knew, she'd made much more of an impression on him than he had on her.

Joanna's green eyes widened, and her lips parted on a gasp of disbelief. *"Adam?"*

So she did remember. He cleared his throat before speaking, keeping his tone as even as possible. "Hello, Joanna. This is a surprise."

"You could say that." Her right hand fell on the boy's shoulder. Her face had paled—though he couldn't say whether it was from leftover concern for her son, shock at seeing him or a combination. "What are you doing here?"

"He works here," Simon piped up. "Does that mean it's okay to talk to him?"

Adam saw her fingers tighten on her son's shoulder before she replied. "Yes. It's okay. But you're still not allowed to come outside without my permission."

The boy pointed. "There's a tide pool on the other side of that big rock. Can I go look in it?"

Without taking her gaze from Adam, Joanna nodded. "Stay where I can see you."

It shouldn't be this hard to think of something to say to her. Though meaningless small talk would never be Adam's strong suit, he'd gotten better at it during his three years working at the resort. He made it a personal rule not to get intimately involved with guests, so he avoided that awkwardness. Still, this wasn't the first time in his life he'd unexpectedly run into a woman he'd slept with, and he was usually able to manage a few polite words. Apparently, none of those other women had affected him in quite the same way Joanna had.

He settled for the mundane. "How have you been, Joanna?"

She moistened her lips, visibly nervous. Was she still on edge because of her son's early disappearance? He couldn't imagine why running into Adam again would elicit such a dramatic response. They'd had nothing more than a few days of fun. Laughed, danced, walked, swam, enjoyed each other in bed a few times. A few damned good times. But thinking about that wasn't making this encounter any less awkward.

"I'm—um." She pushed her blowing hair out of her face, and he could see that her hand wasn't quite steady.

Seeing him again wasn't a happy surprise for her, apparently. Was she worried he would make things uncomfortable with her husband? Okay, he could understand that. How could he let her know that he was willing to pretend their fling never happened?

Giving her his most impersonal smile, he took another step back. "As your son told you, I'm on staff here, so if you or your family need anything at all during your stay, just let us know."

Her gaze darted from him to the boy and back again. She moistened her lips again. "Thank you."

She'd changed little in appearance, but something was definitely different about Joanna. The woman who'd drifted on occasion through his memories had been confident, animated, flirty. If there was, indeed, a husband waiting for her, he could understand why she wasn't flirting now, but he couldn't figure out why she seemed so stiff and nervous. The only explanation that made sense was that she was concerned he might interfere with her current relationship.

He made a sudden decision. "I've got a few vacation days built up." More than a few, actually. Despite his employer's encouragement, he hadn't taken more than a handful of days off in the past three years. "I'm thinking about taking a week off. If I don't run into you before I leave, it was nice seeing you again, Joanna."

Though he'd have to scramble to make arrangements, maybe things would be easier for her. It was for a similar reason he'd slipped away after their long-ago weekend together, to save her—okay, to save them both—from awkward partings. At least this time he'd said goodbye.

He started to turn, but paused when Simon ran up to him again, another shell clutched in his hand. The boy gazed up at him eagerly, his steel-gray eyes squinting against the brightness of the rising sun. "Do you know what this one is?"

Man, there was just something about this kid's eyes...

"That's a banded tulip," Adam said automatically. "Got a little chip out of it, but it's still a nice shell for your collection."

Simon repeated the name under his breath as if committing it to memory, then asked, "Will you help me look for a starfish?"

"Um—"

"It's time for breakfast, Simon. We need to go back to the suite and get dressed for the day."

The boy heaved a huge sigh but didn't

argue. Probably didn't want to push his luck after sneaking out earlier. "Can we come back after breakfast?"

"Yes, we will."

Simon held out both hands toward Adam, a shell displayed on each little palm. "Banded tulip. Lettered olive," he recited slowly, nodding to each in turn. "Right?"

"Very good."

"I still want to find a starfish. And a Scotch bonnet. My friend Liam found a Scotch bonnet once and I want to find one, too."

Once again, Adam was impressed by how well Simon expressed himself for being such a little guy. Was he small for his age? "How old are you, Simon?"

"Five years and three months. Have you ever found a Scotch bonnet?"

So, a little older than he'd first thought. "I have, yes. I hope you find one during your stay. There are lots of shells in the gift shop. You can buy them there or study them to learn the names."

"Okay. But I want to find my own."

"Of course."

"Simon, let's go, please." Joanna sounded as though she was losing patience quickly.

"Okay. But…just one more second. I think I see another shell over there." Without waiting for permission, Simon dashed a few yards away and bent down to dig in the wet sand.

Joanna made a low, strangled sound of frustration.

Cute kid, Adam thought. She must have had him soon after...*oh, damn.*

He'd always been good at math, but it didn't take a CPA to figure out that adding nine months of pregnancy to five years and three months took him back exactly six years. Feeling suddenly like the world's biggest idiot, he realized why he'd thought the kid—Simon—had looked so familiar.

It had been like looking at a childhood photo of himself.

JOANNA ZIELINSKI WAS aware of almost the exact moment when the truth hit Adam. His head snapped back, his jaw tightened and his eyes narrowed as if against a blast of overbright light. He must have felt as though he'd just been poleaxed.

She knew the feeling. Seeing Adam here on this beach talking with Simon had stunned her into near incoherence—an uncharacteristic response from a trained psychologist used to giving lectures to college students. She always prepared thoroughly for those presentations. She couldn't have practiced for this.

She'd had no clue that the man who'd slipped out of her bed six years earlier now worked at the very resort where they'd accidentally conceived a son.

"Simon," he said, his voice a taut growl now.

It wasn't a question, but still her first impulse was to shake her head. To lie about her son's parentage. Her second, and almost overwhelming, instinct was to snatch up her child and run back to the happy home she'd created for him on her own.

Her last encounter with Adam had turned her meticulously outlined, fiercely pursued life plan upside down. Something told her this unexpected reunion would have similarly far-reaching and life-changing consequences. For her, for Adam and for Simon.

She banked down her seething emotions and squared her shoulders. She'd always taken pride in her integrity, and she wasn't going to abandon her principles now.

"Yes," she said in answer to the question he hadn't uttered. She kept her voice low so her words wouldn't carry to Simon. "I didn't know it for a couple of months afterward, but I was pregnant when I left here six years ago."

"By me."

That didn't seem to be worthy of a response, so she let it pass.

He pushed his left hand through his hair, and she thought she detected a slight unsteadiness in his fingers. This was obviously hitting him hard. Understandably.

Suddenly self-conscious, she smoothed the hem of the purple tank top she wore with purple-and-green plaid shorts. It certainly wasn't the first time Adam had seen her rumpled from sleep, but that seemed like another lifetime now.

She noted Adam wasn't wearing a ring, which didn't mean he wasn't married or otherwise committed. Was he thinking of the awkward discussions he might need to have with his wife? Did Simon have siblings? If so, how would this development affect them? How was she going to explain all this to her son?

Adam moved his hand to the back of his neck. His tousled dark-coffee hair was longer now. Thick. Touchable. He'd gained a few pounds in the ensuing years, but they looked good on him. Really good.

It shook her again when their eyes met. His were the same smoke-gray as Simon's. Exactly as she'd remembered, though she'd always pictured them gleaming with a smile. He wasn't smiling now.

"Did you even try to find me?" he asked, his voice low and gruff.

Her chin rose. "You didn't leave me an address, if you'll remember." Or even a goodbye, she added silently, her chest clenching with the memory of waking up and realizing he was gone. That the fantasy was over.

She couldn't do this now. She needed time to gather her thoughts, to get her nerves under control. She took a quick step backward on the damp sand. "Simon needs his breakfast. If I don't see you again before you go on vacation…"

His eyes narrowed sharply. "I'm not going anywhere. We have to talk. You owe me that much."

Six years of emotions flooded through her—shock, stress, joy, exhaustion, wistfulness, laughter and tears. Her voice was barely audible even to her over the wind and waves and seagulls when she responded, "I don't owe you anything."

With that, she turned and hurried to her son's side, taking his hand to lead him back to their suite. Simon cooperated without protest, probably sensing this wasn't the time for rebellion.

She doubted she had completely avoided a painfully awkward conversation with Adam.

She'd postponed it, at best. But at least he wasn't trying to detain her, which would give her a chance to prepare for whatever was to come.

JOANNA SETTLED SIMON at the table on their balcony where he could look over the resort while he ate the breakfast of fruit, yogurt and granola she served from the kitchenette in their two-bedroom suite. They had a spectacular view of the beautifully maintained grounds, which were centered around a small, natural-looking lake decorated with blooming aquatic plants, fish-feeding piers and paddle boats. Masses of colorful flowers and shady trees lined winding paths. The sprawling U-shape of the resort allowed a glimpse of the ocean from their balcony through clearings in the trees.

To keep Simon occupied for a few extra minutes, Joanna set up her computer tablet in front of him with an educational video about seashells, his latest intellectual passion. Screen time during a meal was a rare treat for him, and he was obviously delighted. She left the sliding doors open when she went inside, but she moved across the room so he wouldn't hear her when she made a call.

Her sister answered on the second ring,

though her groggy voice made it clear she'd been roused from sleep. "Joanna? What's wrong?"

Finally letting go of the tight rein on her emotions, Joanna blurted, "Maddie, he's here."

"What? Who's there? Are you okay?"

Hearing the sudden anxiety in her younger sister's voice, she drew a deep breath and tried to speak more calmly. "I'm okay. Mostly. I'm at the resort with Simon. And…and Adam's here."

"Adam? Wait. *The* Adam?"

Joanna swallowed hard and nodded, then remembered Maddie couldn't see her. "Yes."

"Oh, my gosh, what's he doing there?"

"He works here."

Maddie gave an incredulous laugh. "You're kidding."

"Do I sound like I'm kidding?"

Her sister grew abruptly serious. "No. Sorry. You must have been shocked."

"That's one way to describe it." The feelings swirling inside her were so fierce, so complicated that she hardly knew how to define them. Honestly, she'd never expected to see Adam again. It had never even occurred to her when she'd booked this trip that Adam would be here, especially not on staff.

"Did he remember you? Do you think he

knew you were coming this weekend? Maybe he saw your name on the reservations list?"

Remembering the look on Adam's face when he'd said her name, Joanna replied, "Yes, he remembered me. But I think he was as stunned as I was when we ran into each other this morning. I'm pretty sure he didn't expect to see me here again."

Especially with his child in tow, she thought, biting her lower lip.

Their brief affair had been unplanned and intense. For the first time in her focused and responsible twenty-seven years, Joanna had felt completely unfettered. Passionate, desirable, spontaneous, adventurous. So unlike her usual self. They'd met on the first night of solitary long weekend vacations for both of them and had been inseparable afterward. They'd spent hours walking on the beach, talking, laughing and holding hands. Flirting. Dining. Dancing. Making love. Just having fun, with no strings or expectations on either side.

She'd thought they'd been careful despite the playfulness of their time together. She'd discovered a few weeks after returning home that they hadn't been quite careful enough.

"Does he know yet? About Simon, I mean," Maddie clarified unnecessarily.

"He sort of leaped to conclusions when he

found out how old Simon is. Maybe he saw the resemblance. Simon really does look just like him, Maddie. I've always known that, but seeing them side by side…well, it's almost spooky."

"Oh, my gosh. So, what now?"

"I don't know," she admitted in little more than a whisper.

"What did he say? Was he happy? Mad? Skeptical? What?"

"Honestly, I don't know. I didn't give him much of a chance to say anything. I told him I had to make Simon's breakfast, and I bolted. He said he wants to talk later. I could tell he was shocked, of course, but the only question he asked was whether I'd tried to find him."

As the only person to whom Joanna had confided all the details of that vacation fling, Maddie was indignant. "This from the guy who ghosted you without even a 'Hey, babe, I'll call you sometime'?"

"Which is basically what I told him," Joanna agreed, grateful her sister understood so well. There'd been a time when she'd never have believed she and Maddie would have this mutually supportive relationship. This closeness was one of the two good things that had come of her brief affair with Adam.

She'd always planned to tell Simon the truth

about his parentage at some point. She'd even thought this trip would be a good time to tell him that she'd met his biological father here, if it seemed appropriate. She'd planned to leave it up to him to decide if, when he was older, he wanted to find his father. Not that she'd have been able to assist him much. She and Adam hadn't exchanged many personal details during their time together.

Maybe she could have located Adam before now, had she put in more effort. She could've persisted in her request for resort records. As a professor, she had strong research skills. There should have been ways to track him down, though his name was common enough to have made it difficult without more information. She could have even hired a private investigator, for that matter. She'd found plenty of reasons to rationalize her choice not to pursue the search. For one, Adam had been clear from the start that he'd had no interest in commitments. He hadn't elaborated, but she'd gotten the impression he'd had important plans for after his vacation.

Having just defended her doctoral thesis and on the verge of beginning a new phase of her chosen career, Joanna hadn't been looking for a serious relationship, either. She'd simply asked him to assure her he wasn't married.

Though she'd been amenable to a no-strings vacation fling, sleeping with a married man would have crossed a line for her. He'd promised her he was single and unattached, and she'd believed him. Foolish, perhaps, but she'd sensed from the beginning that Adam was trustworthy.

"How did it feel? Seeing him again, I mean?"

Joanna still didn't know how to answer that question. It wasn't as if she'd been in love with Adam. She hadn't known him long enough for that. Of course, she'd thought of him since; after all, she lived with a daily reminder of him. And maybe she'd wondered if the blazing sexual chemistry between them might have led to more had the timing and circumstances been different. Their situation seemed even more problematic now, considering everything that had happened in the intervening years and the big life changes looming for her and Simon.

"Do you think he'll want to be part of Simon's life now? Is he going to cause you problems? If so, he'd better damned well be aware that he owes six years of back child support. Is he married now? That could be awkward, huh? Will he—"

"Maddie," Joanna broke in quietly. "I don't know any of those answers yet."

And it was the not knowing that had her stomach tied in tight knots.

"Mom? Is there more yogurt?"

"Yes. Just a sec," she called back to her son. "I should go, Maddie. I just needed to hear your voice."

"Do you want me to come? I can be there in a few hours."

Because she knew her sister would absolutely drop everything and rush to her side, Joanna blinked back tears. She was so very thankful they'd set aside their early differences and had become friends as adults. "I appreciate the offer, but I can handle it. I'll call you later, okay?"

"Good luck, Jo."

"Thanks." She was pretty sure she'd need it.

"Mom?"

"Coming," she said. She put down her phone and moved to get the yogurt from the kitchenette fridge. Pausing in the open doorway with the container in hand, she studied her son with an ache of love in her heart. He looked so serious and sweet dawdling over his breakfast, a frown of concentration on his face as he memorized everything he was seeing on the tablet screen.

He was her everything.

Panic momentarily closed her throat. Her muscles quivered with a strong, if ill-advised, urge to run. She could be packed and checked out in less than twenty minutes. She could leave a note for Adam, which was more than he'd left her. Would he try to find them now that he knew about Simon? That would hardly be difficult if he worked for the resort and had access to her address. Would he disrupt the comfortable life she'd made? Or would he be relieved, instead, if she made it clear she'd ask for nothing from him?

No, she thought, moving forward to spoon a dollop of yogurt over the fruit remaining in Simon's bowl. She wouldn't run. She owed it to Simon, if not to Adam, to deal with this directly. As for her own emotions about seeing Adam again—well, she would try to sort those out later.

"You knew that man on the beach, didn't you, Mom?" Simon asked, glancing up from his bowl with a smear of yogurt at the corner of his mouth.

She smoothed a cowlick at the back of his head. "Yes, I know him."

"What's his name?"

"Adam." She saw no need just then to add the surname.

"Did you meet him last time you were here?"

She'd told Simon when she'd booked this vacation that she'd visited the resort once before, though of course she'd left out the details. What on earth had made her come here again? When she'd made the reservation just after her son's fifth birthday, she'd assured herself Simon would like what she remembered about the place—the quiet beaches, the pools, the day programs for kids. She'd told herself it was time to deal with her memories of her son's father, to see the place again through a fresh, more realistic perspective. If she'd had any idea of what—who—she would find here, she wasn't sure she'd have had the courage to follow through. "Yes, I met him then."

To her relief, Simon's attention moved on now that she'd satisfied his curiosity. "When do I leave for the aquarium?"

She smiled, pleased that he seemed eager for the arrangements she'd made for him. Through the resort reservation website, she had enrolled him in the Explorers Club, a program for kids his age. Each afternoon this week, he would join five other children and two certified teachers for field trips and activities based on introductory oceanography. She'd thought Simon would be less likely to be bored with the mother-son vacation if he interacted with other kids in an educational setting. Her bright, inquisitive child was always excited by learning new things. As an academic herself, she wanted to encourage him to continue to view learning as fun.

"You'll leave right after lunch. One o'clock. What would you like to do in the meantime? Go swimming? Walk on the beach? Build a sandcastle?"

He nodded abstractedly. "Okay, but first can we look up lettered olives on the computer?"

"Lettered olives?"

He picked up the shell he'd found on the beach that morning, a smooth, mottled cream-and-tan cylinder. "Mr. Adam said it's a lettered olive shell, and he said it's from a snail, but that's all I know. The video I just watched didn't talk about lettered olives. Can we learn more about it?"

Mr. Adam. She felt a wry smile twist her lips in response to the name. "Yes, but we're not going to spend all of this beautiful morning on the computer."

Which Simon would happily do if she let him. He loved surfing kids' sites and watching educational videos, many of them geared to children several years ahead of him in school. Though he would start kindergarten in the fall, he was already reading at a third-grade level and was several grades ahead in math.

While doing her best to promote her gifted child's intellectual development, Joanna made sure he stayed physically and socially active, which was another reason she'd signed him up for the day camp program. She also needed some time on her own to rest and prepare for an upcoming job change that was exciting but would involve a major upheaval in their lives. She'd promised that she would take advantage of at least a few of those free hours just to pamper herself. She'd put in too many long hours during the past year, spending every spare moment with her son, and she craved the downtime she'd arranged for these precious vacation days.

She grimaced as it occurred to her that she'd rationalized her holiday fling with Adam in much the same way six years ago, considering it a reward to herself after the grueling months of preparation for her doctoral defense. She'd booked the trip a few months earlier with her then-boyfriend, Tim. They'd planned it as their first getaway together, a step forward in a relationship that had seemed promising at the time. They'd broken up a few weeks before leaving, when Tim admitted he wanted to see other women and she'd realized that didn't bother her as much as it should have. Rather than cancel her reservations, she had decided to celebrate both her degree and her newfound independence in her own way. And she'd made the most of that heady freedom with Adam.

Things were much different now, of course. She'd been young and completely independent then. Now there was Simon, and nothing was more important to her than being a good mother to him.

She just wished she knew what she was going to say to his father.

MADDIE ZIELINSKI HAD a hard time focusing on her work Monday. Her thoughts were with her sister and the trepidation she'd heard in Joanna's voice that morning. Understandable. If there was one thing Maddie could say for certain about her older sister, it was that Joanna adored her son. For that matter, so did Maddie.

As unplanned as he'd been for Joanna, as unsettling as the circumstances of his conception had been to their parents, little Simon had brought Maddie's immediate family closer than they'd ever been. And she hated the thought of some stranger—even if he was technically his father—coming from out of the blue to disrupt the comfortable rapport they'd developed.

Would Adam want to insert himself into the boy's life now that he'd learned of his existence? She conceded reluctantly that she could understand if he did, but how did they know if this would be a good thing for Simon? The child had been sheltered and cherished his whole life, given every advantage Joanna could provide for him, raised with love and encouragement and judicious guidance. They knew nothing about Adam.

Maddie had no doubt he was personable, good-looking, reasonably intelligent—how else could he have charmed her usually straight-laced sister into bed within a few hours of meeting her?—but for all they knew, he could be a real piece of work beneath a slick facade. Regrettably, Maddie had more experience with the type than Joanna. Joanna might have met a few players in academia, but as a defense attorney, Maddie encountered them every day. She'd gotten involved with some real jerks in her personal life, too. Fallen for a few before she'd decided she'd rather be single and sane than hooked up and stressed out. She might be the younger sister, but when it came to the dating game, she considered herself more worldly and realistic than her sister.

Despite Joanna's assertion that she could handle this, Maddie wondered if maybe she owed it to both her and Simon to make sure their best interests were protected. She wouldn't call herself an objective party, of course, since her full loyalty was squarely with her sister and nephew. Maybe Adam was a decent guy—maybe he'd be a great role model for young Simon—but being naturally cynical and experience-hardened, she felt compelled to find out for herself if he could be trusted.

# CHAPTER TWO

"ADAM? YOU WITH ME, bro?"

Frowning, Adam realized he'd been lost in his own thoughts during his meeting with Trevor Farrell, owner of the Wind Shadow Resort. Despite his efforts to pay attention, he'd heard maybe every other sentence Trevor had spoken during the past half hour. Shaking his head in apology, he murmured, "Sorry, Trev. Got a lot on my mind today."

It wasn't like him to be distracted, so he wasn't surprised when his employer asked, "Is everything okay?"

Adam started to brush off the question, then hesitated. Trevor would surely run into Joanna and Simon at some point during their stay. Would he remember her from that long-ago weekend? Considering Trevor's phenomenal memory, it was entirely possible.

"Do you remember when we met six years ago?"

Trevor lifted an eyebrow. "Of course."

Adam had won an all-expense-paid, long-weekend visit to the then-new resort in a raffle to benefit a veterans' charity group. Somehow Trevor had found out Adam was headed overseas for a tough deployment soon afterward, and he'd gone out of his way to greet him. He'd encouraged Adam to let him know if there was anything he could do to make the vacation more enjoyable. Having served a four-year hitch himself before opening the first in a planned chain of American beach resorts, Trevor was an enthusiastic supporter of the military. He'd encouraged Adam to look him up if he needed anything when he got out. Though Adam hadn't really expected to take advantage of that offer at the time, he'd somewhat impulsively headed this way when he'd been looking for a job after his honorable discharge. Trevor had hired him on the spot.

Adam had thought he'd stay long enough to build a little nest egg and get used to civilian life again, then move on to the next adventure. Somehow, he'd ended up as Trevor's unofficial second-in-command instead. And in the midst of that development, he and Trevor had become friends.

"Do you also remember the woman I met while I was here?"

A fleeting smile tugged at Trevor's lips. "Her name was Joanna, and she was…memorable. I could tell you were mesmerized by her, and it was no wonder."

Mesmerized. That was one way to put it, though hardly a comfortable description for Adam. Always respectful of his privacy, Trevor had never asked about Joanna during the past three years, nor had Adam mentioned her. But it seemed she'd made an impression on both of them.

He leaned forward in his chair, bracing his forearms on his thighs. "She's here. She's staying at the resort."

After a moment of silence, Trevor tapped a few keys on his computer. "Joanna Zielinski," he read from the screen. "She and a companion have a third-floor, ocean-view suite in Seafoam Lodge until the end of the week." He looked up, meeting Adam's eyes. "Awkward."

"Her companion is her son. Simon. He's five years, three months old."

Trevor could do the math just as well as Adam. His blue eyes widened, the only sign of shock he allowed himself to show. "So..."

"He looks just like me, Trev."

"That's not quite as reliable as a DNA test." His friend frowned now, obviously weighing all the potential consequences. Trevor tended to be suspicious, so Adam wasn't surprised when he asked, "Do you think she came here looking for you?"

"I'm almost certain she was as surprised to see me as I was her."

"*Almost* certain."

Adam nodded. Was Joanna really a good enough actress to have so convincingly pulled off that look of stunned dismay? He didn't know her well enough to be sure, but her reaction had certainly looked real enough.

"Did you ask if the boy's yours?"

Adam swallowed hard. "She said she was pregnant when she left here six years ago."

"Which doesn't mean she wasn't pregnant when she arrived," Trevor pointed out.

Was it possible she…? No. Adam pictured Simon's face again and doubted it was coincidence that the kid was his spitting image.

"She just happened to show up at the resort where you work almost exactly six years after you met here? With a child who could be your son?"

Clearing his throat, Adam nodded. "From what little I could determine in a very brief encounter, yes, that's her story."

"Should we put Walt on alert?"

Walt was another of their friends. Another veteran. And an attorney.

After a moment, Adam shook his head.

While he understood and appreciated Trevor's concern, he preferred to handle his own problems as much as possible. "Not yet, thanks. I need to talk to Joanna first. Find out what's going on."

"That's fair. So…how do you feel about all this, Adam? Are you okay?"

He wasn't quite sure how to answer that one. He was still reeling, still a long way from coming to terms with the potential consequences of this morning's shock. "I guess I'm kind of numb. Not sure how I feel about it yet. Like I said, I need to talk with Joanna."

"And if the boy is your son?"

*His son.* The very words sent a tangle of emotions through him that he couldn't begin to identify. As much as he hated to admit it, he suspected fear was among the strongest ones.

"I'll deal with it."

Somehow.

THE CHAUFFEURED VAN for the field trip was already parked beneath the spacious porte cochere of the guest relations building when Joanna and Simon made the short walk from their suite. In addition to the concierge desk, a soaring lobby and a well-stocked bar, this large, three-story structure held a coffee and pastry shop with patio seating, an arcade, a tech center, conference rooms and an extensive gift shop. The management offices were located on the top floor.

The three guest-quarters buildings were all designed in a style similar to this one, distinguished by thematic names—Seafoam Lodge, Sandy Shore Lodge and Gull's Nest Lodge. Joanna had stayed in Gull's Nest during her previous visit but had specifically requested Seafoam this time, only partially because it provided the best views.

Another boy and four girls clustered around the van, getting to know each other and the teachers who would escort them to the aquarium. Simon appeared to be the youngest of the group, or at least the smallest, but he was accustomed to that. The other boy seemed relieved not to be so outnumbered now.

Joanna spoke with both the teachers and a few other parents hanging around to make sure the van got away safely. She was pleased to see her son and the other boy talking, their heads bent over the shell in Simon's hand as Simon shared everything he'd learned about lettered olives that morning. The other boy seemed interested, and one of the girls edged closer to listen, so Joanna was reassured that Simon would make friends here.

Two men stepped out of the building, both

dressed in the emerald polo shirts and light-weight khaki pants that identified them as staff of Wind Shadow Resort. One was Trevor Farrell, the owner. Though she hadn't seen him since arriving late yesterday, she recognized him from her previous stay.

Adam stood at Trevor's side. They made a striking pair, both tanned and fit, Adam dark-haired and gray-eyed, Trevor a fraction taller, his hair lighter, his eyes blue. They wore the same basic uniform as all the resort staff, but it was obvious to her, at least, that these men were in charge. She wondered what Adam's job was and when he'd started it. He certainly looked at home.

She was having a hard time drawing her eyes away from him. But then, she'd had that same issue last time, too. As it had before, his smile made her heart race. She hoped her cheeks weren't as flushed as they felt.

Ever the gracious host, Trevor stopped to greet the assemblage. "Good afternoon," he said, his smile pleasant and practiced. "Getting ready to leave for the aquarium?"

One of the teachers, whose nametag identified her as Miss Deborah, grinned and nodded, making her blond ponytail sway. "We're just about to load the van. As you can see, the children are excited."

"I know you'll have a great time," Trevor assured them, then glanced at the cluster of parents. "For those I haven't met yet, I'm Trevor Farrell, and this is my associate, Adam Scott. If there's anything we or any of the staff can do for you during your stay, I hope you won't hesitate to ask."

Joanna chewed her lower lip as Trevor and Adam moved among the group, shaking hands and making small talk. She clasped her hands in front of her, wishing there was a way to make a quick escape before they came to her.

As the other children were being strapped into the van, Simon broke away to rush back toward her, holding out the shell. "Will you keep this for me, Mom? I don't want to lose it."

"Of course."

Trevor and Adam reached them then. Adam's expression was inscrutable behind his nonrevealing, professional smile.

Trevor spoke first. "Ms. Zielinski. What a pleasure to see you again."

"You, too, Mr. Farrell." Did he really remember her, or had Adam alerted him?

Out of the corner of her eye, she noted that Adam's attention was focused on Simon. Her fingers tightened around the shell until the edges dug into her palm. She loosened her grip before she crushed the treasure entrusted to her care.

"I'm Simon," her son piped up excitedly. "I'm going to the aquarium."

Trevor glanced down automatically. Joanna saw his smile flicker slightly when he studied the boy. She figured the resemblance to Adam had to be obvious to anyone, and especially to someone who apparently now knew Adam well. "Hello, Simon. It's very nice to meet you. I hope you have a great time."

Simon looked eagerly at Adam. "Did you know the lettered olive shell comes from a predatory snail that eats small crust— crust—?"

"Crustaceans," Joanna supplied quietly. He probably would have come up with the word on his own, but he was being summoned by the other ponytailed teacher, Miss Molly. Joanna gave him a gentle nudge. "They're waiting for you, Simon. Have fun. I'll be right here when you get back."

"A predatory snail?" Trevor murmured, watching as Simon dashed toward the van. "And he's only five?"

Joanna was accustomed to this question when people heard her son speak. "He's academically advanced for his age."

"I would say so. Cute kid." Trevor's expression revealed little of his thoughts.

"Thank you."

Adam shifted a step closer to Joanna. "I'll catch up with you later, okay, Trev?"

Trevor nodded and turned to leave without further comment. The van drove away with the eager children waving from the windows, and their parents scattered. Joanna was left alone with Adam for the first time since he'd crept out of her bed all those years ago.

He looked at her for a moment, then waved a hand toward the walkway leading to the lodges. "I'll walk you back."

Wanting desperately to refuse, she scrambled for a reasonable excuse. But because that made her feel spineless, she tamped down her nerves and nodded. Without another word, she turned and headed briskly toward her building, leaving him to follow if he chose.

Seafoam Lodge opened into a beautiful courtyard filled with flowers, benches and a small koi pond with a center fountain. No one else was in the courtyard at the moment. Stopping beside the koi pond, Joanna pushed her hands into the pockets of the yellow sundress she wore. She tended to dress in tailored dark garments at the medical school where she taught in the rehabilitation department.

She'd packed comfortable, breezy clothes for this vacation she'd foolishly predicted would be fun and stress-free.

Adam stood in front of her, looking strong, solid and all grown male even as the steady breeze ruffled his hair, lifting a cowlick very much like the one she'd smoothed on her son's head earlier. Unwillingly assaulted by memories of running her hands over that long, hard body—and of him doing the same to her—she bit her lower lip.

The silence between them was growing oppressive, but Joanna left it up to him to speak first. She didn't know what to say, but she also wanted to judge his state of mind. He appeared to be doing the same thing, which led to an awkward standoff. She caved first, motioning toward one of the benches nestled into the landscaping. "Maybe we should sit down."

He lifted one eyebrow. "You really want to talk about this out here?"

As if in response to his words, a silver-haired couple dressed in tennis clothes and carrying rackets appeared from the direction of the courts, greeting Adam familiarly as they strolled toward the lodge entrance.

With a sigh, she conceded the point. "Let's go up to my suite," she said, aware that it was hardly a gracious invitation. Judging by his expression as he fell into step beside her, he understood why she'd spoken so curtly.

Her hand wasn't quite steady when she swiped her key card. She led him inside, then crossed the room to open the French doors to the balcony. The living area was spacious enough, with comfortable seating, a big-screen TV and the kitchenette on the other side of an eating bar. Yet it felt vaguely claustrophobic with Adam seeming to take up so much room. "Why don't we sit outside? The balcony should be private enough."

After a momentary hesitation, he moved past her through the doors to the table where Simon had eaten his breakfast. He reached down to pick up something from one of the chairs, straightening with a slightly ragged stuffed dragon in one hand. "Almost sat on this."

Their fingers brushed when she took the toy. She felt the impact all the way to her toes. She was aware of the heat in her cheeks when she took a too-quick step backward, but she hoped Adam didn't notice. If he did, he had the tact not to mention it as he sank into his seat.

Settling into the chair across from him, she made a concerted effort to speak lightly, with an ease she was far from feeling. She was afraid if she let her composure slip now, she'd have a hard time reclaiming it. She set the stuffed dragon on the table. "This is Norbert. Simon's usually more careful with him. I guess he was excited about the field trip."

"So. Simon."

Another faint tremor went through her, but she thought she controlled it better this time. She met his gaze. "I realized I was pregnant a few weeks after I returned home six years ago. It was quite a shock. I thought we'd been so careful. And before you ask, there was no chance that I was already pregnant when I met you. You were the only man I was with when he was conceived."

A muscle twitched in his jaw, which she took as confirmation that the question had occurred to him.

She moistened her lips. "I named him Simon Eryk Zielinski. Eryk was my grandfather's name."

Adam pushed a hand through his wind-tossed dark hair, and she could see the tension that gripped him. They hadn't exchanged a lot of personal information when they'd met before, but she'd assumed he was close to her own age. She was now thirty-three, but the passing years had aged him more. Not so much in appearance. He was as fit and as attractive, if not even more so, as he'd been then. But beneath the polite smile he'd worn among the resort guests, she'd detected a solemn gravity that hadn't been present before.

She wondered again how he'd ended up working here, what else he'd done since she'd seen him last. She wondered what he was thinking. Feeling.

His stormy gray eyes met hers and she swallowed hard. For a moment, she felt a bit intimidated. Shaking off the feeling, she lifted her chin and squared her shoulders, waiting for him to speak.

"You didn't really answer me earlier," he said in a low voice. "Did you try to find me?"

She spread her hands. "You made it clear when you left that you weren't interested in future contact. When I found out I was pregnant, I called the resort, but the woman in the office wouldn't give me your information. Short of hiring a private investigator, I didn't know what else to do."

His eyes sparked and for a moment, she thought he was going to tell her that was exactly what she should have done.

She spoke forcefully again before he had a chance. "Do you remember what you said to me that first night, when we ended up in my bedroom after walking on the beach?"

He frowned as though he wasn't sure where this was leading. "Not specifically."

"You said there was no need to exchange contact information because you had plans that didn't include a relationship. You made it clear a little vacation fun was all you wanted. As I told you then, I wasn't looking for anything more, either. I figured the way you left proved you hadn't changed your mind."

He had the grace to wince at the reminder of the way he'd slipped out. "I had an early flight that day, and it seemed easier to skip goodbyes. Of course, I had no idea—"

She shook her head. "I'm not asking for an apology. You were never anything but honest with me. I was just as happy to avoid any awkwardness."

Which was true, for the most part. Once she'd gotten past the disappointment of waking to find him gone, thinking she would never see him again, she'd decided he'd chosen exactly the right way to end things. The brief affair had been spontaneous, hot and fun, and it wouldn't have felt right to wrap it up with a perfunctory hug or a bittersweet kiss. She'd told herself she didn't regret a thing, that their time together would be a memory she would privately cherish for years to come.

Then she'd realized she was pregnant, and

she'd known the memories wouldn't be so easy to tuck away.

"I wasn't apologizing," Adam said curtly. "Did you really want me to leave with a handshake?"

She was taken aback by how closely his words echoed her own thoughts.

Their gazes held for several long moments. Was he replaying some of the same memories that had crept out of the past to haunt her now? Was he hearing sounds of quiet laughs and soft moans, of hungry kisses and exultant gasps? How many times had she woken in the middle of the night after dreams filled with the rush of the ocean and the touch of his hands?

Those rare but vivid dreams had taken her by surprise each time. She'd have sworn she'd long since put the weekend behind her. But then again, she lived with a daily reminder of her days and nights with Adam, so it was only natural she'd have thoughts of him from time to time. Right?

Swallowing hard, she rose to her feet. She craved a few moments to herself, just a chance to clear her thoughts, to lock away the memories again. "I need a glass of water. Can I get you anything?"

He looked as though he were going to decline, but then seemed to change his mind. "Yeah, water sounds good. Thanks."

She doubted he was any thirstier than she was, but maybe he, too, thought it a good idea to change the tone of this conversation. To focus on what needed to be their priority.

Their son.

TOO RESTLESS TO SIT, Adam stood when Joanna did, then turned to lean against the railing and gaze moodily out at the view. The suites were arranged to maximize privacy with palmettos and flowering trees between the balconies. Vacationers milled on the beach in the distance. A young couple strolled hand in hand through the courtyard below, seemingly oblivious to anyone around them.

He vaguely remembered what that felt like.

Absorbed in their own pursuits, no one looked his way. And even if they did glance up, they couldn't know that his entire life had changed since he'd set out for a jog that morning.

He had a son.

Despite Trevor's warnings, Adam had little doubt the boy was his. He suspected DNA tests would merely confirm his gut instinct, though he wouldn't object to the formality. He still found it hard to believe Joanna had deliberately sought him out now for any of the reasons Trevor had implied—for *any* reason, actually. In fact, she seemed poised to run, taking her—taking *their*—son without a goodbye. He could hardly blame her for that impulse, considering.

She'd claimed to be unable to locate him. Obviously she hadn't tried very hard. He wouldn't make the same mistake if she were the one to vanish now. They had some things to settle before going their separate ways again. He just wished he knew what the hell he was supposed to do next.

A sound from behind him made him turn to find her approaching with a glass of ice water in each hand. She set the glasses on the table, then wiped her palms on her dress, drawing his gaze. She had great legs, long and shapely. He remembered with unexpected clarity exactly how they'd felt wrapped around him. He cleared his throat and shifted his weight, giving her a curt nod. "Thanks."

Any nervousness that might have been present in her expression earlier was hidden now behind a look of determination. Obviously she'd used the brief time inside to reinforce her defenses. It bothered him that she'd felt it necessary to do so.

"You're angry with me," she said.

"No." His response was automatic.

She held her ground. "Yes."

He sighed and shoved a hand through his hair. "Okay, yeah. Maybe a bit."

"You think I could have tried harder to find you."

He met her eyes. "Yes."

Her mouth tightened, but she continued. "Even considering the way you left? No phone number. Not even a note."

Despite the truth of her words, he refused to be placed on the defensive. "I've already told you my reason for that." Part of the reason, anyway. "But you had to have known everything changed with the pregnancy."

"Everything certainly changed for me," she said in a strained whisper, looking away. Her right hand went to her stomach, as if in subconscious memory, and he found his mind filled with images of her swollen with pregnancy. His throat tightened painfully.

"I was six weeks along before I realized I was pregnant, or at least before I admitted it to myself," she said, her hand falling to her side. "You'd made no effort to contact me, so I assumed you'd moved on with your plans, whatever they were. As I said, I did try to reach you through the resort, but I couldn't get anywhere. Adam Scott is not an uncommon name. I didn't even know what state you lived in."

He grimaced. "I was in Afghanistan."

Her eyes widened. "Afghanistan? You were in the military?"

"Army."

She moistened her lips, drawing his attention to her soft mouth. "I wondered at the time if you'd served a tour. There was something about your haircut and the way you carried yourself. But you didn't seem to want to talk about it, so I didn't push. I had no idea you were on your way overseas."

He shrugged. "It was my second deployment. And you're right, I didn't want to discuss it. The whole point of taking that vacation was to get away from military talk for a few days."

He'd relished the few days of luxury and relaxation, but he hadn't been overly concerned about his upcoming assignment. He'd been aware of the dangers he would face, of course, and had considered himself rather noble for leaving no one to worry about his safety. Still, he'd fully expected to return as relatively unscathed as he had from his first, far-less-traumatic mission. Remembering that almost cocky naïveté now made him grimace, though fortunately Joanna didn't seem to notice.

"How long were you deployed?"

"Ten months." He didn't add that it had been a twelve-month tour cut short by an explosive device.

"Which would have made it even harder for me to contact you," she pointed out.

"It would have been possible," he muttered. He'd had the right to know about his child, even though he had no clue how he'd have reacted. "Five years, Joanna. Five years I've had a son I didn't know about."

Her eyes glittered, and the sight of her tears punched him in the gut. His throat ached with the emotions he was choking down. Pain and regret hovered between them as they stood there, gazes locked, both struggling for words.

His phone beeped with a text, shattering the tense moment. The sudden sound startled them both. Unsure whether he was more annoyed or grateful for the interruption, he glanced down at the screen and cursed softly. "There's something I have to deal with now. Work."

"Of course," she said, a bit too readily. "We can talk later."

He looked up from the phone with a frown. "We *will* talk later. We still have a lot to discuss."

She gave a resigned nod. "I'd rather not tell

Simon anything about this until after you and I have had that discussion."

He knew exactly what he felt this time. Relief. He wasn't at all ready for the boy to know who he was. "Agreed."

Pushing the phone back into his pocket, he started to turn, then paused, looking over his shoulder. "You're not going to run, are you?"

She held his gaze when she answered lightly, "Not yet."

He wished he could take more reassurance in that reply.

SIMON RETURNED FROM the field trip chattering a mile a minute about everything he'd seen and learned. He hopped out of the van clutching a reusable water bottle imprinted with the aquarium logo in one hand, and a slightly crumpled craft project in the other. Joanna dutifully admired the blue cardboard ocean covered with stickers of all the specimens he'd seen that day. She smiled when she saw that he'd drawn shells on the glitter-embellished "sand" at the bottom of his ocean, including a fairly credible lettered olive.

"This is great, Simon. I'm glad you had a good time."

"We had a wonderful time," Miss Molly

volunteered, overhearing the comment as she mingled among the reunited kids and parents. "You have a very bright and well-behaved son. He asked such smart questions that I can tell Deborah and I will have to stay well prepared for each day's lessons."

Joanna was pleased that Molly seemed more impressed than impatient with Simon's endless questions. That wasn't always the case.

"See you tomorrow, Simon, when we'll go to the maritime museum."

"'Bye, Miss Molly." Falling into step beside Joanna, Simon continued to recap his field trip, barely pausing to take a breath as he leaped nimbly from one sandy stepping stone to the next.

She tried to interject the occasional response or question, just to let him know she was paying attention. It was difficult to focus on anything other than her dilemma with Adam. "What was your favorite exhibit?"

He puckered his lips in thought for a moment, then said, "The archer fish! They shoot water out of their mouths at insects sitting on branches above them. The bugs fall in the lake and then the fish eat them. We saw them when the aquarium people put bugs in the tank."

"That's a very clever fish."

Simon grinned up at her. "Bet the bugs wish they were dumber."

She chuckled. "I'm sure you're right."

She loved teasing with her bright little boy, making each other laugh with silly jokes. His laughter could make her smile even after the hardest day. Just standing beside his bed and watching him sleep brought her a deep sense of joy she could never have imagined before she'd had him. They'd been happy in their tidy house in a suburb of Atlanta, their own small refuge.

The idea of sharing him with someone else made her stomach tighten in rejection. Because she recognized the selfishness of that reaction, she shoved it away, assuring herself she wanted only what was best for Simon, whatever that might mean for his future. Of course, she would protect him fiercely from being hurt if she suspected that might happen, but there was no need to borrow trouble. For all she knew, Adam had no interest in fatherhood, no desire to have his bachelor life complicated by a five-year-old.

She wouldn't be surprised if he offered financial assistance, regardless of how involved he wanted to be in Simon's life. Granted, she didn't know Adam well, but she'd pegged him as a man of honor. She wouldn't accept a dime for herself, of course, but she supposed it would be only fair to allow Adam to open a trust account or make some other financial arrangements for the boy. She couldn't let her own pride interfere with her son's best interest, as grating as it would be to surrender even that modicum of parental control. As for any other interaction…she swallowed hard, telling herself again to take it one step at a time.

"I'm sure you're a little tired after your busy afternoon," she told Simon. "Would you like to rest awhile before dinner?"

As she expected, Simon shook his head. "I'm not tired. But maybe we could go to the beach and I could build a sand castle?"

"We could absolutely do that."

Fifteen minutes later, she reclined on a low beach chair with her bare legs stretched in front of her, reading a book on her tablet, and with an insulated tumbler of ice-cold water beside her. Above her, a blue umbrella fluttered in the steady breeze, shading her from the late afternoon sun. Only a few people milled on the beach and in the waves. Others were out on the fishing pier many yards to the south.

With the beach relatively empty, Simon had plenty of room to play. He sat cross-legged on the damp sand near Joanna's chair, his sunscreen-shiny face creased in concentration. He'd dumped a bag of brightly colored beach toys around him—shovels and pails, sand molds, a plastic bulldozer and a construction vehicle with a scoop bucket on a bendable arm. Imitating the beeps and other mechanical noises he'd heard on his favorite construction-themed videos, he focused on building a road to the sand mound he'd already prepared for his planned castle.

Joanna divided her attention between her busy son, the gripping novel and the natural beauty surrounding her. She thought wistfully that this was exactly what she'd envisioned when she'd booked this vacation. She'd known there would be bittersweet moments, of course, but she'd been prepared to deal with them. This was all she'd wanted—quiet time together outdoors in the sun and surf.

Another young boy ran up to watch what Simon was doing. The child immediately grabbed one of Simon's plastic shovels and plopped down to dig with it.

"Cody!" a male voice called out. "That doesn't belong to you."

Noting that the boy, who looked to be close to Simon's own age, had Down syndrome, Joanna prepared to caution her son to be patient, but she should have known it wouldn't be necessary.

"It's okay," Simon told the boy's father, who was hurrying over. "He can play with me."

The dad looked at Joanna, the expression on his broad, ruddy face questioning. She smiled and nodded. "Let him play for a few minutes if he wants to."

Accepting that his son had settled in, the man chuckled wryly. "Thanks. To be honest, I wouldn't mind sitting a bit to catch my breath. Cody insisted I carry him on my shoulders all the way down the beach and back while my wife takes a nap. I'm Ken McGee, by the way, and this is my son, Cody."

"I'm Joanna Zielinski, and this is Simon." Setting her tablet aside, Joanna motioned for Ken to sit on a towel she'd spread nearby for Simon.

He accepted the invitation, settling on the towel with his legs folded beneath him. "You can play just for a few minutes, Cody, but then we have to go join Mommy for dinner, okay?"

Engrossed in a lesson from Simon on how to pack damp sand into a mold, Cody gave no sign that he'd heard his father, though Joanna believed he had. She and Ken exchanged a few remarks about the beautiful weather and the resort facilities. Standard stranger small talk.

Ken glanced toward the boys. "Your son is good with Cody."

Watching as Simon helped the other child dump the mold and tap out the sand, Joanna smiled. "One of Simon's friends at our church back in Georgia is a little girl with Down syndrome. He's very fond of Michaela. She's a sweetheart."

Cody scooped a shovelful of sand and tossed it in the air, giggling when the sand rained down on him. Leaning back to avoid having a face full of grit, Simon looked wryly at his mother. "I think Cody likes demolition better than construction."

Ken's laugh sounded a bit weary. "You can say that again."

As if he realized how his words could be interpreted, he added quickly, "Cody's a great kid. I—my wife and I don't mind the challenges. Wouldn't trade him for the world."

"Of course not," Joanna replied gently, trying to avoid the psychologist's penchant of reading more into statements and expressions than the speaker had intended. "It's obvious he's a precious little boy."

"He is," Ken agreed with a more natural smile, though she still thought she detected signs of stress in his eyes. "And he's been making great strides lately developmentally. I—we're doing great."

She merely smiled, pretending not to notice

either the slip of words or the too-hearty tone. Nor his repetition of the word *great*.

Ken stood then. "C'mon, buddy, let's go find Mommy. She'll want to clean you up before dinner."

"See you around, Cody," Simon called after them, earning a wave of a chubby hand in return.

"You were very sweet with Cody, Simon," Joanna commented, proud of her son.

He was already making repairs to his road and castle. "He's like Michaela, isn't he?"

"Yes, he has Down syndrome, which means he doesn't learn things as easily as you do. But he still likes to play with toys and other children, so it's nice of you to share and to be patient helping him."

"Yes, it is." Adam stepped into view from behind her, his gaze on Simon. "Cody's become a favorite around here in the past couple of days."

Joanna's pulse rate sped up, and she realized ruefully that for all the time that had passed, she still turned into a smitten schoolgirl whenever Adam strolled into view.

# CHAPTER THREE

"Hi, Mr. Adam. I'm building a road and a castle."

Joanna looked through her lashes at Adam, wondering how he felt about having his son call him "mister." Whatever the emotions, he had them well hidden. "It's looking great, Simon. Nice digger you've got there."

"It's an excavator. The boom is hydraulic," Simon replied off-handedly before going back to playing, making impressively realistic sound effects.

Adam looked at Joanna with a raised eyebrow. She smiled faintly as she rose to greet him. "He likes to watch educational videos about construction equipment."

"Yeah? You like heavy equipment work, Simon?"

"I like seeing how things are made," Simon replied, dumping a load of sand from the bucket.

Adam glanced at Joanna, and for a moment she thought she detected a hint of emotion in his eyes. Wistfulness, perhaps? Regret that there were so many things he didn't know about his son? Or was she projecting how she might feel in his position?

Before she could decide, he schooled his expression and spoke evenly. "So, Trevor and I are having dinner at Torchlight tonight. He wanted me to invite you and Simon to join us."

Her first reaction was to be alarmed by the seemingly innocuous invitation. She wasn't ready for a "family" meal with Adam and Simon. Not nearly ready. She looked quickly at Simon, all too aware that he was listening even though he hadn't paused in his play. How could she refuse without arousing his curiosity about why?

"Trevor makes a practice of dining with guests most evenings," Adam added smoothly. "We ate with Cody and his family yesterday."

It seemed to be an attempt to reassure her there was no need to worry about Simon learning anything she wasn't ready to tell him. Still, the whole situation seemed fraught with potential complications. "I don't—"

"Can we, Mom?" Simon piped up, proving he was paying attention. "I want to tell them about the aquarium."

Feeling cornered, she moistened her lips, tasting the hint of ocean salt in the air. Simon would probably enjoy being the center of attention at dinner, as she had no doubt he would be. Other than her father, who believed that children should generally sit quietly unless spoken to, Simon didn't spend a lot of time with men. She'd always been very careful not to let him get too close to the few men she'd dated to protect him when the relationships ended—as they always had after a fairly short time. She simply hadn't met anyone who'd felt like a good fit. And now that Adam was here, she found herself instinctively wanting to protect her son again. Not to mention her own heart, which she feared was unexpectedly vulnerable.

"Mom?"

Trapped, she somehow managed a smile. "Thank you, Adam. Tell Mr. Farrell we'd be happy to join you. What time?"

"Does seven work for you?"

It was a little later than Simon usually had his dinner, but he'd had a snack before they'd come out to the beach, so she figured he'd last until then. And it would give her time to get them both cleaned up. "Yes, seven is fine."

He lingered a few moments longer, watching Simon play, and then he met Joanna's eyes again. "See you later, JoJo."

The offhand nickname shook her to the core, making her bare toes curl into the sand. She flashed to the memory of his voice in a darkened bedroom, husky in her ear as he'd laughed softly and murmured, "Just let yourself go, JoJo. You know you want to."

She *had* let herself go with him, in a way she'd never done before or since with anyone else. Just remembering their lovemaking made her weak in the knees.

Adam was studying her too closely. His stormy gray eyes darkened and narrowed, as though he could somehow see the steamy images in her mind. They stood staring at each for what seemed like minutes, though it was probably only a moment or two. They were jarred into motion when Simon made a sudden explosion sound, sweeping a hand to crash down one wall of his castle.

Adam didn't jump, but he sounded a bit startled when he asked, "What was that?"

Simon grinned up them from amidst the scattered remains of his construction. "Earthquake."

Chuckling, Adam took a step back. "I'll get out of the danger zone, then. I have a few more things to do this afternoon, so I'll see the two of you at dinner."

With one last glance, he turned and strode

away. She couldn't resist watching him. She'd almost forgotten his distinctive walk, a rolling, ground-eating gait that was as efficient as it was sexy. Pulling her attention away from the all-too-intriguing sight of his backside, she shook her head and began to gather her belongings, telling Simon to put his toys in the carry bag. They had to get ready for dinner. This was no time to dwell on how attractive Adam Scott still was to her.

ADAM AND TREVOR were waiting when Joanna led Simon into Torchlight just before seven. The resort included two dining options that were more casual than this upscale restaurant, so this was a special treat for her son. As they entered the restaurant, she reminded Simon to use his best manners and his indoor voice—something he sometimes forgot when excited.

Both men rose when she and Simon were escorted to their table. Joanna didn't quite meet Adam's eyes as she greeted them. After being seated, she was given a menu, but neither Adam nor Trevor requested one. Hardly a surprise. She was sure they had the menu memorized. She was offered a children's menu, which she handed over to Simon, to the apparent surprise of both Trevor and Adam.

"You can read the menu, Simon?" Adam asked.

Studying the menu gravely, Simon nodded. "Most of it. What's gira—giran—"

Joanna looked over his shoulder to read the word he pointed to. "Girandole. It's a type of pasta, shaped like little spirals. It says it's topped with a light creamy sauce with peas and chicken or shrimp. This is a very nice children's menu," she added to Trevor after glancing at some of the other choices.

He smiled, looking pleased by the compliment. "Our chef has four kids. He says it drives him crazy to take them out to eat and have them offered only burgers or chicken nuggets or peanut butter and jelly sandwiches. Kids can have all of that here, of course, but we make sure there are always other options for our more adventurous young diners."

"I can recommend the girandole," Adam said with a nod to Simon. "That cream sauce will make you want to lick your plate—though I doubt your mom would approve."

"You doubt correctly."

Simon giggled. Adam smiled at Joanna. His gray eyes gleamed like polished steel in the flickering candlelight. She swallowed hard and dragged her gaze away.

"I want the girandole," Simon announced, mangling the pronunciation only slightly. "With shrimp."

"Excellent choice, sir," Trevor affirmed, making the boy giggle again.

Brought back to the present, Joanna placed her own order for a scallops and risotto dish she hoped she'd be able to swallow, considering how tight her throat felt. She then made an effort to mask her discomfort during this deceptively innocuous dinner with their host. She doubted very much she was the only person at the table aware of the undercurrents swirling beneath their lighthearted small talk.

At least she didn't have to figure out how to make conversation. Trevor took care of that by asking Simon to tell them about the aquarium visit. Simon happily launched into a detailed play-by-play recount to which, to give them credit, both men listened graciously, inserting appropriate comments and questions. Joanna was content to sit quietly and let her son be the center of attention. She supposed this was a good way for Adam to get to know Simon a bit, in a public setting with no pressure or expectations on either side. To Simon, Adam was just one of two nice men with whom he was having a special dinner.

She glanced at Adam's face to see if she could judge how he felt about that, only to find him looking back at her. He appeared to be dividing his focus equally between her and Simon. Was he still annoyed with her, despite the dinner invitation? Still suspicious of her? Did he doubt that Simon was his son? Could he really look at this boy and not see himself sitting there?

He talked easily with Simon, and not in an overly patronizing tone her bright son found annoying. A pang went through her as she watched Simon respond eagerly to the male attention.

Simon would have enjoyed dinner with just her at the buffet, too, she assured herself. She and Simon never had trouble having fun together or making lively conversation. But maybe she should have made more of an effort to find more male role models for him. She'd planned to sign him up for some sort of team sports when he got older, but five seemed so young.

Perhaps she really had been selfish. Her mouth suddenly dry, she reached for her water glass, looking at Adam over the rim as she took a drink. How much would she have to share her son with this man she barely even knew?

SIMON WAS AN amazing kid. Well-behaved. Funny. Smart. Almost scary smart for his young age. Adam figured the boy would probably be designated as gifted. From what he'd read, kids like that could be challenging to parent, trying to keep them both intellectually stimulated and socially engaged. Joanna appeared to be handling the balance well, judging by what he'd seen so far. Simon was obviously eager to learn, and he'd seemed to mix well with the other kids on the outing earlier. Adam had been impressed with how well he'd interacted with Cody, a child with far different needs.

He was frankly fascinated by Simon, finding himself searching the boy's face for familiar features, wondering what Simon had been like as a baby, as a toddler, what he would look like as an adult. Fatherhood was one of the things Adam had written off, something he'd taken care to avoid. Or at least, he'd believed he had. He thought he knew himself too well to trust he'd settle in easily to routine domestic life. Despite the three years he'd worked relatively happily here at Wind Shadow, he didn't consider himself the type to stay in one place for long, or to live up to the lofty expectations of others. With little particularly positive experience with family in his past, he'd never regarded himself as daddy material.

He was the type who slipped out in the night rather than face hard goodbyes.

He looked at Joanna, who picked delicately at her scallops while listening to her son's cheery babbling. He'd reluctantly agreed with Trevor's suggestion that a casual meal in a public setting would be a safe way to get acquainted with the boy and learn a bit more about Joanna's agenda, if she had one. Still, this meal had to be as uncomfortable for her as it was for him, though she was doing a good job of hiding her emotions behind a fixed smile. He couldn't help comparing it to the genuine, happy smiles he remembered from before—smiles that lit her eyes and crinkled her nose, pushed shallow dimples into her cheeks and were often accompanied by infectious laughter.

Even with the more forced expression, she looked beautiful this evening, her features illuminated by the candles on the table. She'd brushed her hair to a glossy chestnut curtain and accented her striking green eyes with what looked to be minimal makeup. Her sleeveless peach-colored blouse was cut just low enough to give a tasteful glimpse of creamy skin. He shifted in his chair and stabbed his fork into his steak.

"So, anyway, the aquarium wasn't as big as the one back home, but it was still really fun," Simon concluded when he'd shared all he could think of to report about his outing.

"There aren't any aquariums in this country as big as the one in Atlanta," Trevor replied with a chuckle. "I haven't had the pleasure of touring that one, but I've read about it."

Adam glanced again at Joanna to see if she reacted to hearing Trevor mention her home city. Obviously, as owner of the resort, he had access to his guests' records. Did she wonder if Adam had snooped into her personal information? Because she would be wrong. This was the first he'd heard that she and Simon lived in Georgia.

"Atlanta, huh?" Adam said, dragging his gaze from Joanna back to the boy. "That's where you live?"

Simon chased a pasta spiral with his fork. "We live in Alpharetta. But we go to the aquarium in Atlanta sometimes. And to the zoo. And the children's museum, and the science center with the planetarium. That's my favorite."

"It sounds as though you stay busy."

"We do things on weekends, because Mom doesn't usually work then. And sometimes my school takes field trips. When I don't have school and Mom's working, my nanny, Rose, takes me places. Mostly the park. I like to feed the ducks there. Mom says there will be a lot of parks when we move, too. And a lot of boats and museums and..."

Joanna cleared her throat. "How's your dinner, Simon?"

He scooped another forkful of pasta and shrimp into his mouth and said around it, "It's good."

She smiled and handed him his napkin. "I'm glad you're enjoying it. But don't talk with your mouth full."

"Where do you work, Joanna?" Trevor asked conversationally, earning a quick look from Adam. They'd agreed before Joanna and Simon arrived that this meal would be pleasant and friendly, no interrogations. Yet he suspected Trevor had proposed this casual gathering as a way to scope out Joanna's motives, which his suspicious friend still questioned. Still, Adam supposed this was an innocent enough topic.

Her reply was indirect—not where she

worked, but what she did. "I'm an assistant professor of psychology."

Adam felt his fingers tighten around his fork in response. It probably shouldn't surprise him that she was an academic, but he was still a bit taken aback.

"So it's Dr. Zielinski?" Trevor asked.

She smiled faintly. "Just call me Joanna."

Adam reached for his wineglass.

Trevor seemed intrigued. "Psychology, huh? Have you worked in a clinical setting, or solely in academics?"

She toyed with the scallops remaining on her plate. "I've had a few private clients, but teaching has been my main focus until now."

"Considering a change?"

"Yes." She sounded as though that was all she wanted to say about it. Thinking of the way she'd interrupted Simon when he'd mentioned an upcoming move, Adam frowned.

But Trevor wasn't quite finished. "Are you from the Atlanta area originally?"

"I am, yes."

"Gram and Grampa live in Buckhead," Simon inserted, making an effort to stay involved in the conversation. "My mom grew up there, didn't you, Mom?"

Joanna nodded. "I did."

"Grampa's a surgeon. He cuts people open

and fixes their hearts," Simon added artlessly. "He says I can be a surgeon, too, but I
want to be a marine biologist. Or an architect.
Grampa says architect is just a fancy name
for a carpenter who can draw, but that's not
right because they use computers and math
and physics and design stuff. I saw a video
about them. I think I'd like being an architect,
but marine biology sounds fun, too. Mom said
when we move, I'll get to—"

The pasta Simon had balanced on his fork
while he'd chattered fell with a plop onto his
lap. He winced and looked quickly at his
mother. "Sorry. It fell on the napkin, though."

She was already helping him clean up the
small mess. "Just be more careful, okay?
Don't try to talk and eat at the same time."

She didn't seem annoyed by the accident,
Adam noted, drawing his fascinated gaze
away from the precocious kindergartner. Was
she actually a bit relieved that Simon had been
interrupted again when he'd started to mention a move?

She didn't seem to want to discuss her plans,
whatever they were. Was she reluctant to talk
about them because she didn't want him to
know where she and Simon would be living?
She wouldn't go to that extent to keep him
away from his son, would she? That hardly

seemed to fit with Trevor's concern that she'd had ulterior motives for showing up here this week. So far, she seemed to be doing everything she could to hold Adam at arm's length. Frankly, it was beginning to annoy him.

"What would you like for dessert, Simon?" Trevor asked. "Cheesecake? Pie? Or we have an excellent chocolate lava cake that you can order à la mode, if you like."

"That means with ice cream! I like à la mode."

Adam had to give Trevor credit. In his easy manner, he'd drawn out quite a bit about Joanna during this deceptively simple meal. They'd learned that she was a professor. The daughter of a surgeon. Adam was no expert on Atlanta, but even he recognized the expensive neighborhood Simon had mentioned so casually.

No wonder Simon was such a genius. He might've gotten Adam's gray eyes and cowlick, but the rest had come straight from his mother. Adam wasn't looking forward to the prospect of telling Joanna or Simon about his own dysfunctional family background.

Was there anything this kid needed that he didn't already have? Especially anything Adam might have to offer?

TIRED FROM HIS busy day, Simon was already drooping by the time he'd finished his dessert. Still, after politely thanking their hosts for dinner, he wanted to linger at the small amphitheater near the lakeside bar to hear the calypso band. Relieved that the meal had gone relatively well, Joanna had kept her goodbyes polite but brief. It had been left unspoken but taken for granted that she and Adam would be seeing each other again soon. Adam had looked as though he wanted to say something more before they parted, but after a glance at Simon, he'd merely wished them good-night.

A handful of people danced around the tiny stage, their rhythm enhanced by a few too many tropical drinks. Simon was fascinated by the movement and the bright colors and the steel drum. Joanna sat next to him on a low bench and he snuggled against her to watch the festivities. Before the end of the second number, he'd fallen asleep.

Enjoying the party herself, she waited a few minutes before trying to rouse him for the walk back to their cabin. She was tempted to order a piña colada to sip while Simon dozed in her lap, but she knew she should get him ready for bed. He would need his energy for tomorrow.

"Looks like your date conked out on you."

Moistening her lips, she glanced up to find Adam standing nearby, watching her and Simon without smiling despite his light words. He stood mostly in shadow, one side of his face illuminated by a tiki torch. The flame flickered in his dark eyes, seeming to mirror the inner turmoil he'd probably experienced that day. She knew her own emotions were pretty well shredded after the past fifteen hours.

"He's had a full day."

"Starting very early."

She remembered the jolt of panic she'd felt when she'd woken at dawn and seen Simon's bed empty. The relief when she'd found him. The shock when she'd identified his companion. "Very early. He wanted to listen to the music for a while before turning in, but he didn't last long."

"So he inherited your appreciation for music?"

Her thoughts drifted in response to the question, back to moonlit hours spent snuggled on a bench much like this one—if not this very one—listening to other bands. Getting up occasionally to dance in the sand, their fingers laced, bodies pressed together, mouths close enough for the occasional kiss. Until the tension had built too high, and they'd slipped away to find privacy. And a bed.

That all felt like another lifetime now.

She swallowed hard. "Yes, he loves music."

Adam studied her face. Was he thinking back to the same things she was? Had he remembered their previous encounter as fondly as she had, or had she been nothing more to him than a pleasant diversion he'd forgotten about since? Still, he'd immediately recognized her face and knew her name on the beach this morning. She supposed there was some gratification in that.

But it was getting late. Looking down at Simon, she jostled him gently. "Come on, honey, let's go back to the cabin. You need to get to bed so you can rest for tomorrow."

"I don't want to go yet. I want to hear the music," Simon roused enough to respond, a hint of whine in his protest. As well-behaved as he generally was, he could be a pill when he was tired, which he certainly was now. She hoped he wasn't about to show one of his rare flashes of five-year-old temper here in front of…well, in front of everyone.

Adam motioned toward the lodges. "As it happens, I'm headed that way myself. How about a lift, buddy? You can ride on my shoulders if you like."

Distracted and intrigued, Simon lifted his head to peer at Adam. "I'd be really high up, wouldn't I?"

Adam smiled faintly. "Yes, you would. You'd be able to see a long way."

Simon promptly climbed onto the bench and held up his arms. Joanna felt a ripple of dismay at the sight of her son reaching out to the man he didn't know was his father. And something else...maybe a little possessiveness? Or was it fear of something she couldn't quite define?

Adam crouched in front of the bench while Simon climbed on, then straightened with the boy high on his shoulders.

Giving her a slightly crooked smile, Adam asked, "Ready, JoJo?"

From his lofty perch, Simon giggled drowsily. "That's a funny name for her. Aunt Maddie usually calls my mom Jo, but sometimes she calls her Joey."

Joanna fell into step beside them. "Not if she wants me to respond."

"Maybe I should call you Dr. JoJo."

She lifted an eyebrow. "Not if *you* want me to respond."

"Oh, I absolutely want you to respond," he said lightly.

Something about his tone made her miss a

step on the pebbled pathway. She pulled herself together sharply with an admonition that she had to keep her wits about her this week. She couldn't think clearly if she allowed herself to be dazzled again by infatuation—or whatever it was she had once felt for Adam, if only for a weekend.

It didn't help to see him with her—*their*—son on his shoulders, both laughing when Adam bobbed and weaved to give Simon a more entertaining ride. Her fingernails dug painfully into her palms. As appealing a picture as they made, what would be the consequences of bringing this man—this virtual stranger, really—into their lives?

Adam glanced down at her, and whatever he saw in her expression made him stop smiling. "Are you okay?"

"I'm fine. Just tired." More tired than she'd realized, apparently, she decided, considering the dramatic turn her thoughts had taken. She'd be able to think straight tomorrow, after she'd had a chance to rest and process this change in their circumstances a bit more.

They'd arrived at their building, so she reached up to help Simon down, too vividly aware of each time she brushed against Adam in doing so. "Good night, Adam. Thank you again for inviting us to dinner."

"I'll see you tomorrow, Mr. Adam?" Simon asked hopefully.

Adam ruffled his hair. "Sure, buddy. See you tomorrow."

He turned his head to look at Joanna then. "I'll see you tomorrow, too."

She nodded in resignation, knowing they still had a lot to talk about. "Simon leaves for his field trip at one."

"Right. I'll find you."

Was that a promise...or a warning? She was too exhausted to decide.

MADDIE WAS GRATIFIED to see her sister's number on her caller ID Tuesday morning. She'd been on pins and needles wondering how everything was going between Joanna and Adam. It had been all she could do not to hop on a plane yesterday after Joanna's frantic call, but she'd forced herself to take some time to make responsible arrangements for her work obligations. Still, family came first. As she'd learned during the past six years, a family didn't have to be perfect, just mutually supportive.

"Jo? Is everything okay?"

"It's...nerve-wracking," Joanna answered. "But it's okay, I guess."

Hearing some odd beeping noises in the

background, Maddie asked, "What's going on? What are those sounds?"

"Simon wanted to come into the arcade after breakfast. I figured you'd be impatient for a report, so I'm taking the opportunity to talk while he's engrossed in a pinball machine."

"Pinball, huh? That kid's probably already figured out the geometric trajectories of the balls to get the best scores," Maddie said with an indulgent laugh.

Joanna's answering chuckle sounded strained. "He's working on it."

Maddie really did adore her funny nephew. The way her own love life had fizzled lately with one disappointing date after another, Simon could be the closest she would ever come to having a kid, something she hadn't realized she wanted before spending so much time with Joanna and Simon. She just didn't want to make babies with any of the guys she'd been out with lately.

"So? Have you talked to Adam again?" She'd waited as long as she could to ask.

"We had dinner last night," Joanna said, then added quickly, "Not alone. We ate with Simon and Trevor Farrell, the owner of the resort. So we didn't talk about anything important, just small talk."

Even mentioning the man's name added another layer of tension to Joanna's voice, something Maddie noted with a deepening frown. "So how's Adam acting? Is it weird with the two of you? Is he trying to get to know Simon? He totally believes Simon is his kid, right?"

"Yes, it's weird. And yes, he believes me. Or he says he does. He seems sort of fascinated by Simon. Maybe even intimidated by him. Like he's not quite sure how to behave."

Maddie supposed that all made sense. Had to have been a shock for the guy to find out suddenly that he had a kindergarten-age son. She cleared her throat before asking the next question. "I don't suppose you've told Mom and Dad that Adam is—"

"No!" Joanna interrupted quickly. "And don't you dare say anything until I've had a chance to talk to them."

"You know I won't. Trust me, I want nothing to do with that conversation."

Henry and Gail Zielinski still hadn't recovered from the shock of having their most responsible and previously compliant daughter return from vacation pregnant and unmarried. They'd wrung their hands and asked—within Maddie's hearing, of course—what they'd done wrong to be the parents of not just one but two rebellious daughters.

Maddie shook her head at the memory of that conversation. To give them credit, their parents had supported Joanna's decision to raise the child, and they'd welcomed Simon with as much warmth as their reserved personalities allowed. Still, Joanna had seemed to feel even more pressure to excel in her career and lead an exemplary life to make up for her "lapse in judgment."

Joanna had never quite mastered Maddie's ability to shrug off their parents' disapproval and live the way she wanted, though Jo said she was working on that. The cross-country move ahead should help. Still, Maddie hated thinking about how much she would miss her sister and nephew.

She brought the conversation back to the present. "When are you going to talk to Adam again?"

She could almost hear her sister's swallow. "This afternoon, I think. While Simon's on an outing with Explorers Club."

"What are you going to say?"

"I don't have the foggiest."

It wasn't like Joanna to sound so lost. She was always so efficient and prepared. Maddie felt her own hackles rising in perhaps unjustified annoyance with the man who'd caused this distress. "And if he wants to be a part of Simon's life in the future?"

"I'll deal with it. Somehow. I have to go, Maddie. I'll call you later, okay?"

"You'd better."

After disconnecting, Maddie set down her phone. Then turned to her computer to find the first available flight to South Carolina.

JOANNA MADE IT to midafternoon before she saw Adam. While she'd appreciated having the time to prepare, she'd grown more tense as the minutes ticked past, probably because she knew it was coming and didn't know exactly when.

Maddie had often accused her—sometimes teasingly, others more irritably—of being a control freak, and Joanna supposed that was fair. She liked her schedules, her routines, her notes and outlines and calendars. True spontaneity was a rare indulgence, especially during the past six years, when she'd lived every day with the consequences of letting her hair down once. She wouldn't trade a moment of the challenges for the joy she'd found in her son, but for Simon's sake, she'd been careful not to take any more risks. Sexy, enigmatic Adam Scott was an emotional hazard if she'd ever seen one.

The hour she'd just spent in the spa should have left her relaxed and loose. Though she'd enjoyed the pampering and had appreciated having some of the tension eased by the skilled masseuse, she was still on edge. The reason for her discomfort fell into step beside her only a short distance from the spa.

"Having a nice day?" Adam asked in a casual tone he might have used with any guest.

She shot him a look. "Working on it."

When he merely gave her a bland half smile in return, she pushed her hands into the pockets of her shorts. "How's your day going?" she asked, knowing it was an inane question, but it was also the best she could come up with.

He replied cordially enough. "Good. Busy. It's peak time for us here. Almost every unit is occupied, and we have a few big events coming up next weekend. Two family reunions and a wedding."

Hearing him speak so easily and familiarly about resort business made her pause and tilt her head in his direction. "How long have you worked here? You never mentioned you were even thinking about it when we met before."

"I wasn't considering it then. Trevor told me before I left that he makes a point of helping out vets looking for work. He encouraged me to look him up if I ever found myself in that situation. When I got out of the hosp—out of the military, I remembered what he'd said, and I thought I might as well stop by. His previous assistant manager had to move away for family reasons, so he needed someone to step in. That was a little over three years ago."

He'd covered his verbal stumble smoothly, but she caught it. "You were in the hospital? Were you injured in Afghanistan?"

"Yeah. Obviously, I recovered."

It was clearly not a topic he wanted to discuss, but she couldn't resist asking, "How long were you in the hospital?"

He didn't answer right away, and she wasn't sure he would. But then he muttered, "Six months, counting inpatient rehab. Like I said, I got over it."

Six months. She bit her lip as those words sank in. He hadn't just been banged up; he'd been seriously injured. She couldn't help wondering exactly what those injuries had been, and whether he still suffered from them.

He changed the subject with abrupt finality. "Want to get a coffee? Or maybe walk on the beach for a while? We've got a couple hours before Simon gets back, and I don't have anything pressing to do in the meantime. Nothing that won't wait until later, anyway. And you and I need to talk."

She tucked a strand of hair behind her ear, wishing again that she were anywhere but here, facing a conversation that was going to be difficult at best, but then she nodded. "Let's walk."

Staying in the open should hold back that claustrophobic feeling she'd had when Adam was in her suite yesterday. She was as aware of him now as she had been then, but at least there would be more space around them— and no flashback-inducing beds within sight.

# CHAPTER FOUR

ADAM EXTENDED A HAND, palm-up, toward the path to the beach, signaling for Joanna to lead the way. He strolled beside her, keeping a careful distance between them on the wide walkway. He didn't try to start a serious conversation, and she was too tense to make small talk, so they trekked in silence. They had to move to one side to make way for a couple holding hands and snuggling together, seemingly oblivious to anyone and anything around them. The young woman giggled at something her companion whispered as they disappeared toward the guest quarters, and it wasn't hard for Joanna to guess what they had in mind.

Remembering similar whispers between herself and Adam on this same path six years ago, she cleared her throat, suddenly needing a distraction. "The grounds are beautiful. I've noticed quite a few things that are new since my last visit."

Adam nodded, and she thought he looked pleased by the praise. "Trevor's about run out of room for expansion here. He's opening a second resort on the Texas Gulf Coast next year and has plans in the works for a third in Florida."

She would've liked to know the whole story of the evolution of Adam's job here, but she supposed if he wanted to tell her more, he would. Instead, she kept the focus on his employer, which seemed safe enough. "Trevor's young to have accomplished so much. I got the impression that he's single?"

"He's widowed."

Startled, she slowed her steps. "Widowed? That's tragic."

"Yeah."

"No children?"

"No."

"Did you ever meet his wife?"

"No. It was before we met him."

So, more than six years and Trevor hadn't remarried, though he was probably only in his late thirties. She doubted it was from lack of opportunity. Trevor was handsome, personable, respectable and successful, the type of man most women looked for. Was he still grieving his late wife? The thought saddened her.

She was tempted to ask if Adam had ever been married. She'd have liked to know if there was a woman in his life now, though she'd seen no signs of it. Yet another great-looking guy, good job, sexy as all get-out. The only reason a man like that would be single was that he wanted to be, which must have made his instant fatherhood even more of a jolt.

She clenched her hands and moistened her lips as they stepped out of the tree-lined walkway and onto beach sand. "Will your responsibilities here increase as Trevor becomes busier with his new projects? He seems to have a great deal of faith in you. Would you want to be the senior manager at one of the resorts?"

His face expressionless, Adam shrugged. "I haven't committed to anything at the moment."

Before she could respond, he changed the subject again. So far, they'd been carefully civil, but still the air between them seemed charged with tension. The guarded conversation was beginning to remind her of the pinball games Simon had played that morning. Every time they encountered a topic that made Adam uncomfortable, he bounced to a new one. "You implied to Trevor that you're making a career change, too. Are you looking for something different in Georgia or moving to a new state?"

She tasted a fresh coating of salt when she moistened her lips. "Actually…I've accepted an offer in Seattle. Of course, it means a big change for Simon, so I had to consider it very carefully, but I decided I couldn't pass up the opportunity."

Adam didn't quite stumble, but his steps faltered. His eyebrows drew together when he repeated, "Seattle?"

Was he thinking of how far Washington was from South Carolina? Was he wondering how he could get to know his son at all if they lived three thousand miles apart? Because she certainly was.

She nodded. "I'll be working with patients and their families dealing with long-term disabilities as the result of stroke, traumatic head injuries and other catastrophic health issues. It's always been a particular field of interest for me. I've been to Seattle a couple of times to observe their program, and I think it will be a good fit for me."

His face was hard to read when he asked, "What does your family think?"

"My family has always encouraged me to pursue my career goals." More than encouraged, actually. Her parents had been almost obsessively single-minded about making sure she and Maddie were studious and career-focused from an early age. Their mission had been easier with her than with her obstinate younger sister.

"And they aren't opposed to you moving so far away?"

"My parents aren't exactly the clingy type. They'll expect regular visits home, of course, but they won't try to stop us from going. My sister...well, my sister will miss me," she said with a faint sigh, thinking of how much she'd miss Maddie in return.

She found it rather ironic that it was because of Adam, in a way, that she and Maddie had bonded so tightly during the past years. Maddie had stood by her during her pregnancy, helping her with doctor appointments and nursery preparation, serving as her birthing coach, spending a lot of time with her during those first few weeks of adjustment and sleep deprivation. Their mother was useless at that sort of thing, having mostly turned her own daughters over to the care of nannies during those early months of feedings and changes and colic.

"You never mentioned if you have siblings," she said, looking up at him. Did Adam have anyone who would be excited to know about the newly discovered nephew, or parents who would be anxious to meet their five-year-old grandson?

"No. I was an only child."

"Are your parents still living?" If so, how would he tell them about Simon?

But he shook his head again without looking at her. "They're both gone."

So her sense of him being alone in the world was proving correct. She wondered how long ago his parents had died, but something about his posture let her know he didn't want to get into it at the moment. She didn't press, though if Adam became a part of Simon's life, he would have to tell her more about himself.

Moving a clump of dried sea grass aside with one foot, Adam kept his gaze on the damp sand ahead as he asked, "When are you making this big move to Washington?"

"In a few weeks. I'd like to get settled there before the school year begins so Simon won't have to start after his classmates. This vacation is sort of a last break for us before we have to dive into packing and preparing to resettle."

Adam reached up to squeeze the back of his neck. She considered recommending the spa, but thought maybe he wouldn't appreciate the lame attempt at humor.

"How does Simon feel about all this?"

"He's excited to move to the Puget Sound area, considering his recent obsession with oceanography. He's always eager for new experiences and new things to learn."

"It's a big change for him."

"Yes." She brushed a blowing strand of hair out of her mouth and tucked it behind her ear. "I think I've prepared him as best I can. Of course, now I'll need to prepare him for another change. Once we decide how and when to tell him who you are to him."

Adam didn't respond.

She stopped moving, catching his right arm to bring him to a halt. They'd walked beyond the lifeguard-monitored swimming beach onto a more natural stretch of scrubby dunes and sand. No one else was on the beach, though out in the water two teenagers, a boy and a girl, floated on boogie boards they didn't appear to handle very well. Probably vacationers from inland, she thought fleetingly before turning her full attention to Adam. "You do want to tell Simon who you are, don't you?"

The corners of his mouth tightened. "I need some time, Joanna."

Puzzled, she studied him. He still gripped the back of his neck with his left hand, and she couldn't tell if his discomfort was physical or emotional—perhaps a combination.

"I don't understand. Are you saying you want time to decide how to tell him—or time to decide if you want to tell him at all?"

"I don't know. The latter, I guess."

His reply took her aback. Through all that worrying she'd done about how Adam's presence in their life would affect her and Simon, it had never occurred to her that he might choose not to be a part of that. Even to acknowledge his connection to them.

His voice was emotionless when he said, "Whether or not we choose to clue him in, I realize I have certain financial obligations to the boy. I'll pay my fair share. We'll work something out."

She really didn't want to talk finances, and it annoyed her that he seemed to think that was her priority. As far as she was concerned, there were so many more important issues to discuss. "Is there any particular reason you wouldn't want to tell Simon you're his father?"

Was it for Simon's sake or his own?

"There are plenty of reasons. But honestly, Joanna—do you really *want* to tell him? Looks to me as if the two of you have been getting along very well. Or *is* it just the two of you? Is there someone else in your life? In his?"

"No, it's just the two of us. And we *have*

gotten along very well. To be honest, it's hard for me to consider sharing him with you. With anyone. But that's selfish, and I don't want Simon to resent me for keeping him from his father."

He looked down at her hand on his arm, making her suddenly aware of how close she stood to him. His skin was warm and taut beneath her palm. He met her eyes, holding her in place with nothing more than his intense gaze. Her face was so close to his that she could almost feel his breath on her cheeks— or was that just the teasing ocean breeze?

They'd shared their first kiss on this beach, though their faces had been lit then by moonlight rather than the bright afternoon sun. It had been the night they met, after dinner and drinks and dancing, during a long, slow stroll that had led eventually to her suite.

The memories faded and the silence stretched between them. Heat built inside her, though she couldn't quite determine whether it was irritation or unwelcome attraction raising her temperature more. She was vividly aware that both emotions swirled inside her.

His gaze lowered slowly to her salty, parted lips. Her breath came more quickly when she took another quick step backward. "Adam—"

A scream shattered the moment. They

whirled simultaneously toward the water. The teen girl Joanna had noted earlier was clinging to her board, shrieking. Having fallen from his own board, which had floated out of his reach, the boy floundered in the water, waves crashing over his head and making him bob in and out of sight. Even from this distance, Joanna could tell he was panicking. The girl seemed too frightened to try to calm him down or assist him.

Muttering a curse, Adam kicked off his shoes. His shirt fell on the sand moments before he hit the water.

Running to the edge of the water, feeling the waves break on her sandaled feet, Joanna held her breath as he arrowed through the water toward the teens. He swam strongly, steadily, though he didn't appear to reach out quite as far with his right arm as his left. She could hear him calling instructions between strokes. "Calm down. The current won't pull you under if you just stay calm."

"I can't—" The boy gurgled when another wave splashed over his face, making him thrash again.

The girl screamed, making the situation worse rather than helping. "He's drowning! Save him! My brother is drowning!"

Joanna debated whether to jump in to help,

but the knowledge that she was more likely to get in the way held her back. She could swim, but she had no rescue experience. Should she call for assistance, run for a lifeguard?

But Adam had reached the teens, and she could still hear him talking to them, raising his voice to be heard. She bit her lip as she watched him flinch to avoid a flailing arm, and then he got hold of the boy. She couldn't make out his words, but she heard his deep, reassuring voice as he swam sideways out of the rip current, towing the kid with him.

Joanna clutched her hands to her chest, feeling her heart pounding. She held her breath until she could see that Adam had both himself and the boy under control. The girl was quieter now, though an occasional sob carried on the breeze to where Joanna stood ready to assist as needed. She waded into the water to just above her ankles to help the still-sniffling girl when the drenched trio reached the beach. The girl was shaking like a leaf and nearly dragged Joanna down into the water with her when she stumbled, though Joanna was able to steady them both.

Five minutes later, the subdued, shaken teens ran down the beach with their recovered boards tucked under their arms, having received a kind but firm lecture from Adam on safe ocean swimming. As Joanna had suspected, they hadn't grown up on the coast; they were vacationing with their family from Tennessee. The girl, who didn't give her name, looked as though she wanted nothing more than to find her mother as they hurried away.

Dripping onto the sand, Adam sighed heavily as he pushed a hand through his hair. "Maybe they'll use a little more common sense next time they go into the water. But I wouldn't bet my life savings on it."

"I don't know," Joanna murmured, gazing after the disappearing siblings. "They looked pretty scared. Maybe they learned their lesson."

Adam shook his wet head in exasperation, drops raining down around him. "The kid wasn't even in that much danger from the current, though he could well have drowned from all that wild splashing he was doing. Close to fifty people a year die in rip currents in the US, mostly due to panic. What they need to do is stay calm and swim sideways, like I did, until they're out of the current and can make it to shore. We put literature in all the rooms, warnings are spelled out on signs, but they don't even bother to…"

His voice trailed off, but Joanna barely heard him as she turned back to him and caught sight of his glistening chest. His broad, tanned, badly scarred chest. Those scars hadn't been there the last time she'd seen him shirtless.

Her throat tightened painfully at the evidence of just how badly he'd been injured. No wonder he'd needed months of hospitalization and rehabilitation. She didn't even want to think about how close he must have been to not coming home at all.

Looking suddenly self-conscious, he scooped up his shirt and dragged it over his head, jerking it down over his soaked khakis. She didn't know what to say, but watched in silence as he walked back to his shoes. Noting a slight hitch in his step, she frowned and looked down at the beach behind him. She hadn't noticed him limping before.

Splotches of blood on the white sand marked each step he'd taken. She gasped. "Adam, you're bleeding."

He stopped and lifted his right foot, twisting it to see the sole. Grumbling in annoyance, he reached down to brush it with his hand, hopping a little for balance. "Looks like I got a piece of shell in it. It's fine."

She reached out to catch his arm until he regained his balance. "You probably have sand in the cut now. Maybe more pieces of shell. I have a first aid kit in my suite," she added on impulse, instinctively shifting into caregiver mode. "I'll clean and bandage it for you if you want. Unless you think a doctor should look at it."

"I don't need to see a doctor for a small cut on my foot," he said impatiently. "I need a shower, dry clothes and a bandage. My quarters are here on the grounds. I can take care of it there."

She hesitated a few moments, telling herself she should let it go. Let him deal with it, as he obviously wanted to do. Still—

"You can't even see that cut without doing contortions. Shell cuts can get badly infected. As I'm sure you know," she added sheepishly, remembering where he'd worked and lived for at least the past three years. "I'll come with you and help you tend to it once you've dried off. It won't take long. We only have an hour before Simon gets back from the museum."

After a beat, Adam nodded and shoved his sandy feet into his canvas boat shoes. If the shoe hurt his wound, he managed not to wince or limp as he moved toward the path. "This way."

She had some belated second thoughts about inviting herself to his place, but she supposed that was foolish. She trusted him.

Maybe it was herself she didn't trust to keep her emotional distance from the man who'd once smiled at her on a beach and changed her life forever.

THE TWO-STORY STAFF apartment building was tucked into a secluded corner of the resort, next to the employee parking lot. Signs on the path from the main resort advised that this area was restricted to resort staff, and most of the guests respected those. Adam's place was upstairs at the north end. He couldn't help wincing when he climbed the stairs, trying to keep his weight on the toes of his right foot. He was pretty sure a piece of shell was lodged in his arch, though it could just be residual grit causing discomfort.

He unlocked his door, then motioned for Joanna to go in ahead of him. He saw her glance quickly around when they entered. His furniture was comfortable and functional, unadorned by knickknacks or decorative pillows, though a worn blue knitted throw was draped carelessly over one arm of the couch. A couple of paperbacks were scattered on tables, but otherwise, everything was in place. A utilitarian kitchen took up one side of the main room, separated from the sitting area by a quartz-topped eating bar. Glass cabinet doors revealed his dishes—service for four in plain white ceramic, though he almost never had guests for meals. His pots and pans hung from a rack above the stove.

"Nice place," Joanna commented, turning to look at him as he closed the door. "Very military."

He shrugged, not having to ask what she meant. It wasn't the first time he'd heard similar comments. "I like things neat."

"And maybe easy to pack up when you decide to move on?"

He turned away to avoid answering the too-perceptive question. "I'm going to shower off the salt before we do this. I'll keep it quick. Make yourself comfortable. There's soda, bottled water and lemonade in the fridge if you're thirsty."

He didn't wait for her to respond.

True to his word, he was in the shower less than five minutes. He dressed in a clean resort polo and khakis, combing his wet hair back from his face with his hand. Because the shower had reopened the cut on his foot, he wrapped a hand towel around it and carried the first aid kit into the living room. He could have taken care of this himself, of course, but Joanna had seemed intent on helping, and he supposed it was good to have some privacy. Only to talk, of course.

When he went back to the living room, Joanna was reading the back cover of a paperback sci-fi novel he'd left on the coffee table. "Sounds exciting," she said, putting the book back.

"Not so much. I bailed about halfway through."

She looked from him to the discarded book and back again. "You aren't going to finish it?"

"No." He settled onto the couch beside her. "I've got others waiting to be read. No need to waste time on one I don't enjoy."

Smiling ruefully, she shook her head. "I can't do that. Once I start a book, I have to finish it, even if I don't really like it."

"Well, there's the difference between you and me." One of them, anyway. And a very telling one. "So, do you still want to look at this cut, or do you want me to take care of it? I can, you know."

"I'm sure you can, tough guy, but since I'm available…" She twisted to face him from the end of the couch and patted her lap. "Put it up here."

He lifted an eyebrow. Raising hers in response, she patted again. "Your foot. Let's see it."

Swiveling, he straightened his leg and rested the heel lightly on her thigh. "That sounded a lot like a 'mama voice.'"

She reached for the kit. "I've had a little practice. But for the record, I'm not feeling maternal toward you."

He nodded. For that same record, he had no interest on being mothered by her.

It felt so damned weird to picture her spending the past six years caring for their child. Naming the boy, nursing him, teaching him to walk and hold a spoon and tie his shoes. It made sense, of course, that she'd bonded so tightly with Simon, whereas Adam was still coming to terms with his own biological connection to the kid. He didn't even know what he was supposed to feel.

He was clueless when it came to parenting, couldn't imagine what he had to offer the boy. Maybe one had to be there from the start to gain that sort of knowledge, though his own folks had never gotten the hang of it. If being a competent father was genetic, he'd probably missed out entirely.

Joanna prodded his foot, focusing intently on the task. "I don't see any pieces of shell, but you missed a little sand in the shower."

"Maybe you should've volunteered to help me wash it. Ouch!"

She set aside the alcohol pad she'd just swiped not so gently over his wound. Apparently she hadn't cared for being reminded of the showers they'd taken together. Probably hadn't been the brightest thing to say, but it had just popped out.

Almost everything had changed in the past two days, but one thing was still the same— he couldn't be this close to Joanna without reacting to her. Still. Just having her hands on his bare foot, even as deliberately impersonal as she was being, made his blood warm. Not that they could do anything about it. Not this time.

His life had become complicated enough from simply learning about Simon. Acknowledging his lingering attraction to Joanna could only complicate it more. It would be smarter to put those thoughts out of his mind and concentrate on the boy, whose well-being was paramount.

After cleaning the wound and dabbing antiseptic ointment on it, Joanna smoothed an adhesive bandage into place, then pushed his foot off her lap. "That should do it."

Putting as much distance between them as the couch allowed, he nodded. "Yeah. That should do it."

She closed the first aid kit and carried the trash to the garbage can in the kitchen. Washing her hands in the sink, she asked over her shoulder, "So, is lifeguard one of your titles around here?"

"No." Because he needed something to do with his hands, he crossed the room to pull a bottle of water from the fridge. He felt the thin bandage on his sole, but the cut didn't hurt. Much. "You could call that an unofficial sideline."

"The boy's sister wasn't much help, screaming and splashing the way she was."

Swallowing a gulp of cold water, he nodded. "They were just a couple of young inlanders who shouldn't have been out there alone."

Joanna turned and leaned back against the counter to look at him. "You sound like a local. You never told me where you grew up, only that you'd won that vacation in a charity raffle. Was South Carolina your childhood home?"

He didn't want to get into his childhood right then. Suffice it to say he hadn't been raised in a warm, supportive, encouraging environment like the one Joanna apparently provided for Simon. Neither his detached, nomadic father nor his troubled, chronically depressed mother had taught him much about parenting or selfless reliability, though his overworked maternal grandmother had done what she could to fill in the gaps.

He doubted a woman from Joanna's background would understand. He gave a quick summary instead of anything more detailed. "No. I lived in West Virginia for a while. Kentucky. Mississippi. Joined the army when I was nineteen, served some time in Texas, then a twelve-month tour in the Middle East. I was stationed at Fort Bragg in North Carolina when I met you, before my second tour."

Her gaze fell to his chest, and he knew she was picturing the scars through his shirt. Though he knew it was foolish, he half turned away as if to hide his chest from her, raising his water to his lips again.

Seemingly oblivious to his self-consciousness, she commented, "You moved around a lot as a child."

"Yeah."

She waited, as if to give him a chance to elaborate. After a few moments of silence, she sighed. "Do you find this all as bizarre as I do? We spent a long weekend together six years ago. We never really got to know each other."

"I didn't hear any complaints at the time," he muttered.

She smiled a little wistfully. "I had no

complaints. Then or now. It was a wonderful weekend. We had fun. And though we didn't intend to, we made a child together. But when it comes right down to it…we're basically strangers, aren't we?"

Strangers. The word bothered him more than he could explain, though he supposed technically it was accurate.

He set the bottle down on the counter with a thump and looked at her through narrowed eyes. He shifted his weight, bringing them close enough now that he could touch her with only a slight lift of his hand. "We're not exactly strangers."

"What would you call it, then?" she challenged, sounding suddenly weary. "We really don't know anything about each other."

"I remember a few things about you." Something made him reach out, cup her face between his hands. Something drove him to lower his mouth to only a breath above her surprise-parted lips. To murmur, "I remember that you tremble when I do this."

He brushed his lips across her right cheek, then the left, each time stopping just at the corner of her mouth. And felt her tremble.

"I remember the sound you make when I do this." He caught her lower lip gently between his teeth, then ran his tongue over it.

And heard the faint catch of breath in the back of her throat. A sound he'd heard echoed in a few erotic dreams since he'd left her.

He lifted his head to gaze down at her flushed face with a hunger he was having trouble keeping in check. She might be surprised to know how well he remembered certain things about that weekend. The hell he'd been through afterward, both in his deployment and his long recovery, had changed him in a lot of ways. Maybe Joanna had remained in the back of his mind as a symbol of that one last weekend when he'd felt the brash invincibility of youth.

Six years suddenly felt like a very long time, aging him far more than it should have. As Joanna had pointed out, she really didn't know him now at all—and he didn't know her. Time and vastly different experiences had altered them both, leaving nothing but hazy memories between them.

Well, that and a son, he added with a swallow that burned his throat. Recalled abruptly to his senses, he let go of her, starting to move reluctantly away. Only to be stopped by her hands on his shirt, gripping him, pulling him closer. She rose on tiptoe to meet him when he lowered his mouth again to hers with a muffled groan.

# CHAPTER FIVE

IF SHE CLOSED her eyes, Joanna could almost believe no time had passed since their last kiss. Adam's lips felt exactly as she remembered, moved against hers in the same way, tasted the same. His hands settled on her body with the same confidence and skill and her skin tingled with the same response.

Her mind emptying of all rational thought, she pressed closer, opening her lips beneath his to deepen the kiss. He took her up on that silent invitation immediately and thoroughly, proving she wasn't the only one still susceptible to their attraction. He was hard and solid against her, almost pulsing with a fierce masculine strength.

She'd called him a stranger. How, then, could he still feel so familiar? So right? Was it only that it had been too long since anyone had aroused this rarely-indulged side of her?

Lost in this kiss she had initiated, Joanna ran her palms up his chest. Exploring. Savoring. Despite his scars, his body was as firmly muscled now as she'd recalled.

She raised her arms even higher and slid her fingers into his hair. His thick, soft, still-wet-from-the-shower hair. Long enough now to tangle around her fingers, to tumble over her hands. This, she thought dimly, had changed. It felt so different from the military cut she remembered that she was startled back into the present.

Different. A different time, a different life.

*What was she doing?*

With a gasp, she pushed herself away from him, and he made no effort to stop her. He was probably as unsettled as she was that desire had heated so quickly between them. Not to mention that she'd so willingly fanned those flames.

His expression was grim when she stared up at him. His suddenly hooded eyes concealed his emotions. She suspected her own were written all over her face, and she wished she could be as controlled as he was.

"Okay," she said after a long pause, hating the quaver in her voice. "So we do remember a few things from before. But that doesn't change the fact that we don't know much about each other now."

His voice was rough when he conceded, "You're right, of course. And I can understand why you'd be hesitant to bring a near stranger into your son's life."

She couldn't help noting that he'd said "your" son. It sounded as though he still wasn't certain he would be a part of Simon's future. And even though she had her doubts about introducing him into Simon's life, she felt a jolt of regret at his hesitation, proving he had the power to hurt her—and, potentially, their child—if she wasn't careful.

A buzz from her pocket brought the stressful conversation to an end. "That's my phone alarm," she murmured, silencing it. "Simon will be back soon. He'll expect me to be waiting for him."

Adam nodded, looking almost relieved. "Unless you'd like me to walk with you, I'll hang here for a bit. I have a few calls to make before I head back to the office."

He couldn't have made it clearer that he needed space. From her.

Joanna didn't take offense. She needed a few minutes herself to recover from a kiss that had rocked her all the way to her spa-painted toenails. "No, I can find my way. Thanks."

Without another word, he reached to open

the door for her. He wasn't quite hustling her out…but he wasn't encouraging her to linger, either.

She stepped past him onto the walkway. Before he could close the door behind her, she was struck by yet another ill-advised impulse. "I'm taking Simon to dinner at The Crew's Galley tonight," she blurted before she could stop herself.

Adam seemed startled by the out-of-the-blue statement, but he merely nodded. "He should enjoy that. Food's good. Tell him to try the blackberry cobbler. Preferably à la mode. He said he likes à la mode."

"If you, um, if you want to hear about his outing to the maritime museum, you could—"

He interrupted before she could complete the hesitant invitation. "Trev and I and a couple other members of the staff are having dinner with some travel agents this evening. You know, talking up the place so they'll recommend us to their clientele."

"Of course. I hope it goes well. I'll be seeing you around." As she turned to head for the stairs, feeling foolish about so many things, she told herself it was a good thing Adam had other plans. She'd just as soon have Simon to herself, anyway.

ADAM REALLY WASN'T in the mood to schmooze and glad-hand that evening. Still, he owed Trevor too much to skip out when asked for a favor, and Trevor had requested his presence this evening. Of course, that had been before Joanna turned up with their son in tow. Trevor had asked discreetly before the dinner started if Adam had something else he'd rather do, but Adam had insisted he would fulfill his job responsibilities. Still, he was glad when the perfunctory duties were concluded and he and Trevor were alone again in Trevor's office.

"How about a drink?" Trevor moved toward the small wet bar built into the walnut credenza against one wall. "You look like you could use one."

Adam rarely drank, but for once he decided to indulge. He wouldn't say he needed a drink, exactly, but it sounded pretty good at the moment. "Yeah, thanks. Just a small one."

Trevor took down a bottle of single malt Irish whiskey and splashed an inch into three glasses. Adam was just about to ask who the third glass was for when someone tapped on the door, then entered without waiting for a response.

Adam sighed. "Really, Trev?"

Walter Becker accepted the glass Trevor

handed him and lifted it in Adam's direction. "Good to see you, too, Adam."

"Why are you here, Walt?"

"I invited him, obviously." Trevor gave Adam his drink. "Thought you might want to have a chat with him. Your decision. I haven't said a word about what's happening. If you'd rather not talk about it, we'll stick to baseball. Did either of you catch the Phillies and Blue Jays game last night?"

Walt leaned back against the counter as he took a sip of his whiskey, his dark eyes focused on Adam's face. "If you want to talk, I'm here. As your lawyer or your friend. Whichever you need. And I did watch the game last night, by the way, so we can argue about that idiotic call at the top of the sixth, if you'd rather."

"Trevor really hasn't told you the details?" Adam asked.

Trevor looked mildly insulted. "Of course not. This is your business, not mine. Walt and I are just letting you know you're not alone if you need anything."

Adam wasn't sure if that reminder was reassuring or unsettling. He was comfortable being alone, for the most part. He'd been on his own since he was seventeen.

He'd had pals in the army, and he considered Trevor and Walt good friends now. But by keeping a part of himself separate—the part that had grown up on his own and was comfortable being alone now—he always felt free to move on when the time was right. Handshakes all around, maybe a beer and a few laughs, and then on his way with vague promises to call next time he was in town.

He already owed Trevor for giving him a job. A home. A purpose when he'd desperately needed one. He was reluctant to go further into his debt. Or Walt's.

Still, he supposed it wouldn't hurt to consult a lawyer about how to deal with his financial obligations, whether through support payments or a savings account, whichever Joanna felt best. He didn't have much, but if anything happened to him, he would make sure Simon was his legal beneficiary. He was willing to take whatever official steps were necessary to make those arrangements. He wasn't sure he was prepared to step into the unfamiliar—and, frankly, terrifying—role of active father, but he would fulfill his legal and moral responsibilities to the child he'd created.

"If I ask for your professional advice, I will pay you for your time," he said to Walt, motioning with his still untasted drink. "I'm not asking for any freebies."

Walt took another sip before answering. Squarely built and ruddy complexioned, with salt-and-pepper hair cut close to his scalp, Walt was in his late thirties and looked like the tough ex-marine that he was. He carried himself with a confidence that made others have to take a second or third look to realize that his left arm was a prosthetic. He'd lost that limb below the elbow in a firefight from which he'd emerged as a decorated war hero. Somehow he'd still retained a dry humor and a strong sense of honor.

"Okay," he said, "deal. Will you at least let me offer a veteran's discount?"

Adam gave a weary chuckle. "Hell, yeah. I'm proud, not stupid."

The other men laughed, and then Trevor suggested they sit in the comfortable club chairs at one end of the long office. They finished their drinks while Adam gave Walt a quick rundown of the situation, being as discreet as possible for Joanna's sake.

"So, anyway," he concluded, "I'll want to make everything legal for the boy if, you know, something ever happens to me."

Walt raised an eyebrow. "The boy?"

"Simon." Had he been avoiding the name to keep his emotional distance? Because, if so, it wasn't working.

Call him by name, call him the boy, the kid, whatever, Adam still had a strong reaction to his son. He was grimly aware that one of those instinctive responses was to bolt. And while he would be running from the emotional pitfalls of fatherhood, he suspected he was almost as wary of the boy's too-intriguing mother. A woman who'd called him a stranger and then blown his mind with a kiss, leaving him confused and reeling. How was he supposed to deal with any of this?

Walt scratched his chin thoughtfully. "Before you do anything official, I would strongly recommend paternity testing. It's a simple procedure."

"I don't know that I need a paternity test. Unless it makes everything more legal for Simon."

"Seriously? You have no doubt that this is your child?"

Adam shrugged. "Trevor can tell you he looks just like me. And...well, I don't think Joanna would lie."

"Do you really know her well enough to be sure about that? You said you knew her for, what, a couple of days?"

He understood his friends' concern, but on this point he thought he could be confident. "Long enough to be pretty sure I'm the boy's father."

"We had dinner with Joanna last night," Trevor commented, the first time he'd spoken in a while. "She's a professor—a psychologist—so I doubt she needs the money. She seemed sincere about her surprise at finding Adam working here. There's no reason to suspect she has an ulterior motive."

The lawyer grunted. "In my experience, most everyone has an ulterior motive," he muttered.

Adam set his glass on a table with a thump. "She hasn't asked me for anything, and she's made it pretty clear she has no intention of doing so. If I need any legal assistance, it's strictly for the boy—for Simon's sake—not because I have any reservations about Joanna."

Seeing that his friends were both studying him, he realized he'd spoken more forcefully than he'd intended. Still, he'd meant every word. Whatever happened during the next week, he wanted to be clear that he trusted Joanna, at least as far as the boy's welfare was concerned.

Walt nodded. "So, my advice is for you to arrange DNA testing—just to make everything official—and talk with Joanna about what she considers fair regarding the boy's support. If she won't name a figure, then you should be prepared to make your own offer. Insurance and other medical responsibilities, college planning, estate decisions including guardianship in case of tragedy—all of that will need to be discussed, with contracts drawn up to protect all parties involved. And if you're interested in visitation rights, you'll need to come to an agreement about that, too. I'm telling you, Adam, I've seen these situations get ugly fast, and it's always the kids who suffer in the long run."

"Simon won't suffer because of me. I'll make sure of that." The boy deserved a better childhood than Adam had endured. Even if Adam had to remove himself from the picture to make that happen. "As for visitation, I'm not convinced that'll be an issue. Joanna is starting a new job soon that will take them to Seattle. I can't just leave my job for regular visits there, and it would hardly be fair to the kid to have to fly from one coast to another just to spend time with a father who wasn't even in his life for his first five years."

"Through no fault of your own," Trevor pointed out. "If you'd known of his existence, the situation would have been very different."

Adam squeezed the back of his neck, wondering again what he would have done if he'd heard about Joanna's pregnancy while in Afghanistan. Or if she'd found him in the hospital, working desperately to regain full use of his right arm, still jumpy and surly from what he'd been through. Would he have stepped up then, or would he have relinquished all rights and sent her away, leaving him to concentrate on his own recovery? He had to admit he'd been angry and self-focused then, before he'd been sure he wouldn't lose the arm, before he'd found a new purpose here at Wind Shadow.

Was he any more equipped for fatherhood now?

"Surely you want to get to know your son," Walt commented, looking surprised that it was even a consideration. "To let him get to know you."

Adam swallowed. "Like I said, he seems to be doing pretty well without me. The kid's a genius, Walt. Already reading, memorizing facts about oceanography. Knows about hydraulics and excavation and demolition, just from videos he watched."

"He is advanced for his age," Trevor conceded to Walt. "Carried on a conversation at dinner with the ease of a boy at least twice his age. I don't know if he's a genius, exactly, but he's definitely bright."

He turned to Adam then. "But regardless of how smart Simon is, he'd be lucky to have you in his life. You might not think so, Adam, but you'd be a great dad. Even if you only get to see the kid a few times a year, at least he'd know you'd be there for him."

Though he reminded himself that Trevor was known for his fierce loyalty, Adam couldn't help but be touched by the compliments that arrowed straight to his deepest insecurity. He wasn't sure he agreed, but he appreciated the vote of confidence. "I'll make certain Joanna knows they can always contact me if they need me. Beyond that, well, we'll see."

"I tend to agree with Trev," Walt commented. "A boy deserves to know his father. Mine wasn't exactly perfect, either, but he did the best he could, and I loved him for it. Keep this secret from Simon, and he will find out someday. Then he's going to be mad at both of you for making a decision like that on his behalf."

"I appreciate the advice, Walt." Adam left it at that.

"Just let me know what you need in a legal capacity. We'll get it all worked out."

"Thanks. So, Trev—about that lousy call last night in the sixth…"

His friends went along with his not-so-subtle change of direction. Within a few minutes they had a spirited, good-natured sports debate underway. Adam had to force himself to participate fully, but he was satisfied he made a credible attempt. If nothing else, it gave him something to focus on other than how much kissing Joanna had shaken him.

Getting tangled up with her again, as tempting as it might be, would be even less likely to end well this time.

"THE BLACKBERRY COBBLER was really good, Mom," Simon raved as Joanna tucked him in that night. "I think blackberry cobbler à la mode is my new favorite dessert."

Sitting on the side of his bed, she laughed softly. "Last night you said chocolate lava cake à la mode was your new favorite dessert."

He grinned. "Last night it *was* my favorite."

"I think you mostly like the à la mode part."

"Who doesn't like ice cream?"

Nestling Norbert into the pillow beside him, Joanna nodded toward the nightstand, where an impressive ship in a bottle was displayed. The square plastic bottle had been cut and glued back together with a rope trim hiding the seam, and the ship was made of Popsicle sticks and construction paper stuck on a sea of blue glitter. Simon was quite proud of that day's craft project. "That's going to look good in your bedroom. We'll have to wrap it carefully for the drive home."

"I bet we make something that has to do with sea turtles when we go see the turtle beach tomorrow. We'll have to pack one bag just with my shells and crafts, won't we?"

She smiled. "Yes. Which is I why I brought an extra bag just in case."

"Can we play minigolf in the morning, before Explorers Club?"

"Of course." She smoothed his hair. "You're having a good time here?"

"The best."

She felt her smile waver a bit before she asked, "Would you be terribly disappointed if we had to go home a couple of days early?"

The way his eyes widened provided the answer. "But Mom—you said we could stay until Sunday. Tomorrow's the turtle beach with Explorers Club. And the next day we're going to learn all about tide pools. And Friday you're going with me and the other kids and parents for the crab boil and the dolphin tour, remember? And I still haven't found a starfish. Or a Scotch bonnet. And what about—?"

"Calm down, Simon. You won't miss any of your plans, although I can't guarantee you'll find a Scotch bonnet," she added, touching the end of his nose with one fingertip as she gave in. "It was just a suggestion. But since it means so much to you, we'll stay for the full vacation. Okay?"

He nodded, gripping his stuffed dinosaur tightly against his chest with his lower lip still quivering. "You always keep your promises."

"I always try very hard to keep them." She leaned over to kiss his soft, sweet cheek, her heart so full it ached a little. "I love you, Padawan."

Amused by the teasing reference to one of his favorite sci-fi film series—introduced to him by his aunt, Maddie, of course—he giggled sleepily. "Love you, too, Jedi Master."

Feeling like the worst mother in the galaxy, she left the room, turning off the light behind her.

Though the windows were open and a breeze blew off the ocean, the room felt suddenly stuffy. Joanna stepped out onto the balcony and leaned against the railing, staring out over the moonlit grounds. She shouldn't have mentioned her fleeting thought of leaving early to Simon. It had been a cowardly impulse, fueled by kisses that shouldn't have happened. But damn, they'd been good. Just as she'd remembered. Maybe even better.

"Playing Juliet? That didn't end well, you know."

Adam's voice had drifted up from below the balcony, and for a moment she thought she'd imagined it. She leaned farther over the railing to find him standing some thirty feet below, gazing up at her from the shadow of a rustling palmetto. His face was half in darkness, giving him a mysterious, rakish appearance that elicited a wholly feminine jolt in her.

Seeing him again after their kiss that afternoon was as unsettling as she'd predicted, the very reason she'd been tempted to run. At least there was a healthy distance between them this time, so neither of them would be tempted to touch or taste.

She cleared her throat. "What are you doing down there?"

He motioned vaguely with one hand. "Just heading back to my quarters after that god-awful PR dinner."

He'd raised his voice only a little for her to hear him, which worked because no one else was in the courtyard. She could hear the sounds of music and voices from the bar area, but Seafoam Lodge was quiet for now. "I take it you didn't have a good time?"

"Lots of things I'd rather have been doing."

Something about his tone made her bite her lip as her head filled with images of alternatives. *Stop this, Joanna.* "Well—good night, Adam…"

But he wasn't quite ready to end the balcony chat. "How was your dinner at the buffet?"

She leaned over a bit more. "It was very good. Simon loved your dessert suggestion."

"Glad to hear it. Is he in bed?"

"Sound asleep. He's worn out from his busy day." She glanced around again. She still didn't see anyone, but that didn't mean they were truly alone. "Should you really be calling up to me this late? What if the people below me are trying to sleep?"

Adam's brief laugh was quiet, but she heard it, anyway. "JoJo, it's not even nine o'clock. That's only late at a vacation resort if you're five."

"Oh." Wrinkling her nose, she shook her head in bemusement. "Of course. I'm still in mommy mode, I suppose."

"Are you ever not in mommy mode?"

For a few reckless minutes that afternoon, she hadn't been. She'd been focused on Adam. On herself, as a still young, healthy woman with very natural desires. "Occasionally."

Their gazes met, and the distance between them seemed to shrink. Her hand twitched on the railing as she fought the impulse to reach out to him. And then he nodded and took an abrupt step back, deeper into the shadows. "I'd better get going. Good night, Joanna. Sleep well."

"You, too."

From her perch, she watched as he disappeared down the pathway toward his quarters. It was as if his departure triggered an end to an oddly quiet interlude. Muffled teenage laughter drifted on the breeze from the beach path. Two middle-age couples appeared from the pool area and ambled toward the building entrance below, their lively conversation and laughter easy and maybe a little rum-fueled. A wistful sigh escaped her, hanging in the fragrant, salty air when she turned to go back inside her darkened suite.

TORCHLIGHT OFFERED A breakfast menu and The Crew's Galley served a big buffet, according to the promotional material, but when given the choice Wednesday morning, Simon opted for the coffee and pastry shop patio outside the guest relations building.

Joanna agreed, but only with the condition that he order something healthier than a sweet pastry this time. He conceded cheerfully. Selecting a veggie wrap and coffee for herself, she followed Simon to a table close to the patio railing so he could people-watch while he ate. Swinging his legs beneath his chair, he chattered eagerly about the day's plans.

"Look, Mom. There's Mr. Adam."

Her heart skipped, but she kept smiling as she glanced over to where he indicated. Standing by a fountain a few yards away, Adam was in deep discussion with two maintenance workers holding toolboxes. Adam pointed and talked while the other men nodded, obviously taking instructions. A woman in the resort uniform stood with the small group, waving a hand as if to add her own input.

It was the first time Joanna had seen Adam in his leadership role, and she could tell he was a natural at it. No surprise that his employees smiled as they conferred with him. Adam was both personable and likeable in his own quiet, steady way.

She'd bet he got along very well with the staff here, which had no doubt accelerated his career. It was obvious that Trevor depended on him—and liked him. She was glad Adam had such a good friend. He'd seemed so solitary when they'd met.

She bit her lip. As she'd just observed, Adam didn't have to be alone. It had to be his choice.

How many hearts had he broken when he'd walked away?

She wouldn't let him break hers. And she damned sure wouldn't let him break her son's.

As though he sensed someone watching him, he looked around then, and waved when he saw Joanna and Simon. Simon waved back. Adam said something else to his coworkers, then turned and headed toward the coffee shop.

"Good morning," he said, pausing on the other side of the patio fencing.

"Hi, Mr. Adam. I'm having a breakfast sandwich and chocolate milk."

Adam's lips quirked as he took in the boy's chocolate milk mustache. "So I see."

Joanna handed Simon a napkin. "Wipe your mouth, honey."

After a quick swipe that smeared as much as it cleaned, Simon spoke to Adam again. "We're going to play minigolf after breakfast. And after lunch Miss Molly and Miss Deborah are taking me and the other kids to see sea turtles."

"Sounds like a fun day."

Adam bobbed his head in agreement. "After I get back from seeing the sea turtles, Mom's driving me into town for dinner, and we're going to a fun center with go-carts and arcade games and some kids' rides. Mom found it online and she asked if I wanted to go and I said yes. I like it here at the resort, too," he added earnestly as if to make sure Adam's feelings weren't hurt, "but I want to check out the fun center."

"I don't blame you," Adam assured him. "I've met the owner in passing, and I've heard it's a great place. Most kids your age like the bumper boats ride. You should give it a try."

Simon's face lit up in a way that was all too familiar to his mother. Before she could step in, he'd blurted, "You should go with us, Mr. Adam! Mom's not crazy about go-carts and if you go, I can ride with you in the big ones, not just the kiddie carts. And you can see your friend who owns the center."

"Oh, I—"

"Mr. Adam might have other plans this evening, Simon. Don't pressure him." *Take the hint, Adam.*

Adam hesitated so long, she decided he was having trouble figuring out the best way of politely declining Simon's impulsive invitation. So she was shocked when he said instead, "Sure, why not? It's been a while since I drove a go-cart, but I think I remember how."

While Simon bounced in his seat in anticipation, Joanna shot a questioning frown at

Adam. He shrugged, acknowledging her surprise. "What time were you planning to go?"

Faced with no other choice, she answered graciously. "Simon gets back from his field trip at four. I'll let him rest and freshen up, and then I thought we'd head out at about six."

Adam nodded. "I'll meet you in the Seafoam courtyard then. Have fun today, Simon. Beat your mom at minigolf, okay? I played with her once a long time ago. As I remember, she's not very good at figuring out where to aim the ball."

Simon laughed. "She's really not."

"I'm right here, guys."

Both grinned at her, and the eerie similarity of their smiles made her throat tighten. When Simon was this close to Adam, the resemblance was all she could see. She found almost none of herself in his features.

Adam sketched a little salute and stepped back. "I've got to get back to work. See you later, Skipper. JoJo."

Simon watched Adam disappear toward the entrance to the staff offices. "He called me Skipper. Like he calls you JoJo, huh?"

She forced a smile. "I guess he likes giving people nicknames. What made you invite him to join us tonight, Simon?"

"I like him. He's nice." He drained the last

of his milk, then set down his empty glass, suddenly frowning. "Is it okay that I asked him, Mom? Did I do something wrong?"

Was she dismayed by the invitation because she'd looked forward to spending a mother-son evening, just the two of them? Or because Adam Scott would be the third member of the party? Stupid questions, considering she knew the answer.

"No, Simon, you didn't do anything wrong."

"You like Mr. Adam, don't you?"

"Yes, of course."

"Are you almost done with your coffee? I'm ready to play minigolf."

There was no need to dwell on her anxiety about the coming evening. She had a whole morning to enjoy with her son first.

JOANNA AND SIMON had a great time playing minigolf—and while she didn't deliberately let him win, she didn't try very hard to beat him, either. He ended up one stroke below her, a victory he celebrated with a joyful dance that made her laugh.

They went for a prelunch swim in the big family pool—the other was an adult-only lap pool. Simon had a blast on the water slides and tubes and the pirate ship playground built into one end of the pool. She splashed with him for a time, then sat in a lounge chair and watched him play with some of the other children—two of whom he knew from Explorers Club.

Though the pool was well monitored by lifeguards, Joanna never took her eyes from Simon. As she had every day, she snapped several pictures of him playing. She would make a photo book of their vacation for them both to enjoy and remember.

She smiled when she recognized a child splashing cautiously on the pool steps while clinging to a blond woman who tried to get him to go a bit farther into the pool. "Just go down one more step, Cody," his mother urged. "The water feels good. It's just like a big bathtub. Look, you can play with your boat."

Cody whined and turned to bury his face in her thigh, shaking his head.

His mother sighed. "How do you know if you like it if you won't even try it? Look at all the other kids. They're having fun, aren't they? Don't you want to be like the other kids, Cody?"

Joanna almost winced, though she quickly schooled her expression.

Maybe Cody's mother sensed something, anyway. She looked up at Joanna with an expression that could only be described as despairing. "I just want him to have fun. To try new things."

*Like the other children.* The unspoken words seemed to hang in the air around them.

Joanna smiled. "I met Cody and his dad at the beach yesterday. Cody played for a little while with my son. He was obviously having fun. They both were. I'm Joanna, by the way."

"I'm Leah." But Leah didn't appear to be in the mood to socialize. The stress Joanna had noted in Ken seemed magnified in his wife.

It was difficult again to put her career aside and not try to analyze the couple's problems. Not that it took a psychologist to realize that the challenge of parenting a child with special needs was taking a toll on his parents. Perhaps especially his mother.

She wondered when was the last time Leah and Ken had taken a short vacation away from their son to nurture their own relationship. That, too, was important for all parents. All parents who wanted to stay together, anyway, she amended. A whole different set of guidelines had been crafted for coparenting between separated or divorced couples. It was entirely possible she needed to refresh herself on those guidelines soon.

Hoisting her clinging son onto her hip, Leah muttered, "Let's go find your daddy, Cody. You like to play with him."

Giving Joanna a nod, Leah hauled her

son away. Joanna could hear Cody saying, "Daddy, Daddy," as they disappeared toward the lodges.

Shaking her head, she ordered herself to stop being a psychologist and concentrate on her own complicated situation. "Simon, it's time to get out of the pool," she called out, standing. "You need to have a shower and lunch before your field trip."

Ninety minutes later, she walked Simon over to join his group at the van. Sea turtles seemed to rouse particular excitement in the six kids; all of them almost quivered with expectation as they leaped into the van. Joanna waved goodbye and then two of the other mothers, Brenna and Hillary, asked if she'd like to accompany them for cold drinks by the lake while their husbands played golf.

Brenna's nine-year-old daughter, Addison, joined them, and Joanna was amused by how proud the girl was to be included in the women's conversation. Joanna, Brenna and Hillary, who was pregnant with her second child, chatted superficially about a range of topics ranging from motherhood to popular literature to favorite recipes. The others learned during the conversation that Joanna was raising her son on her own.

"Sometimes I feel like a single mom, too,"

Brenna confided. "When my husband's not at the office, he's spending hours on a golf course. But at least this time he brought us someplace we can all enjoy while he hits those stupid balls around."

"I like it here," young Addison agreed. "Everybody's nice. My little sister Cami lost her favorite stuffed unicorn yesterday. Mr. Scott saw us looking for it and Daddy told him what happened, and Mr. Scott found it on the beach. Cami gave Mr. Scott a big hug when he brought it back to her. She almost knocked him down."

Her mother laughed ruefully. "It was quite a family drama. I think Mr. Scott was a bit startled by Cami's enthusiasm. Both he and Mr. Farrell are so accommodating. They and the rest of the staff certainly go out of their way to make their guests feel pampered, don't they?"

Joanna tried to picture Adam being tackle-hugged by a tearful five-year-old. Her amusement had an oddly wistful edge to it. She wondered what these nice women would think if they heard exactly how Joanna was connected to "Mr. Scott."

Addison rolled her eyes expressively when talking about her little sister, who was on the sea turtle outing with Simon and the others, but it was obvious she was fond of the child she called "the brat." Patting her swollen tummy, Hillary said she hoped her daughter, Emily, who was also on the turtle expedition, would get along well with her new brother.

Still trying to stay involved in the adult conversation, Addison turned to Joanna. "Do you have any other kids, Miss Zielinski?"

"No, just Simon."

Addison frowned as if it were hard for her to imagine life without her sister. "Don't you *want* any more kids?"

Brenna cleared her throat. "Addison, dear, your questions are getting rather personal."

Joanna silently agreed but decided a brief answer wouldn't hurt. "I would have loved more children, but it just didn't work out that way for me. Still, I consider myself very fortunate to have Simon."

At thirty-three, she was young enough to have more children—but it wasn't something she wanted to do again on her own. Her career was evolving, she was facing the big move, and she wasn't dating anyone seriously enough to consider having children with him.

"Hi, Mr. Scott!"

Joanna nearly jumped out of her chair as Addison cheerfully greeted Adam standing behind Joanna. Could Fate really have brought him close enough to have heard her speak at just that moment? If so, Fate really seemed to have it out for her this week.

"Hello, ladies."

Though Adam's tone was cordial, Joanna turned her head just in time to see a flicker in his eyes that indicated that he had, indeed, overheard at least part of the conversation. She told herself it was silly to be so self-conscious; it wasn't as if she'd admitted anything embarrassing.

Standing beside one of the employees she'd seen him with earlier, he nodded politely, including Joanna in the impersonal greeting. He and the other man moved on, and Joanna made an effort to pull her gaze away and return her attention to her companions. But she found them all gazing after Adam with admiring expressions, proving the effect his easy smile had on both happily married women and schoolgirls. Not to mention Joanna herself.

She still wasn't sure why he'd accepted Simon's invitation to join them that evening. Had he felt cornered, unable to decline? Did he see it as a way to spend more time with Simon, and if so, was he banking memories before they went their separate ways? Or did he want Simon to get to know him better before they revealed that Adam was his father?

She supposed the only way to find out was

to flat-out ask him at some point tonight. They couldn't continue to dance around each other like this. He'd had a couple of days to adjust, and now it was time to get some issues settled. At least where Simon was concerned.

The impromptu mocktail party ended then, and Joanna parted from her new friends with good wishes all around. She spent a pleasant hour afterward in the resort shops, where she perused a colorful selection of tote bags, scarves and jewelry. She wasn't avoiding another encounter with Adam, she assured herself. It was simply nice to have the opportunity to browse at her leisure. Simon would have been thoroughly bored.

She found her attention drawn to a display of boys' clothing, in particular a bright green T-shirt bearing the resort logo. The shirt was very similar to the polo worn by resort staff. She knew Simon would like it, but still she hesitated before adding it to her purchases. She had no doubt he'd wear the shirt often when they were back home. Every time she saw him in it, she'd notice that it made him look even more like Adam. But then, she would always be aware of that resemblance, anyway, she thought, and added the shirt to the items she'd already selected.

# CHAPTER SIX

ADAM ALMOST CANCELED half a dozen times during the afternoon, finding at least that many excuses for why he shouldn't go out with Joanna and Simon. What had made him accept Simon's invitation? He knew Joanna had hoped he'd decline; the waves of mental suggestion couldn't have been more obvious from her body language. Was he just stubborn enough that those signals had been part of the reason he'd said yes? Or had it been that he'd looked into an eager pair of gray eyes just like his own and hadn't been able to say no?

He hadn't exactly intended to tell Trevor his plans for the evening, but he'd blurted it out when Trevor invited him to sit in on a last-minute poker game with a couple of other friends. Trevor had looked surprised for a moment, but then nodded. "It's a good way to spend some quality time with them. Just friends hanging out at the go-cart track."

"Something like that, yeah."

"Like trying on fatherhood for fit."

Adam shot his friend a hard look. "That's not what I'm doing."

He got a bland smile in return. "Oh? My mistake."

"Damn it, Trev, this isn't easy."

Trevor grew serious then. "I know. I don't mean to make light of it. It's an awkward situation all around."

Adam squeezed the back of his neck. "Tell me about it."

"You'll work it out, Adam. And you know I'm here if there's anything you need."

"I know. Thanks, Trev."

"Enjoy your time with your son."

The words had made Adam swallow hard as he nodded and walked away.

Now it was almost six o'clock and he wondered if it was too late to come up with an excuse. He'd headed out on patrols in a war zone with less anxiety than he was feeling at the prospect of spending a few hours with a five-year-old boy. Not to mention the boy's mother. Thinking of Joanna was almost as unsettling.

She was the one who'd pointed out how odd it was that they'd been lovers, that they'd made a child together, but knew so little about each other. And while he still wanted her whenever he saw her, he wasn't sure how to spend several hours with her knowing from the start that the evening wouldn't end with them in bed together. He'd been comfortable with a casual fling with Joanna, but the idea of co-parenting with her for the rest of his life made him break out in a cold sweat. He'd never committed to anything for that long; could he develop that capability now?

He could still back out of this evening's plans, he thought even as he stepped into the Seafoam Lodge courtyard. He could say that something had come up—he didn't have to add that it was a poker game with Trev. He doubted Simon would be too disappointed, considering the boy barely knew him. Joanna would probably be relieved not to have to keep up a cheery act in front of the kid.

"Hi, Mr. Adam!"

Too late. Adam looked around to find Simon bouncing out of the building and into the courtyard, followed more sedately by his mother. Both were dressed for a casual evening, Simon in shorts, a striped T-shirt and sneakers, Joanna in one of her favored sundresses. She'd twisted her hair into a loose knot that bared her slender neck. Damn, she looked good.

He cleared his throat and dragged his gaze from the woman to nod to the boy. "Hey, Skipper, how was the turtle tour?"

"So fun! We learned tons about sea turtles and we made turtles out of green plastic bowls for shells and plastic cutouts for the head and tail and feet. I'll show it to you later if you want. And Mom bought me a shirt that looks kind of like the one you wear when you work. It's green and it says Wind Shadow Resort and it has the little sailboat and everything. I like the shirt you're wearing now, too, but it doesn't say Wind Shadow."

"That's because I'm not working tonight."

Simon drew a hand from behind his back, revealing a sheet of paper gripped in his little fingers. "I made you something."

"Um—" Caught off guard, Adam blinked a couple times. "You made something for *me*?"

Grinning broadly, the boy nodded. "Do you like it?"

Adam examined the sheet he now held. Using crayon and pencils, Simon had created a colorful scene depicting features of the resort. He'd drawn buildings and fountains, figures in a swimming pool, an ocean in the background with fish on top of exaggerated waves, even a fairly recognizable van driving away with smiling faces in the windows. Two other figures—one a woman in a yellow dress, the other a man in a green shirt and light brown pants—waved goodbye to the van. Were those people supposed to be Joanna and him?

The page was completely filled with the artwork, but on the back, Simon had written in shaky block letters, "To Mr. Adam, from Simon Z."

Adam tried to speak lightly, as if he hadn't just been rattled by a five-year-old's friendly gesture. "This is really great, Skipper. Thanks."

"You're welcome. I like to draw."

"I can see that. You're quite an artist."

Simon giggled, preening with pride.

Taking advantage of the boy's momentary silence, Adam looked at Joanna. She was chewing her lip, a habit he recognized as a sign of nerves. He gave her what he hoped was a reassuring smile before asking, "How was your day, JoJo?"

As if realizing what she was doing, she released her lip and managed a credible smile in return. "Very nice, thank you. I did some shopping and chatted with a couple of other day camp moms. I heard about your heroic rescue of Cami's stuffed unicorn, by the way."

He grimaced at the reminder of yesterday's dramatics, and a semihysterical little girl who'd all but taken him down with a too-fervent tackle when he'd returned her toy.

"Yeah. I never know what I'll be doing from one day to another."

Mostly he sat in meetings, set schedules and placed orders, double-checked others' work, kept an eye on vendors and subcontractors—whatever Trevor asked of him—but when a guest asked for help looking for a stuffed unicorn, he pitched in if he could. Kept things interesting, he supposed.

"Mom said we can have pizza for dinner, if it's okay with you. I like vacations because we don't always have to eat healthy," Simon said with a laugh. "Do you like pizza, Mr. Adam?"

"Who doesn't like pizza?"

Simon beamed. "I know, right? But Grampa hates pizza. He said it's just junk food and nobody should eat junk food."

"Simon." His mother placed a hand on his shoulder. "That's enough information for now."

"Oh. Sorry, Mom."

She smiled down at him. "I know you're excited. But save a few words for later, okay?"

The boy grinned up at her. "I'm sure I'll have more words to say."

Laughing, she gave him a hug. "I have no doubt."

She really was a great mom. Adam could tell she and Simon had a special relationship.

They were very close, but there was still no question about who was in charge.

Adam had lost his own mother a long time ago, but his relationship with her hadn't been as tight as Simon's with Joanna. She'd moved him place to place and gotten involved with one loser after another, only to spend weeks moping in her room after each relationship crashed. He'd been closer to his maternal grandmother, who'd been the only steady adult in his childhood.

He'd seen his footloose father only sporadically through the years. His dad had died in a car accident while Adam was still in boot camp, leaving him with no immediate family members and few extended ones. The army had become his family, and then the resort his home. For now, at least.

He'd never expected to find himself suddenly dealing with another very close relative. His son. Who knew him only as "Mr. Adam."

"Would you like to go in my car?" he offered to Joanna.

"Thank you, but Simon's booster seat is in my car, so it's probably best if we take that."

"I have to ride in a booster seat until I'm eight," Simon clarified, always eager to chime in. "I'm kind of small for my age, but Aunt

Maddie says I'll probably have a growth spurt and someday I'll be taller than her and Mom."

"Yeah, I was pretty scrawny at your age, too. I shot up in high school, so you'll—" Realizing what he was saying, Adam shot a quick look at Joanna, who was frowning. "Kids grow at different rates," he amended awkwardly. "I'm sure your aunt is right about that growth spurt."

Joanna relaxed and Simon seemed satisfied, already chattering about pizza and go-carts as they turned to move together toward guest parking.

Adam had the uncomfortable feeling that he was walking on eggshells rather than a pebbled path. He told himself he was going to have to be more careful than that in his interactions with the boy, at least until he and Joanna had another chance to talk privately. Which, of course, came with yet another set of potential pitfalls.

Swallowing a sigh, he shook his head at the complex situation he'd become tangled up in. Which only became more complicated when a little hand slid into his and he looked down to find Simon grinning up at him.

Was the boy this open and chummy with everyone? Adam's less trusting nature made him believe Joanna would have to warn Simon about that. Maybe the boy felt safe with him because he represented the resort, or because Joanna had acknowledged meeting him before. Or maybe Simon felt some vague bond he couldn't quite explain. Maybe Adam wasn't the only one who had gazed into a pair of gray eyes and felt a sense of recognition.

He looked up to find Joanna glancing back at them as she led the way to her car. He couldn't completely read her expression, but he thought she looked worried. He supposed he understood. She didn't want her son to be hurt. That was one sentiment with which he agreed completely. Adam didn't want any kid to be hurt, disappointed, injured—but most especially, he realized, this particular kid.

His kid.

JOANNA HAD EXPECTED Simon to keep the conversation moving during the outing, and he didn't let her down. Over dinner in a noisy, bustling pizza parlor, he shared with Adam every minute detail he'd learned about sea turtles and other aquatic life on the Carolina coast. He talked so fast he barely seemed to breathe, pausing only occasionally to take big bites of his Hawaiian pizza.

To give him credit, Adam didn't look bored. He listened intently and asked encouraging questions, though she couldn't be positive whether it was because he was so genuinely interested or because, like her, he was letting Simon control the conversation.

"Obviously you learned a lot today, Simon," he said after a while. "You want to be a marine biologist? Sounds like you're getting a good start."

Wiping pizza sauce from his chin with a napkin, Simon nodded. "Mom says I'll learn a lot about marine biology in Seattle. We'll live in an apartment close to Puget Sound. That's part of the Pacific Ocean."

Adam kept his expression pleasant but not particularly revealing. "I've heard it's nice. I've never been there myself."

"I haven't, either. Mom's been a couple times, and she showed me lots of pictures. Grampa said it rains all the time, but Mom helped me look it up on the internet, and Seattle just gets thirty-seven and a half inches of rain a year. Atlanta gets an average of fifty inches of rain a year, so that's even more. Mom says people think it rains all the time in Seattle because it's spread out more and in smaller amounts than the big rainstorms we get in Atlanta."

Adam looked suitably impressed. "That's interesting. It's great that you like learning new things. And that you remember what you learn so well."

Simon nodded earnestly. "It's fun to learn. And Aunt Maddie says I just like to talk," he added with one of the impish grins that always went straight to his mother's heart.

Adam laughed, a rich, warm sound that also affected her a bit too strongly. "Yeah, I got that impression."

Simon giggled and took another bite of his pizza.

Adam turned to Joanna while the boy was busy chewing. "How about you, JoJo? Did you want to be a psychologist when you were a kid?"

She answered candidly. "I thought I wanted to be a surgeon, like my father, or a high school administrator, like my mother. When I got to college, I realized I was chasing someone else's dreams rather than my own, and I focused on what most interested me. By the end of my sophomore year, I'd already set a goal to earn a doctorate in psychology."

"Which you did."

"Yes. My first vacation here was my reward to myself for doing so. I saw an online ad for the resort and it looked so nice, I couldn't resist booking a reservation."

The mention of that previous trip made Adam's easy smile fade a bit. "You were young for a PhD. I had no idea you were already a doctor."

So many things they hadn't known about each other then, she thought wistfully. So many things they still didn't know. "I was twenty-seven."

His eyelids lowered, but not before she saw something that made her frown. "How old were *you* when we met?"

His mouth twisted into a wry smile. "I was a couple months away from turning twenty-six."

"Oh." Why did it rattle her to find out he was more than a year younger? As she recalled, Adam had looked older than twenty-five then. He looked older than thirty-one now. Not in a bad way. In fact, in a damned good way, she thought, her gaze tracing the firm line of his jaw, the intriguing curve to his sexy lips. Lips that had so recently captured hers.

She raised her eyes to meet his again, and his expression now made her cheeks warm. Had she looked at his mouth longer than she'd realized? He smiled, shrugged, then turned back to Simon to share a few more facts about sea turtles the boy hadn't learned on the expedition earlier, to Simon's delight.

The server brought their check and set it down automatically in front of Adam. Because she'd come up with this plan, Joanna reached for it, but Adam gave her a look that made her draw her hand back.

"Least I can do," he muttered, and pulled out his wallet.

"You're supposed to say, 'Thank you, Mr. Adam,'" Simon said to Joanna in a stage whisper, giving her a nudge under the table.

"Thank you, Mr. Adam," she parroted with a forced smile, making her son laugh and Adam chuckle.

The sprawling fun center was a kids' fantasy complete with colorful rides, flashing lights and cheerful music. The rides included a small Ferris wheel, bumper boats in a concrete "lagoon," a merry-go-round and whirling ladybug cars. Four go-cart tracks twisted around the central arcade building, each designated for different ages and skill levels of drivers. Simon's eyes were wide as he gazed around, trying to take it all in at once.

"What do you want to do first, Skipper?"

Gazing up at Adam, Simon spread his arms. "All of it."

Chuckling, Adam put one hand on Simon's shoulder and one on Joanna's back. "We'd better get started, then."

Joanna felt the warmth of his hand through her thin cotton dress. The fabric might as well not have been there, considering the way she responded to his innocuous touch. During the years they'd been apart, she'd thought of him, of course, as Simon's biological father. But she'd almost forgotten how strongly she'd reacted to him during those heady days they'd had together. Reminding herself that they were now surrounded by children—including her own—she tried to push the hormones and erotic memories aside.

For the next hour, they played with Simon, making sure he had a wonderful time. And Joanna enjoyed herself, too, though her awareness of Adam simmered beneath the surface all evening, fueled by fleeting touches and lingering glances. Anyone watching them would assume they were a family—mom, dad, son. They would be right, of course, though she doubted any of them could imagine the circumstances. She knew Adam was equally aware of the impression they gave. True to his word, Adam took Simon for rides in the go-carts. Both snugly strapped in, they sped around curves and up and down inclines, to the boy's squealing delight. Afterward Adam stood with her on the sidelines and called out suggestions when Simon drove the kiddie carts. The boy basked in his attention.

She propped her elbows on the low fence beside Adam, watching as Simon maneuvered the small blue car with an expression of intense concentration. "He's having a wonderful time. He's pretty good at driving that thing, isn't he?"

"Yeah. Ten years or so, he'll be wanting a real one."

She groaned. "Don't remind me."

"You're doing a hell of a job with him."

The off-handed compliment shouldn't have pleased her as much as it did. "You're good with him, too," she said a bit hesitantly. "He likes you."

Adam kept his eye on the boy in the blue car. "Yeah. His new buddy, Mr. Adam."

She moistened her lips before asking quietly, "Would you rather he called you Dad?"

She couldn't actually hear him swallow over the roars, buzzes, beeps and shrieks surrounding them, but she sensed her question had made him uncomfortable. She wished she understood better why he was so intimidated. Was it the daunting responsibility inherent in fatherhood—or the difficulty in walking away from it once accepted? Whichever, he pretended like he hadn't heard her. Flushed and windblown, his cowlick sticking straight up, Simon ran up to them after his ride ended. "That was fun. I drove good, didn't I?"

"You were the best driver on the track," Adam assured him.

The way Simon's face lit up in response to the compliment cooled Joanna's irritation a bit. "Really?"

"No doubt."

"Adam? Adam Scott?" The man's voice was barely audible over the noise around them.

They all turned to see an older man with a shock of silver hair and black-rimmed glasses above a prominent nose. His neon-yellow T-shirt was emblazoned in orange with the name of the fun center beneath a drawing of a bright red go-cart. "I thought that was you, Adam. Good to see you again."

Adam shook the man's hand. "Nice to see you, too, Leon. Looks like business is going well."

"It is that time of year. How are things out at Wind Shadow?"

"Busy as always."

Leon looked then at Joanna and Simon, giving them a broad smile that revealed a flash of gold crown. "I didn't know you were married, Adam. Your boy looks just like you. Spitting image. Good looking kid."

An awkward silence fell over Adam and Joanna. Simon might have been the only one who didn't notice. He laughed. "Mr. Adam isn't my father. He's our new friend."

"Ah. My mistake." Leon looked quickly from Adam to Joanna when no one contradicted Simon.

Adam filled in the gaps. "Leon, this is Joanna Zielinski and her son, Simon. They're visiting our resort from Georgia."

"Nice to meet you, ma'am. Simon. Having a good time on your vacation?"

"I like your place," Simon gushed. "We've been having fun."

"Glad to hear it." Reaching into his deep pocket, Leon drew out a handful of game tokens for the arcade. "Here, win yourself some tickets. Maybe you'll get a good prize."

Clutching the tokens in both hands, Simon gasped in pleasure. "Thank you, Mr. Leon!"

The older man patted his head. "You're welcome. Have a good time. Come back and see us again."

Fortunately Simon was so excited about the free game tokens that he didn't mention Leon's comment about how much Simon looked like Adam. Still, the encounter had brought home to Joanna—and probably to Adam—that the more time she and Simon spent with him, the more likely it became that the bright little boy would figure out the truth on his own. And that was something neither of them wanted—especially, apparently, Adam.

WORN OUT FROM his busy day, Simon was sound asleep in his booster seat by the time Joanna parked at the resort. She unbuckled him, and Adam reached around her to pick him up. "I'll carry him."

She moved out of the way, letting him take the boy out of the car. She noticed that Adam shifted Simon quickly to his left side, grimacing just a bit when he put the weight on his right arm.

"Do your injuries still bother you?" she asked him, hoping he wouldn't mind the question.

He seemed annoyed with himself for letting the discomfort show, but he answered honestly. "There's still some weakness in the right arm. Can't really lift it higher than my ear. It doesn't bother me too badly. I can still use it for most of what I need to do."

Reminded again of what he'd endured, she bit her lip as she led the way to her suite. She didn't even want to think about how he'd sustained those injuries. All those months of her pregnancy, she'd pictured him being a carefree bachelor who maybe thought of her occasionally. If only she'd known he was in a war zone, then in a hospital…well, she didn't know what she'd have done differently.

She unlocked the door and held it open while Adam carried Simon in. Simon didn't even stir, his limbs loose, his sweet face flushed with sleep. Nor did he rouse when Adam asked, "Where do you want him?"

She motioned toward the bedroom where Simon slept. "Just carry him in there. I'll get him into his pajamas."

Adam lowered the boy gently to the bed, then stepped back. "I'll wait for you on the balcony."

She should have known he wouldn't slip quietly out now. "I won't be long."

He nodded and turned to leave the room.

She joined him on the balcony fifteen minutes later. He leaned against the rail, gazing out over the resort as she had done the evening before. He hadn't turned on the lights, so he stood in deep shadow. Her heart fluttered foolishly at the sight of him there, all dark and brooding and tousled from an evening of playing with their son.

She moistened her lips. "He's out cold. He pretty much sleepwalked through changing into pajamas and brushing his teeth."

"Ran out of fuel, huh? Wish I had half the energy he's got when he's awake."

Laughing softly, she said, "No kidding. Think how much we'd get done in a day."

"You, uh, don't think he read anything into Leon's comment, do you? About looking like me, I mean."

She stopped smiling. "I don't think so. Too much else was going on at the time. And then Leon gave him the free tokens, and that tickled him so much he forgot about it."

"He does look a lot like me, doesn't he?"

"As Leon said—your spitting image," Joanna murmured.

"Did you remember?"

She was confused for a moment, but then understood what he was asking. "Did I remember what you looked like? Yes, of course. For one thing, I had a living reminder."

He let a few moments pass, then spoke again without turning to look at her. "What was it like for you? Going back home to find yourself pregnant, I mean."

"It was…" She hesitated, trying to sum up the past six years in one word. She finally settled on, "…challenging."

After mulling over that response, he asked, "Did it affect your career? Make things difficult for you in that respect?"

She shrugged. "There were some adjustments in my career, of course. I had to arrange maternity leave, and after I went back to working full-time, I had to plan for sick days and school meetings and programs. I was only able to take ten weeks for maternity leave, but I was fortunate enough to find Rose, Simon's nanny, who is a treasure. She took care of him full-time while I worked until he was three, when I enrolled him in a preschool because I could already tell he needed more intellectual stimulation. Now she watches him after school and on school breaks when I have work obligations. He considers her his second grandmother."

"He'll miss her when you move."

It wasn't a question, but she nodded. "And vice versa. They're crazy about each other. I promised to keep in touch and send pictures, and I assured her we'd come see her every time we visit the family."

"So…family. How did they feel about your pregnancy? Your father, the surgeon? How did he react?"

So he remembered Simon's spontaneous chattering during that dinner with Trevor. "My parents are…very traditional." To say the least. "They're only in their late fifties, but both come from conservative Catholic backgrounds. They might have expected something like this from my younger sister, who's always been a rebel and a rule-breaker, but I think I shocked them. To be honest, they weren't happy with me at all, and being so career-focused themselves, they worried that I'd put mine in jeopardy. It took them a few months to adjust, but they came around. They didn't disown me or anything that drastic, but they have a way of making their disappointment known."

Even in the near darkness, she could see Adam's frown crease his face, which was still in profile to her. "How do they treat Simon?"

"They aren't demonstrative people, but they love Simon in their own way, and he knows they do. My sister adores him. He's very close to his aunt, Maddie, and as I mentioned to you before, she and I have grown much closer since all of this happened."

Maddie had confessed late one night during Joanna's pregnancy that their parents' disapproval of Joanna's behavior had made her feel more connected to the older sister who had always seemed such an impossibly flawless model to follow. Joanna hadn't realized until then how pressured Maddie had felt all her life to be more like her dutiful sister. Now that she looked back on their childhoods, she didn't blame Maddie for rebelling against those expectations, or even for resenting the sibling who'd made her life more difficult. Joanna was fond and proud of the strong, independent woman Maddie had become.

Adam brought her back to the present. "You said your mother is a school administrator?"

He never seemed to forget anything she said, even in passing. "Yes, she's the principal of a Catholic high school in Atlanta."

"Another PhD?"

"Yes."

"And your sister? What does she do?"

"She's an attorney."

"Of course."

Raising her left eyebrow, Joanna added, "A public defender."

"Huh. I doubt your father likes that."

She smiled. "I wouldn't say that's why she chose that particular job…but I'm not saying it wasn't part of the reason, either."

"So, a doctor, a school administrator, a lawyer and a psychologist. Come from a family of underachievers, do you?"

She didn't quite know how to respond to the odd note in his tone, so she merely smiled again.

He kept up the low-key inquisition. "What else changed for you after Simon? Did your friends stand by you? I guess your dating life took a hit. You, uh, haven't married or anything along the way, have you?"

"No, I haven't married. I've dated, of course, but not a lot, and never seriously. I didn't want to risk disrupting Simon's life unless I knew there was a future in it. And, well, that's just never happened."

Adam continued to gaze out at the landscape, though she knew he listened intently. Leaning against the railing, she imitated his posture. Though she wasn't looking at Adam now, she was so focused on him that she was only dimly aware of the beauty of the moonlight glinting on the ocean waters ahead of them.

"What about you?" she asked, trying to speak casually. "Never married? Come close?"

His reply was equally offhanded. "No to both. Never really thought of myself as the marrying kind."

She wasn't sure why the statement gave her a jolt. It wasn't as if she expected anything from him for herself; the decisions facing them were all about Simon's best interests.

"It sounds as if you've handled this all very well," he said.

She shrugged. "I'm sure I've made my share of mistakes, but I've done the best I could. I have no complaints. No regrets. Simon has brought me nothing but joy, and I wouldn't trade him for anything."

Perhaps it was the vehemence of her tone that made him finally turn to look at her. She kept her gaze steady, letting him see that she had meant every single word.

After a moment, he nodded. In a gesture that was familiar to her by now, he reached up to the back of his neck. "For what it's worth, I'm sorry for what you went through after I left you."

She moistened her lips, tasting salt and the faint memory of his kisses. "Yes, well, I'm sorry you had to go to war. And that you were so badly injured. Something tells me you were much more alone than I was."

He didn't contradict her. Neither did he look particularly regretful about it. Was he a man who preferred being alone, not held down by family ties? If so, what effect would that have on his relationship, if any, with his son?

"Why did you go with us this evening, Adam?" she asked, wanting to at least try to understand what he was thinking. "If you aren't even sure you want to acknowledge your relationship to Simon, why did you want to spend those hours with him?"

He scowled, drawing back slightly as though

in self-defense. "He caught me off guard. I didn't know how to say no without hurting his feelings."

"You could have made up an excuse."

His frown deepening, Adam shook his head. "I'm not going to lie to him."

Only by omission, she added silently, but decided it wasn't the right time to challenge him. Probably the deception bothered her more than Adam because she knew Simon so much better. It was only natural that she felt protective.

Adam made a muffled sound as though he'd somehow sensed her thought, or perhaps shared it. "Trevor said I was trying on fatherhood for size tonight. I told him it wasn't like that."

She bit her lip for a moment, then asked quietly, "But was he wrong?"

He shifted awkwardly. "I guess I just wanted to get to know Simon a little. He's a special kid, JoJo. You've done a great job with him."

There was no reason for the praise to bring tears to her eyes, but still she found herself blinking rapidly and clearing her throat before she could speak. "Thank you."

"It doesn't surprise me, of course. I suspected when I met you that you were the type."

She felt her eyebrows rise. "The type?"

He shrugged. "You know. Home. Family. Stability. I knew from a few things you let slip that our weekend together was out of character for you. We weren't looking for anything more than a bit of fun for a few days, but I figured even then that you'd want more from someone someday. I didn't mean to screw that up for you."

She shuffled her feet, uncomfortable with his comments. "Like I said, I wouldn't trade Simon for anything. I'm not so sure I'm all that domestic, anyway. I think of myself more as a working single mother."

"Who's going to take care of Simon when you're working in Seattle?"

She supposed the slight note of concern she heard in his voice was understandable. She spoke reassuringly. "He'll start first grade in the fall, and when he's not in school, I'll hire a nanny. I've already gotten a few recommendations from associates I'll be working with there. You needn't worry. My responsibilities to Simon will always take priority over my career or any other part of my life."

He turned his head to look at her then. "I don't doubt that. It was just a question."

Had she sounded defensive? Probably. She dealt with the same qualms and insecurities any working mother faced, perhaps especially any single working mother.

Adam looked away again, his profile stark in the pale light. "I can count on both hands the number of times I saw my dad while I was growing up. Sometimes I wondered if he even remembered he had a son when he wasn't around. My mom had issues of her own, so I was pretty much raised by her mother, my Grams. By the time I was seventeen, I was on my own. I kicked around a while, somehow finished high school, joined the army. With Trevor's encouragement, I've taken a few college business classes since I started working here, but I'm no academic. Never will be."

Apparently she wasn't the only one dealing with insecurities. This was the most he'd told her about his childhood, and it didn't sound like a particularly happy one.

"Not everyone is cut out for academia," she said, trying to speak lightly. "There have been plenty of times when I wondered if I was. I don't care for the politics or the archaic expectations, but I love my work, so I accept the trade-off."

"What I'm trying to say is, I don't know anything about being a father. Never really thought I'd be one—and for sure not the occasional pop-in one like my own. A kid like

Simon—smart, eager, outgoing—well, he deserves more than I had."

She couldn't disagree with him on that. Simon did deserve more than a father who was so stingy with his attention that his son wondered if he even remembered him. She couldn't imagine Adam would become that type of parent, especially considering how disapproving he sounded about his own father's behavior—but did she know him well enough to be sure?

Just because he'd walked out without a goodbye after their casual weekend together didn't mean he would do the same with his son. Right? But she couldn't help worrying; worry seemed to come with the territory when it came to child rearing.

She wasn't sure how Adam interpreted her silence, but he sighed and turned to trace a fingertip along her jaw. "Don't frown, JoJo. We'll work something out. Whatever happens, thanks for letting me tag along this evening. I had a good time."

Her nerve endings tingled in the wake of his touch. Her voice was barely louder than a whisper when she said, "I had fun, too."

His other hand rose so that he cupped her face between his palms. She couldn't see his eyes clearly in the shadows, but she could tell he focused on her mouth. She felt her lips part as she drew in a shaky breath.

His thumbs rotated lazily against her cheeks. "We had a lot of fun together before, didn't we?"

"We did," she agreed, resting her hands on his chest. She could feel his heart beating through his shirt. Strong, steady—maybe a little faster than usual? She knew her own was racing.

His face was close enough for her to feel his breath on her skin. "I know I wasn't there for you, but I never forgot how good it was between us, even if it was only for a few days. If you—when you talk to Simon someday about how he was conceived, I don't want him to think it was just a weekend fling."

When *she* talked to Simon? *If* she talked to Simon? His phrasing added to her unease, but he didn't give her a chance to speak before he closed his mouth over hers with an intensity that implied he'd resisted the temptation as long as he could.

It happened every time Adam kissed her. Her pulse raced, her knees weakened, her skin warmed and tightened, becoming exquisitely sensitized to every point of contact between them. It had been that way six years ago, and time hadn't changed a thing in that respect.

She'd kissed other men in the ensuing years, and some had been quite nice—but she had to concede now that she'd never responded to any other man the way she did to Adam. She couldn't imagine that she ever would, whatever the outcome of this unplanned reunion. There was something special—unique—about the chemistry between her and Adam Scott. Had been from that meeting on the beach.

Because it was so rare, so fleeting, she seized the opportunity to enjoy. To savor. She gripped his shirt in both hands, rising up on her toes to make her lips more accessible to him. He took full advantage, drawing her into the deepest shadows to give them maximum privacy on the balcony, his arms going around her to pull her high against him.

Whatever difficulties his injuries had left him, his arms were hard and muscled, strong bands around her. Supportive rather than suppressive, they gave her a sense of security rather than concern. His mouth was ravenous, urging rather than demanding. And she responded with a matching hunger of her own.

His tongue plunged. Hers welcomed it. His hands swept. Hers gripped harder. Their legs tangled, bodies pressed more tightly, hearts beat frantically against each other.

*This*, she thought dazedly. This was what had been missing.

He raised his hands, cupped her face, lifted his mouth only an inch or so away from hers. His eyes glittered feverishly, reflecting what little light penetrated to the corner in which they stood locked together. "It wasn't a fling," he repeated roughly.

She blinked, their previous conversation almost erased from her mind by his kisses. When it came back to her, she swallowed hard. Her fingers loosened on his shirt. How did this man keep doing this to her? How did he make her want to climb all over him on her balcony with her child sleeping in the next room? That was so unlike her. Unlike her when she wasn't with Adam, at least.

Clearing her throat, she dropped her arms and smoothed her palms down her dress. "You should probably go."

"Yeah. Probably."

But he didn't immediately move away. Nor did she. They still stood close enough that she could almost feel the warmth radiating from him. Or was that coming from her?

It would take her only a half step to be back in his arms. Only a tiptoe to raise her mouth to his. The strength of her desire gave her the control she needed to move back, crossing her arms over her chest. She couldn't have explained why, maybe even to herself, but she was suddenly irrationally annoyed with him—and with herself, for that matter—for making her feel awkward. Out of control. Vulnerable.

"You really should go now, Adam," she said in a low voice as she turned away. "It's getting late." She wasn't looking at him, but she sensed when he drew back.

"Yeah," he muttered. "I guess it is."

"Good night." She didn't look around as she spoke—perhaps for fear of what he might read in her expression. She heard him leave, her hands gripping the railing, her gaze fixed unseeingly on what must have been a beautiful vista in front of her.

# CHAPTER SEVEN

IT WAS ONE of the most beautiful resorts Maddie had ever visited. The grounds were immaculate, the views spectacular, the staff so squeaky clean and cheery they made her teeth hurt. The place was too family-oriented for her taste, but she wasn't surprised Joanna liked it so much. Yet six years later, she was still stunned that her sister had indulged in a reckless vacation fling here. It had been so unlike the prim and proper academic Maddie had known. More like something Maddie might have done—and had, though lately she'd been more selective in her hookups.

Frankly, she'd grown tired of flings and was looking for more permanence as she faced the end of her carefree twenties. She just hadn't found her Mr. Everlasting yet, though she'd always fancied she would know him when she met him. Or maybe she'd just seen too many romantic comedies, she thought with a wry laugh.

She dragged her wheeled duffel out of the

Wind Shadow Resort guest relations building late Thursday morning, a key card gripped in her free hand. She'd been informed when she'd called that there'd been a last-minute cancelation for this weekend, freeing up a one-bedroom suite in Gull's Nest Lodge. Otherwise she'd have had to find a room at a neighboring resort or motel—or crash in Joanna's suite, which wouldn't be fair to Simon. He'd looked forward to this vacation for weeks, and she'd hate for him to give up his bed or feel guilty about his aunt sleeping on the couch.

She wondered if Simon had another aunt on his father's side. She'd grown used to being his favorite aunt—his only aunt—and she wasn't thrilled with the idea of having someone else lay claim to that title. She could only imagine how Joanna must feel at the thought of sharing Simon with a man she barely knew. A man who hadn't even known of Simon's existence until now. Though that wasn't Adam's fault, she added with reluctant fair-mindedness.

Muttering under her breath, she gave a jerk to the duffel. The woman behind the check-in desk had offered to have someone deliver her bag to the suite, but Maddie had declined. She carried her own bags. She looked over her shoulder at her duffel, then turned back to the path ahead, almost too late to avoid colliding with a solid-looking man with a soldier's haircut and a bulldog's expression. His rumpled summer-weight suit looked incongruous in the determinedly casual, tropical surroundings. So did his battered leather briefcase.

"Sorry," he said, though they both knew the clumsiness had been Maddie's. "Are you okay?"

Stopping in her tracks, she stared up at him, struck by the most unsettling sense of recognition and insight. *Well, here you are. Finally.* The words hovered in her mind, as certain as they were spontaneous.

She pushed back the longer side of her trendy asymmetrical bob she dyed a defiantly vibrant red. "Yes, I'm fine, thanks. And it was my fault for not looking where I was going."

Something about the way his deep-set brown eyes studied her face put all her instincts on alert. There was a story here, she'd bet. An interesting one. She was always intrigued by an interesting story. "Are you a guest here, too?" she asked, though he didn't look as though he were on vacation.

His smile lightened his expression, making him look less like a fierce bulldog and more like a friendly—if potentially obstinate—German shepherd. "No, not a guest," he said as the whimsical comparisons flitted through her head. "I'm visiting a client. And you?"

"A client?" she repeated. Was he a lawyer? He looked like a lawyer—and she knew more than her share of those. After a few dating disasters, she'd made it a personal rule not to get involved with attorneys. But then again, she'd always been of the rules-were-made-to-be-broken philosophy.

He tucked his briefcase beneath his left arm, then extended his right hand. "Walt Becker. Attorney at law."

She clasped his hand, noting that it was big and rough-skinned for a lawyer. A hand that had done something other than pushing papers. Just having it wrapped around her smaller, smoother hand made her shiver. She could only imagine how it would feel on the soft skin of her thigh. And other places.

*Whoa, Mads. Slow it down there.* Maybe it had been a bit longer than she'd realized since she'd spent private time with an intriguing man. "Hi, Walt. Nice to meet you. I'm Maddie Zielinski."

His eyebrows rose sharply. "Zielinski? Any relation to Joanna Zielinski?"

"My sister. You've met her?"

"No, not yet."

"Let me guess. You're a friend of Adam Scott?"

"I am, yes. And his legal counsel."

Oops. This could be a problem if things didn't go well for some reason between her sister and Simon's father. "Joanna has her own legal representation. Me. And I think it would be best if you and your client don't talk to her unless I'm present. I'll screen any arrangements on behalf of her son—just to keep everything aboveboard, of course."

She was aware she was making some rather sweeping assumptions on her sister's behalf, but she told herself it was justified. Joanna tended to look for the best in others, whereas Maddie was naturally more cynical and combative. She wouldn't let her sister be either sweet-talked or intimidated into settling for less than she and Simon deserved.

Walt seemed pretty good at hiding his emotions behind a bland smile, but still she thought she saw surprise in his eyes before he masked it. Probably she didn't look quite as much like a lawyer as he did—which, of course, was always her intention. Her hair color wasn't her only minor rebellion against societal expectations and pigeonholes.

"Your client's son has another parent," he reminded her smoothly. "And any demands made on Adam will, of course, be filtered through me."

A surge of energy coursed through her, the adrenaline rush of battle. This wasn't her usual type of legal case, but there was nothing she enjoyed more than a vigorous debate with a worthy opponent. For, um, Joanna and Simon's sake, she assured herself hastily.

"I should find my sister," she said, tightening her grip on the handle of her duffel. She seasoned the smile she gave him with generous dashes of spunk, sauciness and anticipation. "I'll be seeing you, I'm sure, Mr. Becker."

"Yes, Ms. Zielinski. I'm quite sure you will," he murmured.

She didn't look back, but she sensed him watching her as she marched away. She added an extra sashay to her walk, just because.

ADAM SCRAWLED HIS name at the bottom of an official-looking form, then another, and yet a third. That done, he shoved the pile of papers across the desk to Trevor, who waited to serve as witness to Adam's signature.

"What else?" Adam asked after Trevor signed.

Walt tapped the documents into alignment and slid them into his briefcase. He used his prosthetic hand so skillfully that Adam hardly noticed it anymore, though he was continually impressed by how well Walt had adjusted. Having been in danger for a while of losing his own right arm to an infection, Adam had always wondered if he'd have adapted so well.

"That takes care of your revised will, your retirement account and your life insurance," Walt replied. "Simon Zielinski is now your sole heir and beneficiary. You're sure you want to do all of this without getting the results of a DNA test first?"

"Might as well get it all started. You know how I feel about unfinished business." He'd always figured that staying on top of his obligations made it that much easier to get away tidily. Though he sometimes feared he'd inherited his father's restlessness, he never wanted to leave behind the messes his dear old dad had strewn in his wake. "If the DNA test proves I've made a mistake, it's not like any of this is irreversible."

Adam still believed deep in his gut that Simon was his. Call it instinct, genetic recognition or just uncharacteristic gullibility, but he accepted Joanna's account of what had happened. And he would take care of his financial responsibilities without argument, which was the least he could do for the boy.

He thought back to the way he and Joanna had parted last night, after an embrace as arousing as it had been unplanned. He'd thought they were handling everything pretty well, considering. They'd been civil, cooperative, even shared a few kisses in acknowledgment of the attraction that had simmered between them. But something in her tone when she'd sent him away had nagged at him during the hours since.

Maybe she wasn't as okay as she wanted him to believe. For all she knew, he'd been living a carefree bachelor life while she'd raised a child and forged a career on her own. He couldn't blame her for harboring some resentment, even if she hadn't fully admitted those feelings to herself.

"So, with death benefits out of the way—and, we hope, not to be needed for a very long time—we should discuss the next step," Walt said, leaning forward in his seat to interrupt Adam's musings. "I met Joanna's attorney this morning, and I think we should talk about—"

"Wait, what?"

"Her *what*?"

Adam and Trevor had spoken at the same time, both staring at Walt as if he'd lost his mind.

Eyebrows rising, Walt looked from Adam to Trevor and back again. He asked Adam, "She didn't mention this?"

"No, she didn't," he answered stiffly.

*What the hell, Joanna?* Did she really think she needed to pit a lawyer against him? She'd claimed they were basically strangers, and she'd acted oddly last night, but so far she'd given no indication that she wanted anything from him or had reason to mistrust him. So, why the attorney?

"Well, I'm not sure she's paying a retainer," Walt murmured. "Her lawyer is her sister. Maddie Zielinski."

Adam cocked his head, surprised to hear that Joanna's sister had shown up. "Joanna told me Maddie's a public defender."

"You haven't met her yet, I take it?"

"No."

Walt twirled his pen in his right hand. "I met her only in passing on my way in. She seems…interesting."

Trevor frowned, his suspicions obviously

aroused again. "Adam, you need to let Walt do the talking for you. I mean, you have to admit you have a weakness for both Joanna and the boy. And probably some guilt about not being there for them before. I'm not saying Joanna or her sister will try to fleece you—but, well, Walt knows what he's doing."

The thought of sitting across a table from Joanna, flanked by attorneys while they negotiated payments and visitations, made Adam's blood chill. "I'll do my own talking."

Though his concerns were still visible on his face, Trevor made an it's-your-life gesture with his hand and fell silent.

"Fine," Walt said. "You talk for yourself. Just let me look over any paperwork before you sign anything, all right?"

Adam nodded grudgingly.

"So." Walt set his briefcase aside. "About Maddie. What have you heard about her? Is she, you know, married or anything?"

Narrowing his eyes, Adam shook his head. "Really, Walt?"

His friend cleared his throat with an expression that was uncharacteristically sheepish. "What can I say? She's hot. But don't worry. She's way too young and hip for a beat-up old curmudgeon like me."

Trevor tilted his head. "Do people still say 'hip?'"

"Well, there you go," Walt said with a short laugh. "I don't even know the terms these days. I'd better content myself with just admiring the view."

Adam pushed himself abruptly to his feet. "I've got work to do. Thanks for the legal crap, Walt. Have your bookkeeper bill me."

"Right. I'll charge you the usual veterans' legal crap rate," he replied affably.

Leaving his buddies to fret about him if they wanted to, Adam stalked out of the office.

SIMON WANTED TO swim again before lunch, so Joanna settled in the same lounge chair as yesterday to watch him play with the other children. There was no sign of Cody or his parents; had they left the resort already? She hoped they'd found some relaxation on the family vacation, and that Ken and Leah learned to minimize their stress and reconnect with each other. But that was none of her business.

She stretched out her bare legs, enjoying the feel of the sun on her skin. She imagined that anyone seeing her sitting there in her shorts and loose top with a tablet in one hand and a strawberry lemonade in the other would assume she hadn't a care in the world.

That person would be mistaken.

Every time her thoughts traveled back to last night on the balcony, she almost cringed. Not only at heated kisses that should never have happened and had come too close to flaming out of control, but at a parting that should have gone better.

Annoyed by her own vacillating, she told herself she'd play this by ear when she saw Adam, depending on how he behaved. Maybe he understood she'd been overwhelmed, tired and conflicted when she'd sent him away so grumpily. Mostly her irritation had been directed at herself, because after all that had happened in the past six years, all the lessons she should have learned, she still found Adam impossible to resist. Even though there was still a chance, considering his intense guardedness, that they were only passing through each other's lives again.

"Now, that is a serious expression for someone stretched out on a resort lounge chair."

The familiar voice made her whip her head around and then leap from the chair, her tablet falling to the chair cushion, her lemonade forgotten. "Maddie! What—?"

"I decided I needed a vacation," her sister said with a deceptively innocent expression.

Maddie's striking hair and dramatic makeup gave her a quirky and cute appearance that always made Joanna feel a bit staid in contrast. Today Maddie wore a hot-pink sleeveless top that clashed cheerfully with her crimson hair, turquoise capris and glittery platform flip-flops. Big turquoise earrings brushed her cheeks with each movement of her head.

Joanna had never seen a more beautiful sight in her life.

She reached out to hug her sister. "I told you not to come," she said sternly, "but I'm so glad you did."

Maddie returned the hug. "I had a feeling you might need a lawyer."

Extricating herself with a rueful smile, Joanna tucked her hair behind her ears. "Well, I don't think I need a lawyer, but I will always need my sister."

Maddie made her opinion of that statement clear with a snort. "Trust me, you need a lawyer. I met Adam's attorney when I arrived. The guy's a bulldog. Kinda cute—but then, I've always had a weakness for bulldogs."

"Adam's…attorney?"

"His name is Walt Becker. Late thirties, maybe? Ex-military type."

"I haven't met him," Joanna admitted in a low voice.

"You will."

"Aunt Maddie, Aunt Maddie! I didn't know you were coming!" A small bundle of wet boy threw himself into Maddie's arms, flinging water everywhere. Rather than flinching, she laughed and gathered him close.

"Hi, Si-bot. I wanted to surprise you. Have you been having fun on your vacation?"

"So much fun." He beamed up at her. "I'm glad you're here, Aunt Maddie. I want to show you all the crafts I've made and the shells I've found and tell you all about Explorers Club and my new friends and..."

"Whoa, kiddo," she said with a laugh. "Take a breath. I'll see and hear it all, I promise."

She looked over his head to search Joanna's face. "I hope you don't mind that I crashed your mother-son vacation."

"Of course not. Simon and I both love having you here. Besides, we asked you to join us when we made our reservations, remember? You said you couldn't get away."

Maddie shrugged. "Yes, well, things changed," she said. Her expression told Joanna exactly what had been important enough to make her rearrange her schedule.

For Simon's sake, Joanna held on to her

smile, but her mind was spinning as dread built inside her. Adam had retained an attorney. Why? Was it only a precaution? A way to protect himself and/or Simon? Did he want to spell out his rights and responsibilities as a father—or abdicate them? He still hadn't made his wishes clear in that respect. She could understand him having doubts about his place in Simon's life—but her pride prickled at the thought that he might not believe everything she'd told him.

Trying to convince herself that it could be coincidence that Adam was meeting with his lawyer today, Joanna pushed her worries aside and focused on the present. Maddie joined her and Simon for lunch before his afternoon adventures. They sat around a lakeside table beneath a brightly striped umbrella, Joanna and Maddie eating salads while Simon munched fried shrimp and babbled about everything he'd done for the past four days. He spent quite a bit of time talking about the adventures at the fun center, and Joanna doubted that Maddie missed noticing how many times "Mr. Adam" was mentioned.

"So, you had fun with Mr. Adam, hmm?" Maddie asked, confirming the suspicion.

"Maddie."

While Maddie turned an innocent look toward his mother, Simon nodded enthusiastically. "He's nice. He took me in the big go-cart and he drove really fast around the curves. It was fun. And then he helped me win lots of tickets in the arcade so I could get a cool prize. And he knows everything about shells and ocean life and stuff."

"Finish your lunch, Simon." Joanna looked meaningfully at her watch. "You're supposed to report to the van in fifteen minutes."

Simon crammed another fried shrimp into his mouth.

Maddie walked with them to the guest relations building portico. Simon bounced between them, identifying his new friends for Maddie. Joanna greeted the other parents she was getting to know. Both she and Maddie kissed Simon and told him to have fun, then returned the waves he sent them through the van windows as it pulled away.

"He's really having a great time, Jo." Maddie waved one last time at the van, then turned to her sister. "I can see why you didn't cut the vacation short."

Joanna spread her hands. "I couldn't," she said simply. "He's been looking forward to this for months. I asked him about leaving early and he almost cried. Besides, running would only postpone the inevitable."

"Now that Simon's gone, we should talk about some things. You need to be prepared for whatever Adam and his lawyer throw at you. Oh. Speak of the devil, I assume."

Not the devil, certainly, but it was indeed Adam who blocked the path in front of them, along with Trevor and a brawny-looking companion whose slightly wrinkled light gray suit contrasted with their resort uniforms. The lawyer, no doubt. It appeared as if the men had just stepped out of Torchlight, presumably after lunching there.

Adam's expression was somber when he looked at Joanna and her sister, having no doubt heard that Maddie had positioned herself as Joanna's attorney. Joanna met his gaze without flinching. He had some nerve to look at her like that after lunching with his own lawyer. She thought she might see veiled suspicion in Trevor's expression, but as usual, she found it hard to focus on anyone else when Adam was around.

The man in the suit spoke first, addressing Maddie. "Well, hello, there, Counselor. Fancy running into you again."

Maddie's mocking tone matched his. "Hi, Sarge. We were just talking about you."

Joanna glanced at the attorney long enough

to notice that he looked a bit surprised. "What makes you think I was a sergeant?"

Maddie looked him up and down with characteristic flippancy. "Weren't you?"

"He was." It was Trevor who'd spoken, and who first extended his hand to Maddie. "Trevor Farrell. You must be Joanna's sister."

"Maddie Zielinski," she confirmed, shaking his hand. "So that means you're the infamous Adam," she said then, looking at the final member of the trio.

Drawing his gaze from Joanna, Adam turned to her sister. "Adam Scott, though I don't know about the infamous part. Hello, Maddie."

She studied him. "Wow. The resemblance to Simon really is incredible."

He ignored her comment, instead motioning from Walter to Joanna. "That leaves only you two who haven't met, I guess. Joanna, this is my friend Walt Becker."

"Friend?" Joanna murmured as she shook the man's big hand.

"Friend," he repeated. His brown eyes were warm and smiling, but she didn't make the mistake of assuming he was innocuous. She had no doubt he was as tough as he appeared.

Adam made an impatient move. "We need to talk, Joanna."

Maddie took her sister's arm. "My schedule is open today," she said.

Adam flicked her an annoyed glance. "I was talking to your sister."

"I'm speaking for my sister," Maddie retorted, undaunted.

"Maddie," Joanna said, "I appreciate your support, but I speak for myself."

"So does Adam," Walt murmured. "Doesn't mean he'd turn down advice from a concerned friend, right, bro?"

"Tell you what." Trevor said quickly, glancing around at other guests in the area, some of whom were eying the tense-looking group curiously. "I have some things to attend to now, but my personal conference room is available if you'd like to take this conversation inside."

"I've got one more hour free before I have to get back to the office," Walt commented. "Wouldn't hurt to chat for a few minutes."

"Let's do this," Maddie declared, tossing back her hair. "Where's the conference room?"

Walt gestured with his right hand toward the guest relations building entrance. "I know the way."

The two of them headed in that direction side by side on the narrow walkway. Joanna noted that Maddie had an extra spring in her step; there was nothing her sister loved more than a spirited argument.

Adam frowned at Joanna. "Do you really want to do this?"

"No," she replied candidly. "I have no idea why we're having this meeting. But then, I'm not the one who retained a lawyer."

His left eyebrow rose skeptically. "That's not what your sister seems to think."

"My sister is family. She came to see if I needed her, not because I asked her for professional help."

"And Walt is my friend. My version of family," Adam responded evenly. "He volunteered to help me with any legal steps I need to take now that I know about Simon."

"To protect your interests, you mean," she said, remembering the assessing way Trevor had eyed her and Maddie.

Adam shrugged, which only irked her more.

"Fine." She turned to follow the others. "Let's do this."

"Joanna—"

She looked over her shoulder. "What?"

Adam hesitated, then sighed. "Nothing."

He rubbed the back of his neck as he moved to walk with her, the only outward sign that he was no happier than she was.

THE ROOM TREVOR had referred to as his personal conference room was larger than needed for a spur-of-the-moment meeting of four people, but at least it was comfortable and private. Trevor's assistant, Tamar, brought in coffee and a pitcher of water and left them in privacy. Maddie drew a tablet computer from the multicolored shoulder bag she'd carried tucked beneath one arm while Walt set his briefcase on the table and pulled out a legal pad and pen.

Joanna sat beside her sister, chewing her lip and looking stressed. Sprawled in a chair next to Walt at the table that would have easily accommodated ten, Adam made no effort to set her at ease. This meeting hadn't been his idea. The knowledge that it hadn't been Joanna's, either, crossed his mind, but he shrugged it away. She hadn't called off her sister, and Maddie was obviously itching for battle. Her watermelon-colored nails tapped impatiently on the glossy cherry table as she waited for Walt to start, her greenish-blue eyes locked on the other attorney's face in challenge.

Walt let the moment stretch out a bit, probably for dramatic impact, then picked up his pen, holding it poised over his pad.

"I think you should know the steps my friend has already taken on the boy's behalf this morning," he said. He'd asked Adam quietly when they'd settled in their seats if he was free to reveal the legal arrangements they'd made for Simon's future, and Adam had given his consent with a shrug.

While Adam listened without comment, his arms crossed tightly over his chest, Walt quickly summed up the changes Adam had made to his survivor's benefits, naming Simon as his heir. Watching the women on the other side of the table, Adam noticed that Maddie hid her reactions, but Joanna wasn't as able to mask her own shock.

"You did all that this morning?" she demanded of Adam.

He lifted one shoulder slightly. "Over the past couple of days. I figured those were things I should take care of immediately—just in case anything happened. It's not like I have any other close relatives to worry about."

"I suggested he wait until after taking a paternity test before signing the papers," Walt said, making Adam suspect he was deliberately drawing the Zielinski sisters' ire toward himself. "He isn't opposed to a test, but he said saw no need to wait for results. He realizes that anything we've done today can be changed if the test results are…unexpected."

Joanna shot a quick glance at Adam, who, in turn, frowned at Walt.

Maddie's eyes sparked green fire. "You're suggesting my sister doesn't know who the father of her son is? Or that she would try to deceive Adam for any reason?"

So, despite her posturing, Maddie wasn't such an objective advocate, after all. It had to be different for her when her sister was the client.

"I'm not suggesting anything," Walt countered, looking rather pleased with her heated reaction. "Just offering my legal expertise to my friend. It's up to him whether to follow my advice, of course."

Quickly centering herself, Maddie spoke more brusquely. "You'll keep all those documents on file in your office?"

"Of course." Walt slid a card across the table. "My number. Feel free to call it any time."

Adam turned a narrow-eyed look at his friend. Walt gave him a bland smile in return. Either he was deliberately trying to rattle Maddie, or he was letting his attraction outweigh his judgment, despite his earlier protestations that he and Maddie were an unlikely match. Adam supposed he couldn't fault his friend for that; if he himself hadn't been dazzled by sexual attraction six years ago, none of them would even be here now.

He cleared his throat, deciding it was time for him to take a more active role in this discussion. "So," he said, turning to face both sisters, "now that you've heard about the arrangements I made this morning, I think it's obvious why I asked for Walt's assistance. But what about you, Joanna? Why did you feel the need to bring in your attorney without first talking to me?"

"Joanna didn't *bring me in*," Maddie said before Joanna could reply. "She didn't even know I was coming. She called me and told me she'd been accidentally reunited with Simon's biological father, but she did not ask me to come, nor did she ask for any legal advice."

"And yet you introduced yourself to me as Ms. Zielinski's attorney," Walt murmured.

Adam could tell that Walt was getting under Maddie's skin. She eyed him narrowly. "Yes, I did. And if she needs me in that capacity, I'm here for her."

Looking at Joanna's somber expression, Adam wondered if she was beginning to feel as superfluous here as he was. What were they doing, anyway? She hadn't asked him for anything, and he hadn't made any requests in return. Why were they suddenly facing each other across a conference table while these two lawyers argued back and forth?

"Let's cut to the chase," he said, losing patience. "What do you want from me, Joanna?"

Walt cleared his throat and placed his right hand on Adam's arm in implied warning.

Joanna's eyes had gone wide. "Nothing!" she said flatly. "I don't want anything at all from you."

"Jo," Maddie muttered, giving her sister a frown as if to make it clear that she, too, was tired of being ignored. "Don't be too—"

Joanna shook her head, sitting up straighter in her chair, her gaze still locked on Adam's. "If your friends are worried that I'll try to use you for money, they're wrong. I've been taking care of my son quite well on my own. Make whatever arrangements you want to for Simon, but I don't want a dime from you for myself."

"I'm well aware of how much responsibility you've handled for the past six years. And I fully intend to pay my part," he retorted, stinging as usual at her heavy emphasis on the words "my son." Even though he supposed he understood the reason for it. "I'm no deadbeat."

"I would never call you that," she answered evenly, though her eyes still glittered.

"No one's throwing around insults," Walt interjected. "We're just getting some of the legalities out of the way. It's always best to have everything on paper, in terms everyone understands and agrees on—child support figures, discussion of medical and educational expenses, visitation arrangements, that sort of thing."

Adam thought his saw Joanna's face pale at the mention of visitation. Considering that in a few weeks, they could hardly live farther apart, he couldn't blame her for wondering how many more changes lay in store for her and the boy.

And that, he decided, pushing himself to his feet, was where this meeting concluded. He looked at Walt. "I have to get back to work. Joanna, Walt will work up a support agreement for me and send it to you to look over—and Maddie, of course," he added with a nod to her rather combative younger sister.

"Adam, wait. We haven't even talked about—"

"I'm done for now, Walt." He moved toward the door without looking back. "I'll call you with some figures when I get a break later."

Maybe no one else in the room considered him the outsider in this conversation. And it was likely no one was actually attacking him—not even feisty Maddie. Maybe he was just feeling beleaguered, guilty, even a little trapped, and he only imagined he saw those accusations in their eyes as he left. He closed the door to the conference room a bit too forcefully behind him, already pulling out his phone to start checking his to-do list. He needed to concentrate on his work for now. At least he knew what he was doing there.

RATHER SUBDUED AFTER the tense meeting, Joanna went to meet Simon at the bus, saying she would take him back to the lodge to rest before dinner. Maddie assured her sister she could entertain herself quite contentedly for a couple of hours in such a beautiful place before they met up again for dinner later. She headed straight for the lakeside bar, thinking a cool, fruity drink was in order. Her smile broadened when she saw the man sitting alone at the bar, his attention divided between the phone in his hand and the bottle of beer on the teak surface in front of him.

She slid onto the empty stool at his right side. "I'll have a strawberry daiquiri," she said to the instantly attentive bartender.

Walt turned to face her, setting his phone on the bar. "Counselor."

"Sarge."

His steady gaze made her heart beat a little

faster. No one would call Walt Becker classically handsome, but something deep inside her was drawn to him, anyway. She'd never been interested in pretty boys, and this battle-worn vet was neither pretty nor a boy.

"Have you come with terms for me to present to my client?" he asked.

"Actually, I'm off the clock at the moment, and I rarely talk business when I'm trying to relax," she replied lightly, nodding a thank-you to the bartender when he placed a frosty glass in front of her. "What about you?"

"Just enjoying a cold beer and checking my email before heading back to the office. Hard to leave this place on a perfect afternoon," he added.

Enjoying the feel of the breeze against her cheeks, she smiled. "No kidding. A day like this makes you want to stretch out in a hammock and pretend to be independently wealthy, doesn't it?"

He chuckled. "I suppose it does. Can't remember the last time I spent an afternoon in a hammock."

She took a slow sip of her icy drink, then looked at him through her lashes as she murmured, "Maybe it's time for you to indulge yourself again."

She was gratified to see his throat work

as he swallowed hard. "So...are you staying for the rest of the week with your sister and nephew?"

"Yes. I'll drive back with them Sunday morning. I figured I might as well combine vacation with family issues."

"Family issues. That's one way to put it, I guess."

She shrugged. "Like I said. Off the clock. So, tell me, Walt. Is there a Mrs. Sarge?"

He hesitated only a beat before replying. "Used to be. Now she's Mrs. Plastic Surgeon."

Delighted by his dry humor, she grinned. "I won't say I'm sorry to hear that."

He frowned at her, obviously taken aback by her directness. "How old are you, Maddie?"

She tapped her glass. "Old enough to drink this legally. Why?"

"I've got a few years on you."

She shrugged, unconcerned. "Oh, c'mon, Sarge, you're not that old. Bet you haven't even seen forty yet."

"I've caught a few glimpses of it lately," he muttered. "Seems to creep closer every time I look away."

"You know what they say. Age is just a number. And math was my worst subject in school."

She was being brazen, and was well aware of it. But she'd never been one to play at being coy. She knew when a man found her attractive, and she wasn't imagining the sparks between her and Walt.

"So you know this is fake, right?" He held up his convincingly designed left hand.

She flicked a glance at the hand, then smiled back at him. "I know it's a prosthetic, if that's what you mean. Did you leave the hand in Afghanistan?"

"Iraq." He seemed to appreciate her matter-of-fact tone. "I was over there a few years before Adam."

She reached out to touch his right hand, which was still holding his beer bottle. "Maybe you'll tell me about it sometime."

He gave her a narrow look, and she saw suspicion in his eyes. "Is flirting with the opposition a tactic you use often, Counselor?"

She felt her cheeks warm, not with embarrassment but with a quick flash of temper. She reined it in, giving him a cool smile. "You should be relieved that I don't take offense easily. Otherwise, you'd be wearing the rest of my daiquiri back to your office."

"Sorry if I crossed the line," he grumbled.

Her eyebrows rose. "Do you consider that

an apology? If so, you have quite a bit to learn yet."

She stood and trailed a fingertip up his right arm to lightly tap his frowning lips. "As it happens, I'm intrigued by the idea of teaching you. You can start by paying for my drink. See you around, Sarge."

Maddie felt him watch her as she strutted away. She didn't look back to make sure, but she didn't have to.

She'd definitely left him with something to think about.

## CHAPTER EIGHT

AS ADAM HAD PREDICTED, it felt good to be productive after the contentious meeting. To work hard, to know the actions he took and the decisions he made were valuable to the resort and to his employer. His friend. There was satisfaction in feeling tired at the end of the day, aware that a cold beer and a good book waited for him.

True, there'd be no one with whom to share the pleasures, no one to congratulate him for the challenges he'd successfully handled that afternoon, no one to laugh with him over one particularly amusing exchange with a congenial but absent-minded guest. But he was okay with that, right? He knew how to find temporary companionship if he wanted it. He just wasn't in the mood for meaningless interaction this evening.

In addition to the hard work, he'd expended quite a bit of energy not thinking about that meeting with Joanna and the lawyers. Not letting himself dwell on memories of mind-blowing kisses or a child's innocent laughter. The images still haunted him, of course, hovering at the back of his mind like irritating ghosts just waiting for him to let his guard down.

He suspected he'd be spending quite a bit of time battling those ghosts in the near future, after Joanna and Simon returned to their own happy life, but he would worry about that later. Tonight, he'd drink a beer, read his book and otherwise concentrate only on work, the tasks he'd completed and the ones waiting for him to tackle. It was the life he'd led for the past three years, and he'd been in no hurry to make any drastic changes, despite knowing he could at any time. He'd told himself his freedom was more valuable than any rewards or commitments—one of the few lessons his own dad had drilled into him.

He'd begged off on dinner with Trevor and some guests that evening, and Trev hadn't protested. He hadn't heard from Joanna since he'd walked out of the meeting, and he doubted he would hear from her this evening. He'd have to deal with it all again tomorrow, of course, but tonight he planned to just hole up and rest.

Which meant he was unprepared to turn a corner and see Joanna sitting on a bench in a shady alcove, her arm around a sobbing woman, her head bent to hear the words the other woman choked out. At first he thought her companion was her sister, but then he noted the woman's blond hair. She lifted her tear-streaked face toward Joanna, and he recognized the profile. Leah McGee, wife to Ken and mother to Cody, the family with whom he and Trevor had dined earlier this week.

In his brief interactions with the McGees, he'd sensed some tension between Cody's parents. He'd gone out of his way to be friendly and make suggestions of fun things for them to do as a family. Joanna, apparently, had offered an ear and a shoulder, and Leah was taking full advantage. And responding. Even as he hesitated on the path, Adam saw that Leah's tears were slowing, that she listened intently to the no doubt encouraging and supportive words Joanna murmured to her.

Neither woman noticed him standing there. Feeling like a voyeur, he turned and continued quietly on his path.

Joanna seemed to have all the answers for everyone. He didn't know why that suddenly irritated him. Maybe because he had so few answers about what the hell he was supposed to do next. Or maybe because it was uncomfortably easy to imagine sitting there pouring out his problems to her—even though he'd learned a long time ago that in the long run, the only one he could truly depend on to look out for his best interests was himself.

STANDING WITH HER fist hovering over Adam's door, Joanna repeatedly counted to ten, taking plenty of opportunity to talk herself out of this. She'd reached seven for a fourth time when she muttered a curse and knocked. She didn't even know for certain that he was here, but a light shone in the window and she thought she heard the muted sound of a TV inside. That sound shut off abruptly in response to her knock.

Dressed in shorts and a worn T-shirt, barefoot and evening-unshaven, Adam opened the door. "Joanna? What are you doing here? Where's Simon?"

How could he look this drop-dead sexy, even grubby and grumpy? What was it about this man that made her mind go blank—except for a few mature-rated images—every time she saw him?

Forcing herself to concentrate on his question, she said, "It's almost ten p.m. Simon has been asleep for more than an hour. Maddie's sitting with him until I get back."

"What do you—" He stopped, grimaced, then raised his left hand to the back of his neck. "Sorry. There's no call for me to snap at you. Come in."

"Actually…" she said, stepping past him then turning to face him as he closed the door. She drew a deep breath. "…I came to apologize to you."

He looked both surprised and a little suspicious. "For?"

She spread her hands, grateful they were steady. Mostly. "For that awkward meeting this afternoon. For showing up here and making your life more difficult. Basically, for everything that's gone wrong for you since we met six years ago."

After a few silent beats, he dropped his arm to his sides, his mouth twisting into what was probably intended to be a smile. "Thanks, but none of this is your fault. No apologies are necessary."

Her eyes felt hot, her throat tight. Considering everything he'd been hit with this week, she wouldn't have blamed him if he took to his heels. Again. Instead, he'd believed her about her son's parentage and immediately started making arrangements for Simon's future. And while he had good reason to resent the years he'd missed with his son, he had quietly taken his share of the culpability.

She blinked and cleared her throat, pushing aside her conflicted emotions to deal with later. "You have to admit your life was a lot less complicated a few days ago."

"I'll give you that one. Still not your fault."

"But I—"

"Joanna." His hands fell lightly on her shoulders as he gazed down at her. "We've done this already, remember? We agreed to put the past behind us and focus on what's best for Simon."

She looked up at him, her pulse rate already speeding up in response to his nearness, the feel of his hands on her. "We do keep circling back around, don't we?"

He brushed a hand over her arm. "Can't seem to help it."

No, she thought. She couldn't help trembling when he touched her. Or stop her knees from going weak when he stood this close to her. Whatever it was about Adam that made him so fascinating to her—whatever drew her in a way no one else had—she could no more resist it now than she had that first magical night when she hadn't even tried.

She moved abruptly away, needing to put some distance between them. She stopped by his sofa, ruffling the fringed edge of the hand-made throw tossed over one arm. "Did you knit this?" she teased to change the mood, smiling at the whimsical image of him bent over needles and yarn.

He chuckled, though she thought she detected a note of strain beneath the humor. "My grandmother made it for me years ago. A Christmas gift, I think. It's the only thing I still have from her."

She might have asked him a few more questions, but he forestalled her by asking, "Did you tell your sister where you were going?"

She nodded. "I told her I wanted to talk with you. She said she'll be fine in my suite until I get back."

"You mean she trusted you to meet with me without legal representation?"

His tone was a mix of irony and irritation, but she decided to focus on the former. "I had to promise I wouldn't sign anything," she said lightly. "What about Walt? How would he feel about us talking out of court?"

"He'd probably be annoyed that we deprived him of another chance to stare at your sister. I think he's intrigued by her."

She shrugged. "Most guys are."

"Yeah?" He sounded a little surprised. "Huh."

She frowned, wondering if she should be insulted on Maddie's behalf. "You don't think my sister is attractive?"

"Well, sure." He kept his gaze trained on her face when he added, "Just not my type."

Before she could decide how to respond, he changed the subject again. "I saw you earlier this evening. You were with Leah McGee. She was crying."

Startled, she blinked. "Oh. I didn't see you."

"You were occupied with Leah. Is she okay?"

She wasn't sure how much she should tell him. Leah wasn't her patient, but the other woman had trusted her enough to confide in her. She didn't want to betray that trust.

Joanna had been walking back to her suite with Simon and Maddie after dinner when she'd spotted Leah crying in the secluded alcove. She'd sent Maddie and Simon on to watch a movie in the suite while she lingered to ask if there was anything she could do to help the distraught young mother. She'd explained that she didn't want to intrude, but she was trained in family therapy, if that seemed helpful. Her careful encouragement had unleashed a fresh torrent of tears and jumbled words from the woman who had very much needed a sympathetic listener.

"Leah's been going through a rough time," she said after a moment, choosing her words carefully so he wouldn't draw any mistaken conclusions about what he'd inadvertently witnessed. "She lost her mother a few months ago, and she's been dealing with grief and stress and loneliness while trying to be everything to everyone else in her life. She's a strong woman who loves her husband and truly adores her son. She misses her mom and needed to vent. I could offer her that opportunity and suggest a few resources that might help. She'll be fine."

He nodded thoughtfully. "You must be very good at your job. You love it, don't you?"

"I do," she admitted. "I've enjoyed teaching, but I'm looking forward to spending more time working with clients and their families. This job in Seattle looks like exactly what I've hoped to find."

He'd turned away, so she couldn't see the expression in his eyes, but she noticed a muscle twitch in his jaw before he said, "I hope they'll realize how lucky they'll be to have you there."

"Thank you." She sighed, suddenly weary. "I should head back to the suite before Maddie starts looking for me."

"That's really all you came for tonight? To apologize?"

She wasn't quite sure how to explain the impulse. She decided to be candid. "I'm glad we aren't fighting anymore. I never meant for that to happen. I'd much rather leave here remembering the fun we had together."

"So would I." He reached out idly to brush a strand of hair from her cheek. "Not sure how we ended up facing off with lawyers, but I could do without that."

She shuddered. "Same here. Even if our lawyers are my family and your friend, it's still too stressful."

"Look, JoJo." He dropped his hand to her shoulder, his expression grave. "I meant what I said earlier. I intend to make regular child support payments. That's bottom line, no argument. You can spend the money as needed or bank it for Simon or whatever you want. I trust you to do what's best."

"Fine," she said, seeing that he wasn't going to budge. This was obviously important to him. "You can start a new college fund for him."

He gave a chuckle that sounded forced. "The way that kid's going, he might need that in a couple years."

She smiled faintly. "I don't want to rush him through his childhood."

"No. Let him enjoy every minute of it. God knows it doesn't last long enough as it is."

"No, it doesn't," she said, her voice suddenly thick as she thought about how quickly the past five years had sped past. How much Adam had missed in such a short time.

Adam exhaled then, as if reaching a decision. He took a step back, putting both physical and emotional distance between them when he said, "Anyway, I just want you to know that once Walt has set up the payments, his job for me is done. I don't know how much longer I'll hang around here, but wherever I end up, I'll make sure you always have my contact information. You won't have to worry about me causing any problems for you or Simon. Maybe you could text me a picture of him occasionally, let me know how he— how you're both doing—but I won't interfere in your plans."

Frowning, she studied his stern profile. "I don't understand. Are you saying you don't want to be a part of Simon's life?"

"I'm saying I don't want to *mess up* his life. As I've pointed out, you and Simon are doing well. He doesn't need an absentee dad he hardly knows popping in occasionally to confuse him. I told you I grew up that way, with a father who was little more than a stranger to me. I swore I'd never do that to a kid."

She didn't know how to feel about what he was saying. Was he really choosing not to be a father to Simon? To let them leave without making any plans for future visits?

She already knew Adam had issues with permanence, but really? How could he be around Simon and not fall in love with him? Not want to spend even more time with him?

It occurred to her that she should be relieved Adam wasn't going to try to horn in on Simon's childhood. That she wouldn't have to put her son on a plane for court-ordered visitations, or share summers and holidays and other special occasions. Adam wouldn't be a part of Simon's life—or hers. Just the way it had always been. And that was fine. Right? She hadn't really expected a few mind-blowing kisses to turn into a lifetime commitment, had she?

Why was she suddenly so sad? For Adam's sake. For Simon's. And for her own.

"It doesn't have to be like that," she said quietly. "There are ways to stay in touch, for you to be a father to Simon even if you live apart. It's not ideal, but I know other long-distance parents who use video chats to stay in touch. Maybe if the technology had been available when you were a boy, you could have communicated more with your own father."

His mouth twisted. "Phones existed. He knew how to use them. He didn't bother. But

I don't want to talk about my father. He's been dead for years, and I've been on my own since I was a teenager. I learned to like it that way."

She'd never known anyone as proficient at sending mixed signals as Adam. He said he wasn't sorry she was here, but he was already planning for her to leave. He said he trusted her, but he hired a lawyer. He spent time with Simon and seemed to enjoy it very much, but he didn't want Simon to know who he was. He wanted to take care of his son's financial needs, but he didn't want to be a part of the boy's future.

Maybe he was right to walk away again. If he could keep her this disoriented and conflicted, she could only imagine how confused a five-year-old would be. He was correct about that; Simon deserved more.

The saddest part was that she thought Adam deserved more, too. That he was capable of offering more. He was simply choosing not to.

She pushed back her hair. "We'll have to tell him someday. He deserves the truth."

He nodded, still without looking at her. "You'll know when the time is right. Tell him—tell him I want him to have a great life. Tell him I knew you'd make sure he has everything he needs to be happy, safe and successful. Tell him he's a lucky kid to have you for his mother, and I hope he never takes that for granted."

She wondered if it was possible for her chest to hurt any worse than it did at that moment. If this was what a broken heart felt like, she'd been wise to avoid it all these years. And foolish to have let down those defenses with Adam.

Suddenly bone-weary, she said, "I should get back to my suite now."

He nodded and moved to open the door for her, pausing with his hand on the knob. "I'm glad you came by tonight," he said in a low voice. "I didn't like the way that meeting ended, either. This is a much better way to say good—to say good night."

She knew he'd changed his wording at the last moment, but he opened the door before she could try to get clarification. She couldn't just stand there eyeing him suspiciously. Nor did she want him to see the depths of her disappointment.

"Good night, Adam."

He caught her arm just as she reached the threshold and lowered his head for one last, lingering kiss. Another mixed signal, she thought even as she was unable to resist responding. Just one last time, she promised herself.

"Sleep well, JoJo," he murmured, releasing her.

The door closed quietly behind her when she stepped outside and drew a long, shaky breath. The tropical air that had felt so fresh before tasted cloyingly sweet now, reminding her that she didn't belong here. This was only a vacation resort, a place for fantasies that couldn't last forever.

THE RESORT WAS subdued at 1:00 a.m., with few sounds filtering from the outside into Adam's bedroom, where he sat brooding in a chair by the open window. Maybe a handful of night owls were enjoying last call at the bar or taking moonlit strolls on the beach, but all in all, the place was tucked in for the night. Weekends tended to be livelier even at this hour, but this Thursday night—early Friday morning, technically—was peaceful. Adam doubted anyone would even notice if he carried his bags down to his car and drove away.

Just the way he liked it. No one hanging around to exchange difficult goodbyes.

Maybe he should do just that. Maybe he would take a couple weeks of the vacation time he'd accumulated. Or maybe he'd end up back on the road, looking for a new gig in a fresh setting. He could make a decent living doing construction or landscaping, neither of which should be hindered by the limited mobility of his right arm. He could sell cars or sporting goods, or drive a truck and schlep packages. Anything that didn't require a degree, but still paid enough for his basic needs and for weekly contributions to his son's college fund. He wasn't choosy.

He'd never planned to stay here as long as he had. Never expected to rise to a position of responsibility. Never thought he'd be offered a big promotion with a sizable raise, something Trevor had discussed with him just last week. He'd said he needed time to think about it, and even with all his new venture deadlines looming, Trevor had told him to take the time he needed. Adam had spent the past week trying to figure out why the idea of settling into a management position even here at the resort had brought a tightness to his throat that had felt uncomfortably like panic.

How could he be expected to be a stable presence in a kid's life when he couldn't even commit to a job?

His father hadn't offered much in the way of paternal wisdom during Adam's youth. Still, something his dad had said to him on one of those brief visits when Adam was maybe fourteen had stuck with him.

*"Boy, it's a big world out there,"* Doyle Scott had spouted, raising one tattooed hand to smooth back the salt-and-pepper hair he'd worn in a scraggly, leather-tied ponytail. *"Don't let nobody chain you to one little parcel of it."*

With that old echo whispering in the back of his mind, Adam shifted restlessly in his chair. He couldn't help wondering if he'd inherited more than gray eyes from his dad. Why else would the thought of making a commitment—to a job, to a child, to a woman—make him break out in cold sweats and doubt his ability to fulfill any promises?

Maybe he'd stay. Maybe he wouldn't. Whichever choice he made, Joanna and Simon would be gone in a couple of days. A few weeks after that, they'd be on their way to Seattle, as far as they could get from here without falling into the opposite ocean. Joanna could go back to her counseling, or whatever she did, and Simon would excel in school, probably eventually earning an advanced degree well beyond Adam's hard-earned high school diploma and a few community college classes. They'd be fine without him. Better than fine.

His attention was caught by a crayon drawing on the dresser. He stilled, then stood and moved slowly toward the dresser, where he picked up the map of the resort Simon had made for him and looked down at it somberly.

His stomach clenched. His throat felt as though it had been scalded. Shredded. The old, healed scars on his chest seemed to throb with fresh injury. His eyes burned as if filled again with desert sand. He squeezed them closed, but he could still see the childish writing in his mind.

*To Mr. Adam, from Simon Z.*

After several deep, lung-filling breaths, he moved across the room, opened a drawer in nightstand, and dug out a worn leather pouch. The pouch had once closed with a leather strip wrapped around a horn button, but he'd lost the button at some point. He opened the flap and withdrew a wallet-size photograph. He'd taken this photo with his phone six years ago and had it printed. It wasn't of the highest quality or the best artistic arrangement. The glossy photo paper was tattered at the corners and creased down the middle, but all he saw was the smiling face of the subject.

Wearing a bathing suit with a flowered sarong wrapped at the hips, Joanna had stood on the beach, her longer hair whipping around her, her face lit with sun and laughter. Though he wasn't much of a photographer, he'd captured the moment on impulse. He wasn't even sure she'd known he'd taken it. This print had gone with him to Afghanistan, had been stashed in his hospital bedside table and had been with him ever since. He'd considered it one of the few mementoes of his life BND, as he thought of it. Before Near Death. He hadn't looked at the print often, but he'd pulled it out occasionally when he tried to remember what it had been like to be so convinced of his own immortality. A time when he'd remembered how to laugh and have fun with a beautiful woman without thinking about the past or the future.

Very carefully, he folded the crayon drawing and slipped it into the envelope with the photo, stashing the pouch back in the drawer.

"THERE YOU ARE. I've been looking for you."

Stretched on her stomach on a soft beach towel, letting the sun soak into her skin, Maddie opened her eyes in response to the familiar male voice. The first thing she saw was a pair of brown loafers, their spit-shined surface dusted with sand. She raised her gaze up a pair of creased khakis, past a pale blue, long-sleeve shirt to a face that glistened in the afternoon heat, as if he'd tramped around for a while in his search.

She pushed upward and swiveled to sit up

on the big towel, her bare legs bent to one side. Tossing her crimson hair out of her face, she patted the fabric beside her. "I didn't bring a spare towel, but I'm willing to share."

Walt tilted his head. "I'm not sure if I can get back up once I'm down there."

She groaned. "Don't start with the age thing again, please."

Shrugging, he lowered himself to the towel beside her, settling cross-legged on a hot-pink unicorn, yet somehow still managing to look like a tough male. "I'm not accustomed to doing business on a beach towel."

So this was about Joanna and Adam. Tamping down regret, Maddie adjusted her purple bikini top, dug into her straw bag and pulled out a bottle of water. She twisted off the cap, offered a sip to Walt, who waved it away with a smile, then swallowed several sips before setting the bottle aside. "Okay. I'm not exactly dressed for a negotiation, but what can I do for you, Walt?"

"I think you're dressed just fine." He ran his gaze over her scantily clad body, and she gulped as if he'd made that journey with his hand rather than his eyes.

*Whoa.* She almost reached for her water again.

Drawing his eyes back to her face, he gave

her a crooked smile that was part grimace, as if the words had slipped out despite himself. "Sorry. I'm not usually so unprofessional."

She brushed back her blowing hair again, not even trying to hide the fact that she enjoyed making him forget his better judgment. "You don't hear me complaining. But maybe we should wait until business is settled before we pursue this."

He cleared his throat. "Yeah. Uh, business. Adam wanted me to make some arrangements with you and your sister on his behalf. He said he didn't want a repeat of that formal meeting yesterday."

"Seriously? He doesn't even want to be involved in the discussions?"

"Apparently not. He left me a voice mail with instructions at two this morning. I had my phone turned off—some people actually sleep at that hour—but I caught the message a few hours later. He said he wants us to go ahead and set up a fund for Simon that he can contribute to regularly. He said he's taking the day off—a very rare event, believe me—but we're to call him if we have any questions we can't settle without him. He said he'd see us later, tomorrow if not this evening."

"Well, I suppose that's convenient. Joanna's out on an all-day outing with Simon. The last thing she told me was not to talk to Adam if I ran into him today. I think she was afraid I'd start a fight with him or something. I guess she didn't know he was taking a personal day."

Maddie had informed Joanna tartly that she was perfectly capable of controlling herself around Adam, though she'd made no promises that she wouldn't verbally cut him to bits if he dared criticize her sister. "He hasn't taken off, has he? Hasn't run out on her again?"

Walt scowled. "He hasn't run out—and from what I understand, that isn't exactly the way it went last time. He's taking a vacation day, that's all. Said he needed a few hours away from work and people to get his head together. I mean, that makes sense, right? This has all hit him pretty hard."

"It makes sense that he'd have conflicted emotions about finding out he has a son. Jo has a few tangled emotions herself. You think she's happy about having her son's biological father show up? Simon is everything to her, her whole life. She'd do anything to protect him."

"I get that. You're pretty fond of him, too."

"I adore him," she replied simply. "And I'd rip the nose off anyone who ever hurt him."

Walt reached up to rub his nose. "I'll, uh, keep that in mind."

Maddie hit her knee with her fist. "What is it with this guy, anyway? What kind of coward is afraid to acknowledge his own son?"

Walt's expression hardened. "Adam Scott is no coward. He's a decorated soldier who, like me, barely made it back. This development hit him out of the blue, but on the whole, I think he's gone above and beyond to do whatever he can for this boy. Trust me, if it had been up to me, there'd have been definitive paternity test results before any financial offers."

Her eyes narrowed. She drew back in fresh indignation. "Are you implying again that my sister would lie about her son's paternity?"

He held his ground. "Of course I had suspicions when I first learned of the situation. My friend informed me a woman he'd known for only a weekend had turned up with a son she claimed was his, and that he was making the kid his sole beneficiary. You'd have reacted the same if a client came to you with that scenario."

He was probably right, but Maddie wasn't about to admit it. "My sister is not a scammer."

"I'm pretty sure of that now. I only had to talk to her for a few minutes—and to see Simon, by the way—to figure she was telling the truth, at least about his connection to

Adam. But Adam is my friend as well as my client, and he's doing the best he can to deal with this. I won't let anyone call him a coward."

"He won't even let Joanna tell Simon that Adam is his father."

"Maybe he thinks that's for the best. Maybe he's convinced this is better than haggling over visitation and parental rights. I don't know. But having no idea how I'd react, I'm not going to second-guess his decisions."

She bit back any further criticism. Walt hadn't taken that well. Fair enough. She wasn't going to let him say a word against Joanna, either.

She and Walt might have crazy chemistry, but they were very much on opposite sides in this situation. And while she could respect Walt's loyalty, she still found Adam's actions hard to understand.

She sighed and nodded. "Okay, fine. I'll talk to Joanna, but my prediction is that she's not going to be overly cooperative with the legal arrangements. She's no more interested in formal negotiations than Adam is. From what she's said to me, I believe she'll instruct you to advise your client to set up an account for Simon himself and contribute to it as he sees fit in the future. She won't accept a penny of the money to use for her own benefit."

"Your sister is a proud woman."

"A proud, independent and very stubborn woman," she amended.

"Something tells me the two of you are very much alike."

Maddie smiled faintly. "If you'd said that to me ten years ago—even six years ago—I'd have said you were crazy. Joanna was the star student, the dutiful daughter, the one who never broke a rule or even missed a curfew."

"And you?"

She shrugged, relaxing now that the conversation had turned more personal. Maybe Walt irked the hell out of her when he defended his buddy, but she still found him sexy as all get-out. She brought a hint of flirtation back to her voice when she murmured, "I was none of those things."

He eyed her with a renewed wariness. "Why doesn't that surprise me?"

She laughed softly and reached out to trace his jaw. "Can't imagine."

"I, uh, I guess you turned out okay, regardless. Smartass," he added wryly, "but respectable."

Her grin widened. "I'm not so sure my parents would agree with you, but once their perfect older daughter got herself knocked up, I looked a little better to them. Dad's still waiting for me to join a more upscale country club legal firm—or at the very least, become a professor—and both of them wish Jo would concentrate on getting tenure at an Ivy League university rather than going into practice, but they've resigned themselves. I think Jo's picked up a few tips from me about living her own life without worrying so much about pleasing others."

"I've always admired people who learn that lesson early and then follow the beat of their own personal drummers."

Okay, so Walt was on the other side legally. And he seemed to have issues with her age—or was it her boldness that unsettled him? Didn't stop her from melting in response to the open admiration on his face. A few other sun-lovers lounged, strolled, chatted and played on the beach around them while waves crashed and seagulls shrieked, but as far as she was concerned, nothing around them was as interesting as the battle-scarred man sharing her towel, incongruously dressed in business casual.

She eyed him through her lashes. "What about you, Sarge? Whose drums do you follow?"

He gave her a grin that was unexpectedly

roguish—not to mention devastatingly attractive. "The drums that usually lead me into the most trouble."

Oh, wow. If he'd decided to seduce her, he was doing a damned good job.

Studying him, she asked, "Mind if I ask why Mrs. Sergeant Becker decided she'd rather be Mrs. Plastic Surgeon?"

His grin dimmed, and she could tell she'd hit a nerve. Still, he managed to keep his tone droll when he replied, "She said she didn't care for the man who came back from the war."

Instantly indignant on his behalf, Maddie demanded, "She left you because you lost your arm?"

"She claimed I lost a lot more than an arm." He shrugged. "Maybe she was right. Whatever. She preferred the doctor she'd met while I was out of the country. They got married before the ink was dry on the divorce papers. Got a litter of babies now."

Judging by the tone and expression with which he spoke, Walt had accepted the situation. Maddie suspected his feelings were a bit more complex. She wanted to know a lot more about him—but first she supposed they should settle Joanna and Adam's issues.

She wasn't sure how Joanna would feel

about her seeing Adam's friend. His attorney.
But Joanna would be moving to Seattle soon
and Maddie would continue, as she always
had, to make her own choices. Those choices
might well include a few long weekends at the
Carolina coast.

## CHAPTER NINE

"THIS WAS THE best day ever, Mom!" Simon proclaimed as they entered the suite that afternoon. "I had so much fun. I can't wait to tell Aunt Maddie and Mr. Adam about it. We can show them all the pictures we took, can't we? I bet Mr. Adam has seen the dolphins in the ocean lots of times, but I don't know if Aunt Maddie has. I bet she'll like our pictures."

"I'm sure she will." Joanna was tired and a little sunburned, but she'd had a wonderful day with her son. The well-organized outing had begun with an island shell hunt, during which Simon had pounced on the starfish he'd hoped to find all week, followed by a traditional Carolina crab boil lunch with the other families, and concluding with a two-hour dolphin cruise. The dolphins had been playfully cooperative today, putting on quite a show for the delighted spectators.

"I'm hungry," Simon declared, rubbing his tummy. "Where are we going to eat tonight? Can we have fried shrimp baskets again?"

Joanna almost groaned. She was still so stuffed from their huge lunch of crab, sausage, potatoes, corn on the cob, and peach cobbler that she would have been perfectly happy to skip dinner altogether.

"I think we'll find something a little healthier than fried shrimp and french fries tonight," she said, placing a hand on his shoulder. "Maybe the grilled chicken kabobs you saw the other day. You said they looked good, remember?"

"Okay. But can we have fried shrimp baskets one more time before we go home?"

"Yes. One more time. Now you need to go shower and change for dinner. I'll call Aunt Maddie and tell her we're back."

"Okay. Can you call Mr. Adam, too? Maybe he can have dinner with us. I want to show him my starfish."

Thinking of the way she and Adam had parted last night, Joanna wasn't sure Adam would accept. Would he want to spend another evening with Simon even though he wasn't going to have a relationship with the boy in the future? Or would he want the chance to spend every minute he could with Simon before they left the resort Sunday morning?

"I'll ask him," she said cautiously. "But he

could already have other plans, so don't be too upset if he can't join us."

"That's okay. I can tell him tomorrow. But I hope he can come tonight."

Joanna was just going to call Maddie when someone rapped on the door. Though it was probably her sister, she couldn't stop her nerves from tingling a little, just in case it was…someone else.

She told herself she wasn't disappointed when she found Maddie standing there, looking oddly solemn. Apparently Maddie had also been out in the sun that day. Her face and arms were kissed with new color, and her long legs looked golden beneath the short hem of her sleeveless white mini.

"Hi, Jo. Where's Simon?"

"He's taking a shower and getting ready for dinner." Joanna closed the door behind her sister, wondering why Maddie looked and sounded so serious. "I was just going to call to ask you to join us."

"I'd like that. But first—there's something I should tell you."

"What's going on?"

"Walt Becker tracked me down earlier to tell me that Adam took a day off work today, but he left a request for us to figure out a fair child support agreement and submit it to Walt.

Adam will sign it, but he doesn't want any more meetings and he doesn't want to be any more involved than that. He just wants to take care of it through his lawyer."

She kept her gaze on Joanna's face as she spoke. "He left his cell number, said to call if we have any questions, but he made it clear he doesn't want to be bothered unless it's an emergency. He said he needed a few hours to clear his head, and he'll see everyone later."

Joanna didn't know what she was feeling or thinking. Maybe Adam hadn't technically taken off without a goodbye this time, assuming she could believe he'd come back later, but it was clear enough that he'd made his decision. He was choosing not to be part of Simon's life, opting instead to be an anonymous financial donor. The easy way out.

She supposed she should have been angry with him. And maybe she was, beneath the numbness. Of course she was. For Simon's sake—and for her own. Was Adam merely declining fatherhood—or was he rejecting any future with her, as well? Not that they'd even acknowledged the possibility, but still, maybe something real could have developed, had he been willing to let down his defenses. Had she been able to trust that he wouldn't walk out again.

Sure, he'd had a rough childhood. But lots of people had, and plenty chose to deal with the past and move on. It irked her that he wouldn't even try. But mostly…mostly she was just sad. Sad for Simon's sake, though she would continue to dedicate herself to making sure her little boy had a wonderful life, even if he never knew his father. And somewhat grudgingly sad for Adam, despite her frustration.

Maybe her training as a counselor was making her read too much into their interactions, but she sensed a dissatisfaction in him that he probably couldn't have verbalized if he tried. He was missing out on so much, too stubborn or afraid or set in his ways to commit himself to anyone. Whatever painful lessons he'd learned from his absentee father or his time at war or any other difficult experiences he'd survived, she hated to think of him always drifting, always alone, never allowing himself to appreciate what was right in front of him.

She'd known a few people who were content living nomadic lives, without roots or ties. Perhaps Adam's father had been that way. But she wanted to believe Adam secretly longed for more, even if he didn't realize it himself. Maybe he just hadn't yet found the person or the place he could love enough to want to stay. Or maybe she was only fantasizing that he could be the man she wanted, rather than who he really was.

Her sister's voice brought her out of her reverie. "Jo? Are you okay?"

Hearing Simon moving around in his bedroom, Joanna forced a smile. "I'm fine, Maddie. I wasn't really expecting anything else from him."

"Really? Nothing?" Maddie asked skeptically, proving she was aware that Joanna's feelings for Adam had become complicated during this week.

Joanna replied evenly, "I would never force him to be a part of our lives. I won't ask for anything he doesn't want to give. I won't be calling him in the future unless there's an extreme emergency. Adam knows how to reach me if he changes his mind."

"What about Mr. Adam?" Simon asked, appearing in the doorway just in time to hear the last part. His hair was still wet, hastily combed too flat. He'd dressed in the T-shirt and shorts she'd laid out for him, and he carried his shoes in his hand. He looked so young and innocent—and so very much like Adam.

Joanna swallowed hard before saying, "Mr. Adam is busy tonight, Simon. But Aunt

Maddie wants to hear all about our day, don't you, Maddie?"

"I don't want you to forget one detail," Maddie replied a little too cheerily.

"Do you want to see my starfish?"

"Absolutely."

Watching the exchange, Joanna swallowed as she acknowledged how much Simon had bonded with Adam in such a short time. It must be a genetic susceptibility, though Maddie didn't seem to share their weakness. But Simon was very young and eager for new experiences. After all, he didn't even know the real connection between himself and Adam. He'd get over his disappointment and move on with his life, at least for a few years until he started asking more questions about his father. Questions Joanna would need to answer honestly and compassionately.

As for herself—well, she was resigned to carrying an Adam-size hole in her heart. A wistful longing for what might have been between them. At least she had their son to love and to love her in return. Adam was alone—and stubbornly convinced he liked it that way.

"How the hell did you find me, Walt?"

Walt chuckled as he slid onto a bar stool next to Adam. They were about an hour's drive away from the resort. "Trevor. He said he has his magical ways of keeping tabs on you."

Adam snorted. "His 'magical ways' involve asking me where I am and me telling him."

"Hmm. I like his version better. More interesting." Walt ordered a tap beer from the bartender and nodded toward the drink Adam had been nursing. Adam had lost track of exactly how long he'd sat there. "Drowning your sorrows?"

"Just thirsty," he muttered, taking an unenthusiastic sip from his glass.

When he'd told Trevor he was taking the day off, he'd added that he'd have a decision about the offered promotion by the middle of next week. In response, Trevor had asked if he was okay. He'd said he understood that Adam was dealing with a lot and he didn't blame him for needing a few hours to think.

And somehow during that brief conversation, Trevor had pulled out exactly where Adam was going to do that thinking. And had then shared that information with their mutual friend.

"Did Trevor send you?"

Walt shook his head. "No. That was my decision."

"Why?"

"I needed to see my client. In person."

"Nothing's wrong, is it?"

"Other than you being an idiot, you mean?" Walt took a drink of his beer, leaving the question hanging.

Adam scowled. "Don't rag on me, okay? You wouldn't understand."

Rather than taking offense, Walt nodded agreeably. "Yeah, I'd never understand what it's like to come back from war scarred both physically and emotionally, too messed up to keep a relationship together, too jumpy to attend a Fourth of July fireworks display."

Grimacing, Adam shook his head. "Damn it, Walt. That's not what I meant."

"Maybe I understand better than you think. Just saying."

They drank in silence for a while before Adam asked, "Did you talk to them?"

Walt didn't need clarification. "I talked with Maddie. She believes Joanna would prefer that you set up a fund for Simon on your own and contribute to it as you choose. Joanna wants nothing to do with the financial arrangements."

"Doesn't surprise me. She's too proud." And stubborn and independent and smart and caring—in addition to so many other admirable qualities that she could almost qualify for sainthood, he thought glumly. Something no one had ever said about him.

His friend nodded. "That's what I said. Maddie agreed."

Adam glanced sideways at his companion. "You still have a thing for her?"

Walt gazed into his glass. "She's definitely something. But like I said before, hardly in my league."

Remembering his early impressions of spunky, smart-mouthed, slick and chic Maddie Zielinski, Adam didn't try to argue. He couldn't say that Walt and Maddie were any better a match than he and Maddie's competently professional yet still happily domestic sister. The sister he'd overheard saying she would like more children, who seemed to have no issues with commitments or parenthood or tangled family ties. "Maddie's probably too young for you, anyway."

"She doesn't seem to think so. At least, not if I'm reading her signals correctly—and I'm pretty sure I am. She's not exactly subtle."

"Oh." A little taken aback, Adam muttered, "I guess I thought she wouldn't want to be involved with someone who represents the, uh, opposition."

"The opposition? I thought you were the one who insisted there's no conflict. Nobody's trying to make you pay up or sign anything or stay anywhere you don't want to be."

"Then why are you here?"

"Just letting you know you have a friend. I fought my demons a long time ago, Adam. Wouldn't say I won, exactly, but I've got the bastards beaten into submission most of the time. Thing is, I didn't do it alone. You don't have to, either."

Again, silence seemed to be the only response Adam could muster. He'd been alone for so long, he didn't know how to react when told he didn't have to be. His demons had become part of him a long time ago, and he wasn't sure beating them into submission was even an option at this point. Still, he appreciated the gesture. He hid his discomfort with another gulp of his drink.

Walt lifted his glass, gazing into it thoughtfully. "My old man liked his beer. He wasn't a mean drunk. Just the opposite, actually. The drunker he got, the cheerier he became. He was cheery a lot."

He took a sip and set the glass on the bar. "My father wasn't perfect. My mom had her hands full trying to raise me and my sister and still work two jobs to keep food on the table. Pop had trouble keeping jobs. But he was my dad and I loved him. We all did."

Adam pushed a weary hand through his hair. "Yeah, well, I didn't see my father enough to know what I felt about him. He was just some aging hippie who drifted through town to say hello and bum a few bucks to hold him over until his next visit."

"Not cool," Walt said. "So, you're going to miss out on your son's life because your old man was a lousy father? How does that make sense?"

The barb hit home with an accuracy that made Adam wince. "That's not—I just don't want to mess up the kid's life."

"So don't. Be a better father than yours was."

Yeah. As if it were that easy. "They're moving across the country. Even if I knew how to be a father, how am I supposed to do it from three thousand miles away? I could follow them, but what am I supposed to do in Seattle? Even if I could find a job and an apartment I could afford, what would I have to offer a kid like Simon?"

"You're selling yourself short, pal. And I couldn't help noticing you didn't mention Joanna."

Adam's insides churned at the mention of her name. He fought the images that flashed through his mind. He'd spent a lot of time today wondering who unnerved him more—the innocent child or his all-too-knowing mother.

"I've seen you with her, Adam. She's not just someone you casually hooked up with. You have feelings for her. It's possible you always have, even if you didn't realize it until she came back into your life."

Adam made a point of scrubbing a drop of liquid off the bar top with one finger.

Reading too much into that silence, Walt murmured, "So you're scared of her, too?"

"I'm not scared of Joanna," Adam snapped. Lied. "I just don't want to mess up her life, either."

"And you're so sure you would."

His hand clenched around his glass. "Let's just say I learn from my mistakes. Look what happened last time I got involved with her."

Walt's grunt expressed a mixture of disapproval and sympathy. "You don't have to follow them to Seattle, if that's not what you want. You've got a good opportunity here in South Carolina. You're damned good at your job, and Trevor's ready to reward you for that. All you have to do is say yes."

All he had to do. That made it all sound so damned easy.

Setting down the still half-full glass of beer,

Walt pulled money out of his pocket and dropped it on the bar. "Your drink's on me. And now I have to go. Watching you brood has made me think there's someone I might want to get to know better."

"Maddie?"

Walt nodded with a crooked grin. "It might all end in flames, but I won't know unless I try."

"And if it ends in regret? Heartache?"

Walt clapped his right hand on Adam's back. "Then maybe I'll be the one who ends up brooding in a dark bar. It's all part of living, my friend. Not the best part, but it is what it is."

"I hate that saying," Adam grumbled.

Laughing softly, Walt ambled away, leaving Adam to stew. Maybe—just maybe—Walt had been right about a few things.

*It might all end in flames, but I won't know unless I try.*

Adam had never doubted that Walt was a courageous, resilient man. A hero—a word Adam had certainly never applied to himself. But maybe—just maybe—it was time he tried to find some of that fortitude for his own sake. After all, he'd never know if he could do it unless he tried.

Of course, his wasn't the only happiness

he'd be risking this time. And he realized that for once, his greatest fear wasn't for himself—but for Simon and Joanna, both of whom had somehow become entirely too important to him for his peace of mind.

IT WAS LATE when Walt knocked on Maddie's door, but he'd called first, so she was expecting him. After flipping through the clothes she'd hastily packed for this impromptu vacation, she'd chosen a body-hugging summer dress in a deep royal blue she knew was flattering. She'd left her sparkly-nailed feet bare and her hair tousled rather than sleek, applying only enough makeup to highlight her eyes and adding a clear gloss to her lips. Sexy but not trying too hard, she decided as she gave herself a once-over in the mirror before answering the door.

He smiled approvingly when she let him into the sitting room of her small suite. "You look very nice."

"Thank you." He looked damned good himself, in a pale blue-and-white-striped cotton shirt with gray chinos. The shirt was long-sleeved, like the others she'd seen him wear, but turned back to forearm-length, revealing a bit more of the skin-toned prosthetic.

She was curious about his condition, of

course. She wondered how the arm was attached, and if he ever used alternate prosthetics, but his missing hand didn't make him any less attractive to her. Walter Becker couldn't have been more different from the men she usually dated, but something about the way he looked at her made her toes curl. She had a feeling he tackled everything he did with that same intense concentration—and the possibilities were quite stimulating.

She motioned toward the couch, and the open bottle of wine and two glasses on the coffee table beside a bowl of fruit. "I could make coffee, if you prefer. The suite comes stocked with a pretty impressive selection."

"The wine looks good. Just a glass, though. I had half a beer earlier. With Adam," he added.

She paused with one glass half-filled. "Adam? Is he back at the resort?"

"No. I tracked him down. He didn't go far. He'll probably be back in a couple of hours, if not sooner." Walt accepted the wine and watched as she poured another for herself.

She sank onto the couch, patting the cushion beside her. He settled close enough to keep her pulse rate elevated, though she tried to focus on the conversation. "Why did you go to him? Was it to discuss the arrangements for Simon?"

"Not really. Most of that is already settled. I went as a friend. Wanted to make sure he's okay. And to tell him he's an idiot."

"I might have told him a few other things," Maddie said darkly into her wineglass.

She couldn't help remembering the look in her sister's eyes when she'd heard about Adam's impersonal message about anonymous child support. Joanna had made an effort to mask her feelings, but Maddie knew her sister too well to be fooled. She'd seen beneath the impassive expression to the disappointment that throbbed beneath it.

"Adam's hurting, Maddie."

*His choice*, she wanted to retort, but she bit the words back. Walt was worried about his friend. And he knew Adam a lot better than she did. She, of course, was entirely on her sister's side, even though she was well aware that Joanna had her own flaws and insecurities. Despite the prim and proper exterior their parents had trained her to show, Joanna was only human.

All in all, it was probably best if she and Walt just didn't discuss them. Not tonight, anyway. Tonight they could focus on themselves. On the electricity that seemed to

He kissed her throat, the hollow behind her ear, the curve of her breast. She nipped his chin, his ear, everywhere she could reach, enjoying every groan she pulled from him, every ragged breath he drew.

This was one fine, sexy sergeant.

She almost growled in frustration when he suddenly stilled and drew back. "What?"

His eyes stormy, his hard-carved face flushed, he ran his hand over his hair and pushed himself to his feet. "I should go."

Without standing, she leaned back and tilted her head at him, trying to figure out this change in his mood. "Why?" she asked.

He grimaced. "It's complicated. I'm Adam's friend. His attorney."

"This has nothing to do with my sister or your friend," she said flatly. "If you're implying again that I have some ulterior motive for wanting to be with you, then you are very, very wrong."

"I didn't say that." He had the grace to look embarrassed by the suggestion.

She nodded, keeping her tone even, her expression schooled as she drawled, "It's personal, then. Should I be insulted?"

"Hardly."

"So?"

Walt released a gusty sigh. "Look, Maddie,

we just met. I guess what I'm saying is that I'm flattered, but I'm too old for one-night stands. Not that I'm suggesting—I mean, there's nothing wrong with— Anyway."

She was torn between irritation and amusement. She suspected it wasn't like Walt to be so awkward and tongue-tied. She decided to be flattered rather than insulted. "I'm not really into one-night-stands myself these days, Sarge. I'm just not the type who needs a lot of time to know what I want. Or to skirt around the edges when I could be finding out for certain if there's a chance it might be the real thing. If you're not interested in that, say so and I'll back off. No hard feelings. We can even be civil, though I won't promise we'll be pals."

She had no desire to be platonic friends with appealing Walt Becker. As for her other desires—well, she thought she'd made those clear enough. Still, she supposed she could be patient with him taking a bit more time—as long as he acknowledged there could be something lasting between them.

"I didn't say I wasn't interested," he muttered. "Just that I can't see it going anywhere. I mean, you're young and gorgeous and fun and, well…you. And I'm—"

She rose then, placing her fingers over his mouth before he made even more of a mess of this conversation. "You're a strong, fascinating man with an intriguing history and layers I can't wait to explore. I happen to prefer a man who is seasoned and mature. And before you tick me off by implying I'm so flighty and irresponsible that you can't trust me not to toy with you and then take off in pursuit of some slick plastic surgeon, I think you should go now."

"I didn't—"

She rose on her tiptoes, clutching his shirt. "Just so you'll know what you're missing…" she murmured, and then kissed him until she fancied smoke came out of his ears. She could almost feel it escaping her own when she finally drew back, making no effort to mask her arousal. "Good night, Walt."

He blinked dazedly. "Uh—"

Still smiling, she opened the door and all but pushed him out of it. "Sweet dreams, Sarge."

She heard his curse through the door when she closed it between them, which made her laugh again. And then groan when she conceded that he wasn't the only one left with an aching awareness of how the night could have ended.

THE PAINFUL EMOTIONS Joanna had been suppressing broke through the surface with a vengeance in the middle of that night.

She was awakened from a restless sleep by a call from her son from the other room. Blearily noting the time was just after 2:00 a.m., she stumbled into his doorway. "What's wrong, sweetie? Did you have a bad dream?"

"I'm sorry, Mom, but I'm really thirsty. Can I have some water?"

"Of course. Just a second." Clearing her head, she filled a glass for him and returned to sit on the side of his bed. Illuminated by the soft glow of a night-light, he drank with noisy gulps while she watched with an indulgent smile. He really had been thirsty.

"Thank you, Mommy," he said, handing her the glass while he wiped his mouth with the back of one hand.

Her throat tightened for a moment. He rarely called her Mommy these days, having decided a few months earlier that "Mom" sounded much more grown up. She tried to savor each of these precious, fleeting moments while they lasted. "You're welcome."

He decided he should probably go to the bathroom while he was awake, and she promised to wait to tuck him back in. She smoothed his sheets while he was gone, having the bed ready by the time she heard a flush followed by running water. Simon's hands were still damp when he hugged her as she nestled him back into the big bed, but she didn't mind the cold feel of them on her neck. She kissed his cheek and pulled the sheet to his chin. "All set?"

"Mmm-hmm." He sounded sleepy, but she knew from experience that it would take him a few moments to settle down. "Tomorrow's our last all-day here, isn't it?"

"Yes." She kept her voice soft as she stroked his hair. "We'll make the most of it. We'll swim and play on the beach and look for more shells, and you can have a shrimp basket for lunch."

"That sounds like fun." His eyes were already half-closed. "Can I show Mr. Adam my starfish?"

A pang ripped through her, and she had to swallow before she could speak. "I don't know if we'll see Mr. Adam tomorrow, Simon. It's the weekend, you know. I'm not sure he works on weekends. But Aunt Maddie will be here with us all day, and she's going to want you to show her everything she hasn't seen yet. Maybe you'd like to play minigolf with her? Or paddle boats on the lake?"

Simon's eyelids had flown open. "But we

can see Mr. Adam before we leave, can't we, Mom? I don't want to go without telling him goodbye."

Her chest ached. She didn't want to make promises she couldn't keep. If Adam had decided to relinquish parental rights, maybe it was best to start putting distance between him and Simon now, before Simon grew more attached. Before she grew more attached, despite her anger with him. "Mr. Adam isn't a fan of goodbyes, sweetheart. If you don't see him again, we'll just remember how much fun you had with him, okay? I took lots of pictures at the fun center. You can look at them anytime you want."

"It's not the same," he said, his lip quivering.

"No," she agreed, lowering her voice to a soothing murmur. "It's not the same. But happy memories are always the best souvenirs we take home from vacations. Every time you look back on this week, you can think of the fun you had while we were here. All the new friends you made and the things you learned. All the sand castles we built and the pretty shells we found. The good food we ate and the games we played. The sun and seagulls and the boat ride and the funny dolphins…"

She let the singsong words trail off into a

whisper and then into silence when she saw that Simon had fallen asleep. His breathing was deep and even, his eyelashes dark against his cheeks. She thought the slightest frown still creased his forehead, but then he snuggled more deeply into the pillow, and his sweet face smoothed into blissful repose.

Careful not to jostle him, she stood, waiting there a moment to make sure he didn't rouse, then turned to slip silently out of the room, leaving the door open a crack. She moved into her own room, then spent the next twenty minutes trying to hold back the tears she was afraid to release for fear of drowning in them.

Despite the occasional wistful sniffle, she'd never allowed herself to cry over Adam. She'd always told herself it would be foolish to grieve for a relationship that had never existed. Sure, there'd been the odd bout of tears during her pregnancy, but she'd written those off to nerves and hormones. Certainly not to missing the man she'd known for such a short time.

She wouldn't cry now, though she had to dash impatiently at her eyes several times to put a stop to it. But it hurt. It hurt deeply that he seemed to be walking away again, even knowing everything now. He couldn't claim ignorance this time, though he probably thought he was being noble again, acting in her and Simon's best interests. That argument was even more groundless now than it had been before, though she wasn't sure she could convince him of that even if he gave her the chance to try. He was so convinced he was destined to be alone, even to the point of believing it was what he wanted.

Maybe it was just as well, she told herself with a defiant lift of her chin. Maybe it was for the best that she'd been forced to confront the reality of trying to build a relationship, even a tenuous, long-distance one, with a man who wouldn't make even the most basic commitment. Oh, he'd signed papers and set up accounts, made financial promises he would probably keep—but that was easy. Detached, impersonal, no emotional investment or risk involved. A way to assuage his conscience without limiting his freedom to take off whenever he wanted without any of those messy goodbyes.

She'd tried, she assured herself. She'd been willing to work with him. To share the child she'd carried, nursed, taught, protected, loved with every fiber of her being. She'd been cautiously ready to trust him. And he'd shown her just how much pain and disappointment she courted—for herself and for Simon—in giving that trust to a man who wasn't willing to accept it.

Fine. If this was what he wanted, so be it. She could accept that she'd done all she could to make up for the mistakes she'd made six years ago. She wouldn't chase him, wouldn't make any demands. Someday she would figure out how to tell Simon about him, but for now, they were perfectly fine without Adam Scott in their lives.

She just wished this psychologist knew how to heal her own heartache.

SATURDAY MORNING DAWNED with rain. Simon was dismayed at first, certain their last full day at the resort was ruined. He was reassured when Joanna checked the weather app on her phone and told him the rain was predicted to pass very quickly, probably in less than an hour.

"We'll have a great time, I promise," she said, determined not to let the weather or Adam or anything else interfere with this vacation with her son. Soon enough, they'd have to face the demands of a move, new job, new school, making a new life, new friends in a new town—but this week was a celebration of their little family. Their two-member immediate family, she silently amended even as she sent him to dress for a day of fun.

Maddie joined them for breakfast. The rain splashed soothingly against the windows as they ate and chatted, surrounded by other vacationers waiting for the sun's return. Simon didn't mention Adam, and neither did Joanna or Maddie. Still, Joanna had the feeling that his name hovered in the backs of all their minds.

"It's almost stopped raining," Simon announced, bouncing in his seat as he pointed to the windows.

"Yes, but it's still a little wet," Maddie answered. "How about I challenge you to a friendly game of air hockey in the arcade while we wait for the sun to do its job?"

Simon giggled. "You're on!"

Joanna made a show of gazing upward and groaning. "Not again. You two go crazy whenever there's an air hockey table in the room."

Aunt and nephew grinned across the table at each other, and though they didn't look much alike, the fierce heat of competition on their faces was unsettlingly similar.

Joanna shook her head.

Fifteen minutes later, the battle was on. Simon had to stand on a plastic stepstool to have full access to the table, but he didn't let his size handicap him. He threw himself into the game with enthusiasm, whooping and cheering whenever he made a good shot, protesting noisily but being a good sport when a point was scored against him. Standing safely to one side of flailing arms, Joanna laughed and took pictures with her phone. She knew Simon would appreciate having this fun with his aunt memorialized in the photo book.

That photo book would also include pictures of Adam, she thought with a faint sigh. Simon would have too many questions if she didn't add the ones she'd taken at the fun center. And maybe someday, after she'd found a way to explain the truth to him, he would want that reminder of the week he'd spent with his father. Maybe he'd see what she'd seen in those snapshots—the mixture of wonder and regret in Adam's face when he'd smiled down at his son.

They'd made reservations for a horseback ride on the beach that afternoon, something Simon requested after hearing about the activity from one of his Explorers Club friends. Through the guest relations services, Joanna had asked for two horses, one for her and Simon, the other for Maddie. Children under eight were allowed to ride on buddy saddles behind an adult. She expressed concerns to the concierge that she didn't have much experience on horseback, but she was assured the horses were gentle and the guides would take very good care of them.

After spending the remainder of the morning at the beach, followed by Simon's promised shrimp basket lunch, they freshened up in their suites, then met Maddie in the Seafoam Lodge courtyard in preparation for the horseback outing. Joanna had Maddie and Simon pose in front of the pretty little koi pond. They smiled dutifully for her photos, then were distracted by the big, colorful fish swimming around the central fountain. Joanna kept shooting, capturing snaps of Simon pointing out his favorite fat yellow koi while Maddie laughingly prevented him from falling into the water in his eagerness.

She lowered her phone when someone touched her shoulder from behind. Thinking she was blocking another guest's path, she murmured an apology and stepped aside, glancing around to make sure she was out of the way. She nearly dropped the phone when she saw who stood there.

Adam had returned.

## CHAPTER TEN

THOUGH IT WAS probably only seconds, it felt like several minutes passed before Joanna was able to compose herself. She wanted to ask Adam why he'd disappeared the day before, why he'd left terse instructions with his attorney, what the hell he wanted from her—if anything—but this was hardly the time or place for such a confrontation. Nor did she want to reveal how flustered she was to see him again.

Before she could decide what to say, she heard Simon shout, "Mr. Adam!"

A small bundle collided into Adam's legs, making him stagger backward as he caught the boy to accept the enthusiastic hug. "Hey, Skipper. What've you been up to today?"

Simon beamed up at him, causing Joanna to press a hand to her stomach at the happiness on his face. "We've been having fun swimming and playing beach games. It rained this morning, but not for long, and I played air hockey with Aunt Maddie until everything dried off. I almost beat her this time. She says pretty soon I'll be good enough to win every game."

"No doubt."

Maddie had reached Joanna now, and both of them stood there watching Adam interact with his son. Joanna hoped her own expression was less disapproving than her sister's.

"Mom said you might not be here today, Mr. Adam." Simon had stepped back some now, tilting his head curiously.

"Yes, well, I didn't want you to leave without me seeing you again," Adam replied lightly.

"Mom said you're not a fan of goodbyes."

Adam's gaze clashed with Joanna's before he said, "That's true, but sometimes they're inevitable, I guess."

"I'm glad you're here, Mr. Adam. I want to tell you all about the dolphin tour yesterday."

"I'd like to hear all about it."

Joanna glanced at her watch. "Simon, we have fifteen minutes to get the stable if you still want to take the horseback ride."

Simon caught his breath. "Oh, yeah. We're going to ride horses on the beach! I can't ride by myself, but it will still be fun. Come with us, Mr. Adam. Please?"

"Actually, I have some things to attend to this afternoon. Maybe later we can meet for dinner?"

Simon's face fell. And though he nodded in acceptance, his lower lip quivered. Whatever she might have found more comfortable for her own sake, Joanna couldn't blame Adam for adding, "But maybe I could take a little time for a horse ride."

The child's smile returned, along with a delighted intake of air. "Are you sure? It's okay if you can't," he said, "but we'd like it very much if you come, too. Wouldn't we, Mom? Wouldn't we, Aunt Maddie?"

No more immune than Adam to Simon's pleading puppy-dog eyes, Joanna managed a smile. "Of course he's welcome."

Everyone looked to Maddie then. She made a face. "As much fun as that sounds, we only reserved two horses, remember? So maybe you three should go play cowboy while I treat myself to the spa for a couple hours."

"But Aunt Maddie—"

"I wouldn't worry about the reservation, Maddie," Adam interjected. "There are usually extra horses. Besides, I know the owner."

Maddie bent down to meet Simon's eyes. "Seriously, Si-bot, would you mind if I hang here for a nice massage? I promise I'm still on for the after-dinner minigolf game. We'll so beat your mom's score. You know how bad she is."

Simon laughed. "She really is."

Normally Joanna would have had a clever retort to the good-natured insults, but with Adam standing there looking at her, all she could do was smile weakly and say, "Maybe I'll surprise you both tonight."

Straightening, Maddie turned to Joanna. "You don't mind, do you, Jo?" she asked, her back to Adam and Simon as she added in a low voice, "I think it's safer this way. I'm not really in a mood to make nice with Adam."

Seeing that dark look in her sister's eyes again, Joanna asked quietly, "You're sure you're okay, Maddie?"

Maddie stepped back with a toss of her head. "Nothing a massage won't cure. See you later, guys. Have fun with the horses."

Joanna noted that Maddie rather pointedly avoided looking at Adam when she turned to walk away. Thinking longingly that a massage and pedicure would be much less stressful than this horseback ride, Joanna vowed to focus on Simon's fun and worry about everything else later.

ADAM ENDED UP being the one riding tandem with Simon. The good-natured horse plodded along the sand with the string of seven other horses in the group. Adam was pretty sure the horse yawned a few times along the well-known route. Yet from the excitement Simon got from the ride, they might as well have been on a wild steed. The boy didn't exactly bounce in the saddle, which Adam told him wouldn't have been very nice to ol' Dez, but he chattered almost nonstop.

Joanna, on the other hand, was quiet on her equally placid mount beside them. Adam could tell she was making an effort to participate for Simon's sake. She smiled and nodded when Simon pointed out sights, laughed at the boy's running jokes, snapped pictures of Simon and Adam on the horse.

Adam was going to want one of those pictures.

Simon clutched Adam's belt on both sides as though the leather was a second set of reins. Sometimes he got a little excited and gripped too tightly, giving Adam the sensation of being almost squeezed in half, but he didn't mind. Let the boy have his fun.

The ridiculousness of the whole situation struck him, making him chuckle. When he'd woken up that morning in his bed, groggy and a little hungover, he couldn't have imagined he'd end up on a horse with a kid—*his* kid—clinging to his belt. He still wasn't sure what would be best for the boy after the vacation ended, still doubted that having a father he barely knew living on the opposite coast would be a particularly healthy, but he'd figured the least he owed him was a few hours of fun and then a proper goodbye.

"What's so funny?" Joanna's mount, Teenie, had drifted close enough that Joanna had heard Adam's laugh.

He looked at her. "Everything. And nothing."

Somehow she seemed to understand.

Because the well-seasoned horse needed no guidance, Adam let his gaze linger on the woman next to him rather than the path ahead. Everything about her appealed to him. The sunlight on her face, warming her skin, bringing out the green in her eyes. The hair that escaped her ponytail, lifting and dancing in the ocean breeze, caressing her cheeks in a manner he'd have enjoyed doing himself. The thin cotton blouse rippling in that same breeze, hugging her breasts. Her slender hips and long legs wrapped around that poky nag, making him have to turn his eyes away before he reacted in a way that was inappropriate under the circumstances.

The ride ended eventually, of course. Chip, one of the guides Adam knew in passing, swung Simon out of his saddle, then turned to assist Joanna while Adam dismounted. Simon wasn't quite ready to call an end to the outing. While Chip moved on to help others, the boy stood stroking the silky skin of the horse's muzzle, and Dez seemed to enjoy the attention.

"Mom, take a picture of me and Adam with Dez," Simon suggested, looking over his shoulder at her. "I don't think you got a picture of Dez's face."

Adam moved into position beside the horse, who bobbed his head as if he knew the moment was being memorialized. Simon grinned up at him, and Adam felt the increasingly familiar lump develop in his throat.

One of the other riders, a middle-aged tourist in a sun visor, souvenir T-shirt, plaid shorts and sneakers, moved forward quickly. "Why don't you get in the picture, too, ma'am?" he suggested in what might have been a Tennessee drawl. "I'll take a family shot."

Joanna's hesitation was so brief it might not have been noticeable to anyone but Adam. But Simon's enthusiastic nod was enough to make her hand her phone to the friendly man and move into place. She chose to stand behind Simon, her hands on his shoulders with the horse's face separating her and Adam.

"All right, now, everyone say 'ride 'em, cowboy,'" their photographer instructed, making Simon laugh while Adam tried his best to look relaxed and untroubled.

The man returned the phone to Joanna with a motion of his other hand toward Simon. "Y'know, I've got a son who looks a lot like me. But these two have us beat. I guess everyone says you look just like your daddy, don't they, young man?"

And this, Adam thought with a wince, was one of the reasons he'd tried to put some distance between himself and the boy. The more time they spent together, the more likely it was that something would happen to confuse Simon.

But the boy merely nodded, suddenly as adept as his parents at keeping his thoughts to himself. "Thank you for taking the picture, sir," he said.

The man nodded in approval. "Polite kid you've got there," he said to Adam as he moved to rejoin his waiting wife. "Testament to his upbringing."

"Yes," Adam murmured. "It is."

An upbringing he'd had no part of.

Simon slipped one hand into his mother's, the other into Adam's as they walked away from the stables. Maybe the boy was getting tired. He wasn't as garrulous as usual, though he still looked happy enough. Adam glanced over his son's head to Joanna, who was staring back at him. Probably trying to figure out what the hell he was doing, what he wanted from her. From the future.

He wished he knew the answer.

DECIDING HE LOOKED FATIGUED, Joanna insisted on Simon getting some rest before dinner and the promised night game of minigolf on the illuminated course. He claimed to be too old for naps these days, but she agreed to let him sit quietly in the suite and watch a video. She wouldn't be at all surprised if he nodded off.

Adam left them in the courtyard, saying he had some things he needed to tend to for work.

"You'll still have dinner with us, won't you?" Simon asked him.

Joanna frowned in response to her son's tone. He sounded unnaturally subdued, almost pensive. Either he was even more tired than she'd realized or perhaps he had become aware of how little time remained of this vacation that had been so much more momentous than either of them could have expected. Perhaps Simon had just discovered that he shared Adam's aversion to goodbyes.

Adam sent Joanna a searching glance before answering, proving she wasn't the only one to have noticed a change in the boy's mood. "Sure, Skipper. If it's okay with your mom."

She nodded, not even attempting a smile since Simon wasn't looking at her. "Of course. Simon would like that."

He nodded, noting her wording, then ruffled Simon's hair and turned to walk away. Both Joanna and Simon watched him until he was out of sight. Only then did Joanna say, "Okay, sweetie, let's go up to the suite. We could both use a little quiet time, I think."

She set the boy up on the couch with her tablet, a bowl of grapes and a bottle of water, then carried a cup of tea for herself out onto the balcony, leaving the slider ajar. She rested both elbows on the table as she sipped and stared blankly at the ocean in the distance, trying not to think about anything in particular. She was tired of thinking.

Her phone beeped with a text from Maddie.

Everything ok?

Simon's resting. I'm having tea.

It wasn't exactly an answer, but she figured it would suffice.

See you in an hour for dinner. You know how to reach me if you need me.

Joanna set the phone aside and picked up her teacup again. She wasn't particularly looking forward to dinner. The three adults in the group were all going to be tiptoeing on eggshells, and someone was sure to make a precarious mistake.

Maybe they were trying too hard to shelter Simon from the truth. Maybe they should simply tell the child everything and hope he understood this awkward situation. He was so smart, so positive and resilient. In the long run, it would probably be in his best interests to be open with him.

She was beginning to wonder who she and Adam had been trying so hard to protect. Simon—or themselves.

After a few minutes lost in her thoughts, she sighed, drained her tea, and stood to carry the cup back inside. Maybe she'd stretch out on the couch beside Simon and watch the kids' oceanography video with him until it was time to prepare for dinner.

The couch was empty except for the tablet

with the video paused on the screen and the barely-touched bowl of grapes.

Surprised that he'd moved so quietly during the few minutes she'd had her back to the door, Joanna told herself he must be in the bathroom. She carried the teacup into the kitchen and rinsed it out, set it beside the sink and then dried her hands.

Turning back to the couch, she shook her head slightly when she saw it was still unoccupied. Had Simon gone to bed and fallen asleep? She couldn't let him nap long, or he'd be groggy and cranky during dinner. She suspected that Adam might be surprised to see just how crabby the usually sweet-natured Simon could become. He'd seen Simon only on his best behavior so far, attributable in part to the fact that everyone had gone out of their way to cater to his vacation whims. She'd have to be careful about that when they got back to reality; she didn't want her sweet son to turn into a brat.

She moved to his open bedroom doorway, only to find the bed neatly made, its only occupant the stuffed dragon on the pillow. Frowning now, she looked at the door to the small bathroom attached to this bedroom. That door, too, was open, the room tidy and empty.

"Simon?"

She turned quickly to check the other bedroom and bath. There was no sign of him. Nor had he slipped out to the balcony while she'd been in the kitchen. She rushed to the suite door. The deadbolt was unlocked. She knew she'd fastened it when they'd come in earlier.

Grabbing her phone, she threw open the door and looked in the hallway, seeing no one but a maid with a load of fresh towels. The concerned maid denied seeing Simon and asked if Joanna wanted the staff to be alerted that he was missing.

"No," she said after a moment's thought, "I'll call for help if I can't find him in a few minutes. I'm sure he hasn't wandered far."

At least, she hoped he hadn't as she hurried toward the stairs. What on earth was he thinking, slipping out again like this? Didn't he know how much trouble he'd be in, especially after that first morning? He'd promised he wouldn't do it again. Open defiance had never been in Simon's nature—at least, not so far. She'd taken her eyes off him for only a few minutes! She'd never had to worry about doing so before.

He wasn't in the courtyard and when asked, the other guests she encountered there hadn't seen him. Her only guess was that he might have headed back to the beach in search of the

Scotch bonnet shell he was desperate to find. She was already dialing her sister's number for help as she hurried up the path.

ADAM WAS SITTING at the computer in his office, hammering out a to-do list for the coming week, when he sensed someone watching him. He hadn't bothered to close his door, but the corporate offices were pretty much empty at this hour on a Saturday, so he hadn't expected to be interrupted. Still, it wasn't a surprise. It seemed as though there was always something needing his attention.

But it wasn't a coworker he found in the open doorway.

"Simon?" Adam pushed himself to his feet, looking over the boy's head to the empty hallway behind him. "What's up? Where's your mom?"

"She's drinking tea on our balcony. I think I'm going to be in trouble."

Rounding his desk, Adam asked, "Why?"

"I kind of didn't tell her I was leaving," Simon admitted, then bit his lip in a gesture that reminded Adam forcibly of Joanna.

"You mean she doesn't know where you are?"

Simon shook his head, and his gray eyes had turned shiny silver. "I wanted to talk to you."

*Oh, man, don't let the kid start crying.* "How did you know where to find me?"

"I knew the offices were up here and you said you had work to do. I came up the stairs and looked in all the open doors."

"Yeah, okay, you can tell me what you want, Skipper, but you've got to let me call your mom first. She'll be worried sick." Adam already had his phone in his hand.

Heaving a sigh, Simon nodded glumly.

Joanna answered before the first ring finished. He could hear the tension in her voice. Obviously she'd already discovered the boy's absence. Having seen how carefully she watched her son, he figured Joanna must be frantic.

"Simon's with me," he said. "He just showed up in my office. He's fine."

He heard her gasp. "Oh, thank God. What is he doing there?"

"I was just about to ask him."

"I'll come—"

"No," he said, seeing with a grimace that the kid's tears were falling in earnest now. "I'll bring him to you. Just give me a couple minutes to find out what's going on, okay? I'll call you again when we're on our way."

He could tell she still wanted to rush to her son, but she conceded. "He got away so fast," she lamented. "I took my eyes off him for only a few minutes…"

"I know. He's a slippery one," Adam answered. He didn't blame her. She was going to have to be even more vigilant in the future, of course, if Simon didn't learn his lesson this time. "I'll call you, JoJo."

After sliding the phone into his pocket, he turned his attention back to the sniffling child. He pulled a tissue from a box on his desk and held it out. "You might want to blow your nose."

The boy did so noisily and thoroughly, then wadded up the tissue and extended it to Adam. Taking it with two fingers, Adam tossed it into the trash, relieved to see that Simon's tears were drying.

"You, uh, want to sit down?" he asked, motioning toward the two cushioned straight-back chairs.

Simon gazed up at him. "Could you sit down, too?"

Smiling a little, Adam sank into one of the chairs. Whatever made him more approachable from the kid's perspective. Simon climbed into the other, his little feet dangling over the edge as he made a visible effort to sit straight and tall.

"Can I offer you anything?" Adam wasn't

sure how to begin such a serious discussion with a five-year-old, so he fell back on social niceties. "There are some sodas and bottled water in the minifridge in the credenza."

Shaking his head, Simon answered with equal formality, "No, thank you."

"Okay, then what can I do for you, Skipper? Is there a problem I can help you with?"

He half expected a gripe about rules or bedtime or the swiftly approaching end to the vacation. Maybe some worries about the approaching move to Seattle. Some sort of guy question the son of a single mom might have for a man who'd befriended him. All reasonable potential topics the kid might want to talk about.

So, he was stunned when Simon said in a low, uncertain voice, "I just need to ask—are you my father?"

Adam all but reared back in shock.

Okay, so maybe he should have let Joanna come rushing over. What had made him think he could have a discussion with Simon on his own? And what the holy hell was he supposed to say now? How could he possibly explain how Simon had come into being, and why they were both only now finding out about their relationship?

Because the boy was still staring almost

fiercely at his face, and bolting in panic didn't seem like an option—this time, at least—he cleared his throat and stalled. "Um—what makes you ask that?"

Twisting his fingers in his lap, the only sign of childish nerves, Simon continued to look steadily at him. "Everyone says we look alike. Everybody. And I looked at the pictures Mom took of us and they're right. And she said she knew you before I was born, and then Aunt Maddie came and she's been acting funny."

"Did, uh, did your aunt say something about me?"

The boy shook his head. "No. But I could tell something was going on."

The drawback to having a kid this smart was that it wasn't going to be easy to put things over on him in the future. In fact, it wasn't going to be easy right now. "Maybe you should talk to your mom…"

"My mom's been acting funny, too. She looks kind of worried when she thinks I don't see her. I wasn't sure she'd want me to ask her. But you'd tell me, right? If you're my dad, I mean."

Squeezing the back of his neck, Adam figured he had only a few choices for what to do. He could look the kid straight in the eyes and lie his ass off—which he wasn't proud to admit was his first cowardly impulse. Or he could maybe figure out a way to stall until he'd had a chance to talk with Joanna, maybe send Simon off with his aunt while he and Joanna came up with an acceptable story.

Or he could justify his son's trust in him and answer with the truth.

"Yes, Simon," he said, leaning forward to rest his forearms on his knees, vividly aware that he had just changed both their lives forever with those two words. "I am."

*Sorry, JoJo.*

Simon blinked rapidly, as if he hadn't truly expected the answer despite his suspicions. He'd gone pale beneath the pink of his cheeks. Adam could tell the child's clever mind was working hard to make sense of this very grown-up revelation.

"You're probably wondering where I've been the past five years."

Chewing his lip, Simon nodded.

Here was the trickiest part. "It's sort of a long story. Your mom and I did meet here, and we, um, became good friends. But I was in the army then and I had to leave to go to war. Your mom had to go back to her work in Atlanta. She didn't know how to reach me, so I didn't know about you until this week. It was my fault for not leaving your mom my phone number," he added, making sure the blame fell on him. "I'm sorry I wasn't there for you before, Simon. But you're really lucky to have such a great mom. She's made sure you had a very good life."

"My mom is the best." The boy's voice was shaky, but unreserved.

"No doubt."

Chewing his lip again, Simon continued to process the abbreviated explanation. "You went to war?"

"I did."

"Did you get hurt?"

"Yes, but I got better." Obviously. Feeling foolish, Adam shifted in his chair, not sure what to say next.

Simon had plenty more questions, which Adam understood. "How come you didn't tell me before I asked?"

Again, honesty seemed the best policy. "We—I wasn't sure how to do that," he said, again accepting full responsibility. "I didn't want to upset you or spoil your vacation with your mom. I thought maybe we should get to know each other before we tried to figure out where to go from here. It's a complicated situation, Simon, hard enough for us adults to deal with, never mind a kid. I wanted you to concentrate on having fun this week. You did, didn't you?"

"I had a lot of fun. But I wish I'd known you were my dad when we did stuff together."

Adam squeezed his tight neck again. "I'm sorry, Skipper. That was my call. I just thought it was easier that way."

And it made him feel even guiltier to know it had been easier on him, not necessarily the boy.

Squirming around, Simon sat on his feet sideways in the chair, gripping the armrest in both hands as he leaned forward to ask, "Do you *want* to be my dad?"

Again, Adam almost drew back in instinctive self-defense, but he made himself remain still. He struggled to come up with the right words. He didn't want to say something wrong and mess up the boy's life any more than he already had. Questions like this were what he'd been trying all week to avoid.

He took a deep breath. "There is no other kid in the world I'd rather have for a son than you, Simon. You're smart as a whip. Funny and friendly and well mannered. You're excited about learning new things, nice to kids like Cody who have extra challenges, gentle with animals. I couldn't be prouder of you."

Simon had followed along intently, his

young face creased with his effort to follow everything Adam was saying. "I like you, too," he said after a pause.

Adam couldn't help smiling. "I'm glad."

With a sudden frown, Simon tilted his head. "Do I still have to call you 'Mr. Adam?'"

"You, uh…you can call me whatever you want."

"Will you still call me Skipper? I like it when you do."

"Then, sure. Skipper it is." Feeling as if he'd just run through a minefield, Adam looked purposefully at his watch. "I know you're going to have a lot more questions, and your mom and I will try to answer them all. But for now, we'd better get back to her. It's close to dinnertime."

Simon crawled out of the chair. His swallow was audible in the quiet office. "Mom's going to be really mad at me."

*At you and me both, kid.* But all Adam said was, "Yeah, probably. And you have to admit you deserve it, Skipper. You should have asked permission before coming here."

"But I needed to talk to you. And I didn't know if Mom would say yes."

Turning off the office light, Adam ushered the boy into the hallway. "Do me a favor, okay? Promise me and promise your mom you won't ever slip out again without letting an adult know where you're going. It isn't safe. And it's wrong to worry your mom that way. She doesn't deserve that."

Simon gave a sigh. "I promise. It just felt easier to go by myself. I won't do it again."

*Oh, crap.* Hearing the matter-of-fact justification in Simon's innocent voice somehow made it feel even worse. He really hoped the boy hadn't inherited more than gray eyes and a cowlick from Adam. Or from Adam's own restless, walk-away dad.

That was hardly the legacy Adam had wanted to leave his son.

"I STILL CAN'T imagine what on earth Simon was thinking to slip off like that," Maddie said, running a hand through her hair in bewilderment. "He's never done anything like this at home, even with Rose."

"I'm hoping it's a vacation aberration," Joanna murmured, making herself stand still when she wanted very badly to pace the suite.

Why *had* Simon felt the need to sneak out and track down Adam? Was it only that he wanted to spend more time with his new friend? Had there been something in particular he wanted to tell or show Adam? She'd checked a few minutes ago and the treasured starfish was still safely in Simon's room, so it hadn't been that. Maybe he'd forgotten to tell Adam something earlier and had impulsively dashed off to rectify that omission. Or maybe he'd been worried that Adam would disappear again and had wanted to make sure he was still joining them for dinner.

Whatever the reason, she was going to have to make very sure this was the last time he pulled this stunt, which would require some sort of consequence.

"And he went straight to Adam," Maddie said. "Are you sure he didn't overhear you say something?"

"Pretty sure." But Joanna rubbed her arms nervously anyway. She should have known by now never to put anything over on her son.

A tap on her door made her whirl in that direction. She rushed to open it.

Simon and Adam stood side by side, and the identically apprehensive looks on their so-similar faces made her heart leap into her throat. Simon scuffed his toe nervously on the hall carpet. She had the distinct feeling that Adam had to restrain himself from doing the same.

"You, young man, are in trouble," she informed the smaller of the two, ignoring the larger for now.

She didn't miss seeing Adam give Simon a nudge.

Simon wet his lips. "I'm very sorry I worried you, Mommy. I shouldn't have left the suite without your permission and I promise I'll never, ever do it again."

He must have practiced that speech, probably with Adam's assistance, all the way from the guest relations building.

Adam cleared his throat.

"Oh." Simon looked meltingly up at her before quoting, "You're the greatest mom in the world and you don't deserve to be treated that way."

Maddie gave a muffled snicker, then turned hastily away when Joanna shot her a look.

"I accept your apology and I'll trust your word," she said to her son after shooting another hard look at Adam. Obviously he'd coached Simon on what to say. But was there a coded message in there from him, as well? "But there will still be a penalty. Your screen time is cut in half for the next week. And you're getting off very easily with that, considering how badly you scared me."

Simon blinked as if in surprise that the punishment wasn't more severe. It probably should have been, but limiting his already regulated time on the computer had been the first thing that had popped into her mind. With Adam standing there watching, it was a wonder she could think at all.

Adam prodded Simon again.

"Um, okay, Mom," the boy said. "I won't do it again."

That settled, Adam turned to Joanna's sister. "Maddie, would you mind very much if Simon and I talk with Joanna? In private?"

Maddie's eyebrows shot up. She glanced quickly at Joanna. "Okay with you?"

Though her stomach was starting to cramp with worry again, Joanna smiled and nodded. "I'll call you in a bit."

Maddie bent to kiss Simon's cheek on her way past, then poked a finger into Adam's chest. "Do not hurt them," she murmured just loudly enough for Joanna to overhear, though Simon probably hadn't caught the words.

"I'm doing my best, Maddie," he said in return.

Joanna's hands were unsteady when she closed the door behind her sister. She didn't even try to smile when she turned back to Adam. The look on his face—apology? defensiveness? regret?—made her knees go weak, so that she leaned back against the door. "What's going on?"

Simon rushed forward, skidding to a stop

in front of her. "It's my fault, Mom. I made him tell me. Mr. Ad—I mean, um—he said we should wait for you, but I wanted to know. And he told me."

Her heart froze in her chest as she looked from Simon to Adam and back again. "He told you…what, exactly, Simon?"

His mouth curved into a smile he couldn't seem to hold back, despite the gravity of the exchange. "He told me he's my dad."

## CHAPTER ELEVEN

GRATEFUL FOR THE door against her back, Joanna stared in shock and disbelief at Adam. After all his dithering, all their convoluted discussions and attempted negotiations, all her warnings that she wanted to protect her son, he had simply told Simon everything? Without her even being there?

She directed her barely-above-a-whisper question to Simon. "He told you that?"

"I keep saying the kid's a genius." Adam's murmur was rueful, but still carried a hint of what might have been pride. "He figured it out. He came to me to ask. I was honest with him, Joanna. What else could I have done?"

As dismayed and unprepared as Joanna felt, she could only imagine the emotions Adam must have felt when Simon had shown up out of the blue and demanded the truth from him. And while she wished that the life-changing conversation had happened differently, that she'd had more involvement, more control over the details, she could hardly fault Adam for not lying, could she? Though she'd been willing to prevaricate to protect Simon, she had never intended to lie outright.

Too dazed for an immediate response, Joanna moved stiffly to a chair, sank into it and took her son's hands. She focused on his face, trying to decipher his thoughts. His emotions. He gazed artlessly back at her. As far as she could tell, he didn't look traumatized, but this had to be a big adjustment for him. Her own world had just tilted on its axis.

She really hadn't been ready for this, despite the preparation she'd thought she made during the past week. "I know this is a lot of information for you to process. I'm sorry I didn't tell you sooner."

"That's okay, Mom." He smiled reassuringly at her, almost as if she was the one in need of moral support. "Mr.—uh, he explained it to me. How you thought we should get to know each other first. I understand."

"You do?" She shook her head slowly. How had her child gone from five to fifteen all of a sudden?

It hadn't escaped her notice that Simon couldn't seem to figure out what to call Adam now.

"Sure," he said with a giggle that was all

little boy again. "It would be weird if we didn't know each other, wouldn't it?"

She stroked his arm, her eyes prickling with tears as love flooded through her. All she wanted was to do the right thing for her son, to make sure he was happy and safe, secure in the knowledge that he was loved. "Yes, sweetie. I guess it would be weird."

He rubbed his tummy. "Can we have dinner now? I'm really hungry."

And that was that? Utterly baffled, she looked at Adam, who'd listened intently, looking almost as perplexed as she felt. "Um, yes, of course. Go wash your face and hands and we'll eat."

"Okay." Simon started to dash toward his room, then paused to eye Adam. "You're eating with us, right? You haven't changed your mind?"

"I, uh—"

Maybe Adam was tempted to beg off, get a chance to regain his equilibrium—and Joanna could hardly blame him for that—but predictably, he caved when Simon gazed up at him. They were all going to have to watch that in the future. "I haven't changed my mind."

"Don't forget to tell Aunt Maddie we're ready to go," Simon called over his shoulder as he ran out of the room.

"Oh, my God." Joanna stood and raised her hands to her temples, trying to press away the dull headache that had settled there.

"Just so you know—" Adam took a step toward her and lowered his voice with a cautious look in the direction of Simon's room "—the kid kind of scares me."

Still struggling with her own emotions, she couldn't smile at what she assumed was an attempt at humor. "I can't believe he did that. I know it looks bad that he got away from me twice this week, but I swear I was only on the balcony and the door was open between us. I'd looked away for a few minutes. I guess I was too distracted, maybe too wrapped up in worrying about the future, but I…"

Adam was equally serious now. "Joanna. I'm not blaming you. He'd have probably gotten away from me the same way. Who could have predicted he'd suddenly turn into an escape artist this week when apparently he's never done this before?"

"No, never," she whispered, relieved that he understood. "Obviously I'll watch him like a hawk from now on, at least until I'm certain he knows this is unacceptable behavior."

"For what it's worth, I think he meant it when he promised he wouldn't do it again.

But watching him is probably a good idea for a while."

She shook her head slowly. "I don't know how he found out about you. I was so sure he didn't overhear any of our conversations..."

Adam rubbed his neck as if she wasn't the only one dealing with the threat of a migraine. "We weren't giving him enough credit, I guess. Every time someone commented about how much he looked like me, or assumed we were father and son, he was paying attention. He might not know much about relationships yet, but he can put two and two together."

She crossed her arms tightly over her chest as she faced him. "I'm sorry," she said, keeping her voice low. "I know you didn't want it to be like this. You were still trying to decide whether you even wanted to tell him."

She couldn't quite read his expression when he muttered, "He'd have figured it out eventually. Unless you planned to hide those pictures you took of us."

"No. I told him I would make a photo book of our vacation. He'd have had even more questions if I hadn't taken shots at the fun center or on horseback."

"Like I said, Simon's a smart kid."

"So what now?" she asked, half to herself.

"Now..." He glanced around as Simon

bounced out into the room, then finished in resignation, "Now you call your sister and we'll go have a nice family dinner."

EVEN A FIVE-YEAR-OLD had to be aware of the tension lurking beneath the very civil conversation at the table that evening, but Simon chattered as easily as ever, recapping everything he'd done during the week. They saw a few other people they'd met in passing and exchanged greetings and farewells with some of them, but there were a lot of new faces in Torchlight this evening. Joanna figured that many of the guests who'd chosen this same week for vacation had already headed back to their homes and routines. Just as she and Simon would be doing the next morning.

Once again she saw Adam in his professional role as resort employees acknowledged him with respectful nods and genuine smiles that proved he was well-liked here. Guests greeted him with equally telling warmth. He made it clear that he was there to make their stay pleasant and trouble-free, along with the rest of the obliging and thoroughly prepared staff.

Maddie kept looking at Joanna from across the table, as if to gauge her state of mind. She was sure Maddie, too, was still processing this newest development. She'd been visibly gob-smacked when Simon had skipped up to her in the courtyard where they'd assembled before heading to the restaurant and asked with innocent directness, "Did you know Mr. Adam is my dad, Aunt Maddie?"

Maddie had recovered fairly well, considering, telling Simon after a moment that she'd just found out herself. And then she'd given Adam another look that silently threatened his well-being if he did anything to hurt her nephew. Which wasn't, perhaps, the most auspicious beginning to a friendly meal, but for Simon's sake, Maddie made an effort to be her usual vivacious self.

Joanna figured Adam was having as difficult a time as she of staying engaged in the child-centered conversation. Though he did a decent job of holding up his end, she was certain that he was thinking about tomorrow—and beyond—just as she was. She made a concentrated effort to keep the topic focused on the past week rather than the future, and Simon followed along. Perhaps he was still so intrigued by having Adam as his father that he hadn't yet thought about what that might mean. With a child's enviable ability to live in the moment, he probably didn't even want to think about leaving.

She wished she had that ability, at least for an hour or so.

During dessert, Simon looked at Adam with a smudge of chocolate on his face. "Mom and Aunt Maddie promised to play minigolf with me after dinner. We haven't played at night yet, and some of my friends from Explorers Club said it's really cool when all the lights are on. You'll come with us, won't you? We're going to beat Mom's score bad, aren't we, Aunt Maddie?"

"That's not really all that hard, Si-bot. Your mom is, like, the worst minigolfer ever."

"Right?" Laughing, Simon grinned at his mother, who merely shrugged and smiled back.

Simon turned to Adam again. "So will you? I bet you're good at it."

"You might as well say yes now and save time," Maddie advised Adam wryly, the most sociable overture she'd made to him yet. "You know you're going to give in."

Adam swept her with a glance, then glanced at Simon. "I was just trying to save your mother's pride. Now she'll have three other players humiliating her, rather than just two."

To amuse her son, Joanna feigned indignation. "Hey!"

She was rewarded with a peal of happy

laughter. She felt warmth surge through her as she eyed Simon's glowing face. Let him have his fun tonight, she told herself. The challenges that faced them all could wait a few more hours.

They were on their way out of the restaurant when they encountered two more familiar faces. Trevor and Walt had just entered. They paused inside the doorway when they saw the foursome headed their way.

Walt, she noted, seemed to be focused solely on Maddie, which Joanna tended to expect from men when her sister was around. The exception, of course, was Adam, and she felt a little thrill at remembering his sincere-sounding murmur that Maddie wasn't his type. What she found interesting at the moment was the way her sister reacted to Walt, with a slight flush of color on her cheeks, a certain look in her eyes, the restless movement of her fingers. Joanna wouldn't have thought Walt was her sister's type, but there was definitely something going on here. She told herself she had too many issues of her own to worry about Maddie's love life, but she still hoped, of course, that Maddie knew what she was doing. As for Walt—well, if Maddie had decided to set her sights on him, the guy didn't stand a chance.

"Well, hello," Trevor said to them all. "I hope you had a nice dinner."

"It was good," Typically, Simon answered for the group. "And now we're going to play minigolf."

"And who do you think will win?" Trevor asked with an encouraging smile.

Grinning, Simon glanced up at Joanna. "Not my mom, that's for sure."

She growled playfully at him while the other adults laughed.

Simon looked back as he said in an off-handed tone, "My dad will probably win. He's good at everything."

The statement was made in an almost experimental tone, as if he were trying out the sound of the words. Perhaps he'd assumed that since Joanna, Adam and Maddie had already known of his parentage, Adam's friends were in on the knowledge, too. He was right, of course, but it was clear that now that the subterfuge really was over, Simon saw no reason to keep it quiet. Joanna and Adam would have to accept that any decisions they made on Simon's behalf would be done with the boy's full awareness of his parentage.

Trevor looked more startled than Walt at hearing Simon refer to Adam as his dad, but he merely said, "Yeah, he beats me every time we play. But here's a hint for you. He's not so good at the thirteenth hole. Always putts too far to the right of the windmill."

Simon nodded gravely, committing the advice to memory. "Okay, thanks."

Adam spoke then. "Fancy seeing you here again, Walt. I don't remember you hanging around the resort this much before."

Walt smiled faintly but didn't look away from Maddie. "Yes, well, something here just keeps drawing me back."

Maddie tossed her head. "Must be the food. Try the cedar-plank salmon. It's especially tame tonight. Unlikely to cause you any problems later."

"I'll keep that in mind," he murmured.

Joanna noted Maddie trailed a fingertip teasingly down Walt's arm as he passed her into the dining room, and she was pretty sure she saw more in her sister's expression than Maddie intended to reveal. What was it with Adam and his friend that they had such a powerful effect on the Zielinski sisters? And would either of them come out of this week with their hearts intact?

FLUSHED WITH LINGERING excitement from the rowdy game of minigolf—which had come down to a fiercely competitive battle between

Adam and Maddie during the last three holes, with Adam winning by only one stroke—Simon made it clear to Joanna that he didn't want the evening to come to an end. The resort grounds were bustling on this Saturday evening with music and lights and chattering guests. Simon tried to take in everything.

Still, eventually it was time to call it quits. Simon's steps lagged as they approached the Seafoam Lodge. The four of them paused in the courtyard, and he gazed at Adam. "Are you coming up?"

Joanna and Maddie exchanged glances, and Maddie spoke quickly before Adam could say anything. "Hey, Si-bot, how about if you and I head on in and get you ready for bed while your mom and, um, your dad make some plans? I'll read you a story, okay? Remember the book we started the other night? You fell asleep before we could finish, and I'd like to know how the story ends."

With a grateful look at her sister, Joanna nodded encouragingly to Simon. "Go with Aunt Maddie, Simon. I know we have a lot to talk about still, but we'll have plenty of time for that tomorrow, okay?"

A six-hour-plus drive faced them the next day, and she had little doubt the trip would be filled with talk of Adam rather than their usual songs and car games and whimsical stories. At least Maddie would be riding with them to deflect some of the more problematic questions. She'd caught a one-way flight to join them, renting a car from the airport to get to the resort. Normally Maddie could be counted on to provide nonstop entertainment and amusement. But would she, too, have a man on her mind when they left?

Simon's lower lip protruded, but he was probably afraid to push his luck too far after his great escape earlier. "I'll see you before we leave tomorrow, won't I?" he asked Adam.

Adam rested a hand gently on the boy's shoulder. Joanna thought his voice sounded a little huskier than usual when he said, "Of course you will."

"And will you come see us when we move to Seattle? And can we come back and see you here?"

Joanna noted sadly that Simon seemed to accept that he and his newly found father would live separate lives in different states. Perhaps he understood because he had friends at school whose parents were no longer together. One of Simon's best friends, Liam, spent every other week at his dad's house, and Simon had mentioned that on a few occasions. She was sure Simon, too, would grow accustomed to whatever arrangements she and Adam made for him, though none of them would have been what she'd have wanted for her son.

"I won't disappear from your life, Simon," Adam promised.

Perhaps only Joanna understood exactly how much that guarantee cost him. He'd just made the type of commitment he'd spent his adult life avoiding, and because of the honorable man he was, he would make every effort to keep it. Which meant that Adam Scott was now a permanent part of her life, too. In addition to the difficulties she would face in learning to share her son, in preventing him from being hurt—even inadvertently—by a man who had no idea how to be a father, she was afraid she was going to have to protect herself just as vigilantly. She was much too vulnerable where Adam was concerned. And she was well aware that he'd made no commitment to her.

"Say good night, Simon," she said quietly, moving aside to let an attractive couple walking hand in hand pass.

His sweet features were illuminated by the soft lighting around the fountain and koi pond when he gazed upward. "Good night, Dad."

Adam froze. Joanna wasn't even sure he was breathing.

She knew the feeling.

His voice was rough when he finally grated out, "Good night, Skipper."

Simon threw his arms around Adam's waist, giving him a big hug. Adam didn't even hesitate before drawing the boy in, returning the hug warmly. Joanna was gratified that he didn't make Simon's spontaneously affectionate gesture seem awkward.

Maddie hustled Simon inside the building without further delay, throwing a sympathetic look at Joanna over her shoulder as they left. Joanna gave herself a few beats to compose her expression before turning to Adam.

His face was stark in the lamplight. His hand gripped the back of his neck, the sure sign that he was stressed. She didn't know whether she wanted most to comfort him or to give him permission to make a run for it.

Goodness, she was tired. Not so much from all the activity of the day, which she was fairly accustomed to as the mother of an active five-year-old. This weariness was mostly mental and emotional, though it seemed to spread throughout her limbs.

She toyed with the thin gold bracelet on her

right wrist as she looked at Adam. "So, are you sorry you came back today?"

"I have to admit it didn't turn out the way I expected," he said with a dry smile. "I honestly never imagined Simon would take things into his own hands the way he did."

"How could you have?" She pushed her hair behind one ear and asked starkly, "Did you consider staying away until after we'd left?"

"The thought might have crossed my mind," he admitted with a gusty exhalation.

Even though the answer didn't surprise her, it still stung. "Then why did you come back?"

He gestured with one hand, indicating in that one sweeping motion the landscaped grounds, the few guests within sight, the buildings and pools and courts and ocean. "This is where I belong," he said simply. "For now, anyway."

It was still far from a commitment to his job, but like his assurance to Simon earlier, it was as close as she'd heard from him. Maybe he was ready to accept more permanence in his life. Maybe he was learning to battle his old demons successfully and make decisions based on what he wanted, not what he was willing to settle for. It was a philosophy she advocated to her patients, one she'd had to learn for herself in order to find happiness and fulfillment. Adam seemed to be moving in that direction, and she wanted the best for him.

Maybe someday, she thought with a pang, he'd be ready for even more commitment. A wife, maybe more children. He had plenty of time to consider those things. As for herself—well, maybe her close-to-perfect son and her exciting new career path would be enough. At least for now.

"We could go back to my place," he suggested. "Talk some more."

She hesitated, then grimaced, remembering kisses that left her mentally staggering and almost incoherent. "You know what happens every time we end up alone together."

His eyes glinted. "I meant just to talk. But… yeah, I know."

Joanna was sorely tempted, but she made herself stay strong. "I don't think that's a good idea tonight."

"My brain gets that." He reached out to run the back of one hand along her cheek. "Other parts of me are a little slower to catch up. Being this close to you always seems to do that to me."

A smile played on her lips despite herself. She covered his hand with hers. It would be so easy to lose herself in his arms, let the world slip away in a haze of desire and pleasure. It wouldn't solve anything, but oh, it would be so good!

He brushed his smiling lips against her own. Once. Twice. And then neither was smiling as he drew her back into the shadows and the kiss deepened. Heated. Came so very close to melting any last ounce of willpower she had. Every inch of her yearned for him. Every cell responded to him. And that response made her groan into his mouth as she tried to find the strength to resist him. To resist her own traitorous body.

She wished very much that she could forget her better judgment for just one night. But she couldn't. Not while she was so defenseless against him.

She put a hand on Adam's shoulder, applying just enough pressure to let him know she needed him to give her some space. Which he did immediately, though with reluctance.

She stiffened her knees as she frowned up at him. "What do you want from me, Adam?"

He exhaled hard and moved as if to reach up to his neck. Perhaps realizing what the gesture told her, he dropped the arm to his side again. "I'm not asking you for anything. I'm not denying I'm attracted to you, but then, that's always been the case."

"So you want sex, then."

He frowned but answered evenly enough. "Well, I wouldn't fight you off if you dragged me into the bushes, but I wasn't really expecting that, either. It was just a kiss, Joanna."

She pushed a hand through her tousled hair, shaking her head slowly. "I'm sorry. This whole situation has been…difficult."

"Yes."

"It's clear enough that I'm attracted to you, too," she said, knowing it would be both foolish and unreasonable to deny the obvious. "Great sex was enough last time. But it can't be enough now."

He nodded, his face set in hard lines. "Because of Simon."

"Partially. But also because of me. Because I don't want to be hurt. And you could hurt me, Adam."

As she'd expected, he looked appalled by the suggestion. "I would never hurt you."

"No. Not deliberately." She gave him a shaky smile, opting for candor. It was the only way they could go on from here, as coparents, maybe even as friends someday. "You underestimate your appeal, Adam. It wouldn't take much to make me fall for you, and I know that's not what you want."

She patted his arm, much as she would have

comforted her son, though she couldn't have felt less maternal. "There's no need to look so panicky. I don't expect anything from you. I know how you feel about commitments. And you've certainly never led me to think you feel anything deeper for me than attraction. That's okay. We'll work things out for Simon's sake, and there's no reason at all we can't be friendly about it. I just want you to understand why it's best if we keep our distance."

He cleared his throat. Something in his expression took her aback for a moment. But then he moved away another step, letting the shadows hide his face from her. His low voice came out of the darkness, much as it had in her occasional dreams of him. "I thought I'd made it clear that I never saw you as a casual partner. But as for anything more—I just don't have a good track record with that, Joanna. The few times I've attempted relationships ended in disaster, and it was probably my fault. You deserve a hell of a lot more than a guy who doesn't even know what he wants out of life."

"You deserve more than that, too," she replied quietly. "And I hope you give yourself a chance to find it someday. You have a lot more to offer than you realize, Adam."

After several long moments of silence, he

said, "You should probably go to Simon. We'll talk again later."

She nodded. They would talk again, of course. Through phone calls. Texts and emails. Maybe the occasional communication through lawyers if any legal details cropped up in the future. It wasn't the parenting arrangement she'd ever imagined, but it was the one her son had. And she would do her best to make it work, regardless of how much she wished that it could have been different.

"Just promise me one thing," she said in a strained whisper.

"What?" The wariness in Adam's voice caused another ripple of sadness to course through her.

"I know you were pulled into Simon's life before you were ready, but please don't make any promises you don't think you can keep. To Simon, I mean," she added quickly. "I don't want him to be disillusioned."

He stood very still in his cloaking shadows. Had she insulted him? Hurt his feelings? That hadn't been her intention. She was simply trying put Simon's needs first, as always.

"The reason I wasn't sure I wanted to tell him about me was precisely because I didn't want to let him down," Adam said in a low, flat tone. "But I told you, I won't lie to him.

Not today. Not in the future. I'd cut off both my arms before I'd hurt him. Or you," he added roughly.

Forcing back a sudden rush of tears, she swallowed the knot in her throat and nodded. "Thank you," she whispered. "Good night, Adam."

"I'll see you in the morning." With that, he turned on his heel and moved away in long, brisk strides. He didn't look back.

Needing a chance to compose herself before facing her sister, Joanna lingered for a few minutes by the koi pond. She watched the colorful fish swimming lazily through the glittering water lit by tiny multihued bulbs, though she found little solace there. Maybe she'd had enough of meticulously staged escapism for now. Maybe she would find comfort in a return to her work, in the taxing realities of packing and cleaning, moving and settling in, adjusting to all the changes in her life. Changes that included regular contact with the fantasy man who had haunted her dreams for longer than she'd acknowledged. A man who'd become all too real to her this week.

Maddie was waiting in the suite, a glass in her hand half filled with the chardonnay Joanna had stashed in the minifridge for quiet evenings with a book after Simon's bedtime.

This vacation certainly hadn't turned out as she'd expected when she'd arrived.

After taking one look at Joanna's face, Maddie handed the glass to her. "You look like you need this more than I do."

Though she didn't particularly want it, Joanna took an automatic sip, then set the glass on a table. "Is Simon asleep?"

"He didn't make it through three pages of the book. I'm never going to find out how that story ends," Maddie answered lightly, though she studied Joanna's face intently. "You okay, sis?"

Joanna didn't quite meet her gaze. "Oh, sure. Just tired, I guess."

"Crazy day, huh?"

"You could say that again."

"We should have known Simon would figure everything out. I don't think you're ever going to be able to keep secrets from that kid, Jo."

Trying to smile, she nodded. "I suppose that's just as well. I've always tried to be honest with him."

"I didn't expect you back quite so soon. I thought you and Adam would talk longer."

Joanna ran a hand through her hair. "I think we've said all there is to say for now. He needs more time to think about how he wants to proceed. The legalities are all taken care of, as far as I'm concerned. He has all my contact information. We'll see him again before we leave in the morning so Simon can say good bye for now, and then I don't know when we'll see him again."

"He promised Simon he wouldn't disappear," Maddie said with a quick frown in the direction of Simon's darkened room, its door open only a crack.

"I know. And he swore to me he won't make promises to Simon that he can't keep. So I believe he'll stay in touch, one way or another." As for how often he'd want to see his son in person—well, that was to be determined later.

"And what about you?" Maddie asked.

"What about me?"

"Has he made any promises to you?"

"Other than not disappointing Simon, no."

"And is that all you want?"

"It's the most important thing."

"That's not what I asked," Maddie said gently.

Her throat aching, Joanna spread her hands. "What else could I expect? Adam and I still hardly know each other. And he's not the forever-after type, anyway."

Maddie merely looked at her.

With a heavy sigh, Joanna picked up the wineglass again, mostly to have something to do with her hands. She took a sip she didn't taste, then said quietly, "Adam is a great guy, Maddie—you only have to see him with his friends, his coworkers and the guests here to see that. He's been kind to Simon and completely honest with me. But he has a lot of issues. Trust. Commitment. A painful childhood with a dysfunctional family. Probably some lingering effects from the war, being seriously wounded."

She hoped she wasn't revealing too much, but she wanted her sister to understand that Adam had reasons for his actions, or at least believed he did.

Maddie looked thoughtful. "I didn't know he'd been wounded. I guess that's one of the bonds he has with Walt."

"Speaking of Walt…"

Reacting with a wan smile to having the interrogation turned back on her, Maddie shrugged. "He's definitely intriguing."

"Not your usual type, though."

"We both know where my usual type has gotten me," Maddie murmured without taking offense. "I've decided it's time to explore new possibilities. And a new type."

"After only a couple of days? That sounds reckless and impulsive even from you, Maddie."

"You're one to talk." Maddie shrugged. "We're discussing you here, not me. You said Adam has issues. You've got a few yourself. You worry too much, especially when it comes to Simon. You try to control too much, to avoid any complications or messiness in your life. The one time you let loose, you got your heart bruised and ended up with an unplanned pregnancy. And as overjoyed as you are to have Simon in your life, you've been trying to make up for that lapse in judgment ever since. Face it, Jo, you're scared to take another risk."

"Scared to take risks?" Joanna lifted her chin at the accusations that struck entirely too close to home. "I'm preparing to move more than twenty-five hundred miles away from all my friends and family, take my son and resettle in a city I've only visited a handful of times to start a job that's going to be the biggest challenge of my professional life. Frankly, I find that all rather terrifying—but I'm going to do it anyway."

"Okay, I'll give you that," Maddie conceded. "And I still hate that you're moving, by the way. But it's not the type of risk I was talking about. You know you'll both be fine in Seattle, that you'll love the job and you'll be good at it. If it doesn't work out, you know you can quickly find another position. Good therapists are always in demand. But there's more to life than work, you know. And sometimes you have to take a few chances and break a few rules to get what you want outside an office."

Joanna sighed and set down the wineglass again, with a thump this time. There was no use discussing this. As close as they'd become, she and Maddie were still quite different. For one thing, any risks Joanna took affected someone else as much or more than herself, something Maddie didn't have to worry about.

"I'm going to bed. We should head out pretty early tomorrow. We have a long drive ahead of us."

Maddie moved obligingly toward the door, saying over her shoulder, "Get some rest, Jo. And maybe give a little thought to what's best for *you* for a change, rather than everybody else."

Locking the door behind her sister, Joanna thought wearily that what was best for her right now was to go to bed. To lose herself in sleep before facing tomorrow. Preferably dreamless sleep.

THEY HAD BREAKFAST outdoors at the coffee shop. Because it was the last day, Joanna let Simon order anything he wanted. She warned him with a smile that tomorrow morning would mean a return to fruit, yogurt and granola, but he merely grinned and crammed a huge bite of chocolate pastry into his mouth, washing it down with chocolate milk.

Sipping coffee and picking unenthusiastically at an egg white omelet, Maddie shuddered from across the table. "That's disgusting, Si-bot. How can you handle all that sugar this early in the morning?"

"It's never too early for chocolate," Simon replied matter-of-factly.

"Spoken like a true chocolate aficionado." Adam dropped into the empty chair at the table for four, giving Simon a pat on the shoulder as he spoke.

Simon's face lit up with a smile that made Joanna's heart ache. She wondered how Adam reacted to seeing his arrival greeted with such delight. "Hi, Mr.—I mean, good morning, Dad."

Maybe Adam's smile was a little softer than usual when he replied, "Morning, Skipper."

He glanced toward Joanna, and while his smile remained, his eyes darkened a bit.

"Good morning, Joanna. Maddie. All packed up for the drive home?"

"Packed, but not yet loaded into the car," Joanna answered. "I might have to leave a few things behind to make room for Simon's shells and souvenirs."

Simon wrinkled his nose. "I don't have that much, Mom."

She smiled at him. "Just teasing."

"Are you sure we can't stay just a bit longer?" he asked, both hopeful and resigned. "I want to walk on the beach one more time. I never found a Scotch bonnet."

"I'm sorry, Simon, but we have to go." She touched his hand in sympathy, knowing how hard this was for him. "We walked the beach and swam in the pool before breakfast this morning, remember? You were up at dawn to make sure you could play. Now it's time for vacation to be over."

Adam dug into his pocket and held out a hand toward Simon. "I know you wanted to find one for yourself, but I picked this up on the beach last winter. Maybe it can hold a place in your collection until you find your own."

"Oh, wow." Very carefully, Simon accepted the cream-and-tan-spotted shell, which was almost the size of his fist. He ran a fingertip over the pointed end and into the folded-back opening, then traced the tight swirls on the side. Joanna could see that it was a near perfect specimen of the shell Simon had coveted.

He looked up at Adam. "This is great, Dad. Thank you."

A muscle twitched in Adam's jaw, and Joanna speculated that it surprised him to hear himself called "Dad." She knew it jarred her whenever she heard Simon say it.

"You're welcome, Skipper. You can add it to that overstuffed bag of souvenirs. Of course, now your mom will have to leave another pair of shoes behind."

The quip had probably been an attempt to lighten the moment, and it worked. Simon gave a peal of laughter. "The shell's not as big as a pair of shoes, Dad."

"Ah. My mistake."

He met Joanna's gaze, then looked quickly away. Because of what he'd seen in her expression—or because he wanted to hide whatever she might find in his?

## CHAPTER TWELVE

THEY WALKED BACK to the lodge together after breakfast, though Joanna and Maddie left most of their food on their plates. Wanting to give Adam and Simon plenty of time together, Joanna hung back on the path with Maddie, watching as her son skipped ahead, clutching the precious shell in one hand and Adam's hand with the other. She couldn't resist lifting her phone and snapping a photo, capturing them just as Adam looked down and Simon looked up to share identical smiles.

"Adam definitely has a hold on Simon, doesn't he?" Maddie murmured.

Joanna nodded.

"On you both," Maddie added meaningfully.

Joanna saw no need to respond to that obvious fact.

Maddie's phone dinged with a text. She glanced at the screen, then slid it back into her pocket.

"Let me guess." Joanna figured payback was only fair. "Walt?"

Maddie didn't bother to deny it. "Yes. He told us to have a safe trip back to Atlanta."

Turning her head to study her sister's profile, Joanna asked, "Are you going to see him again?"

"Beats the hell out of me. Ball's in his court now." Maddie's sudden laugh was rueful, but sounded genuinely amused. "We're quite a screwed-up pair, aren't we, sis?"

Pushing back her hair, Joanna couldn't help but laugh. "We are that."

Maddie had brought her bags to Joanna's suite earlier that morning, so everything was ready to be packed in the car. Adam helped them carry things down, telling Joanna that his job at the resort sometimes included bellhop service as well as the jobs of lifeguard and unicorn-finder. Reminded of the conversations they'd had that week, she smiled, glad he didn't seem to resent the prickly way they'd parted last night.

He looked around with one hand on the lid of her car's trunk. "Is that everything?"

"Yes," she said simply. "That's it."

Simon would keep his bag of treasures in the backseat with him. A small cooler filled with fruit and bottles of water was stashed behind the driver's seat. She could think of no other excuse to delay their departure.

She placed a tender hand on Simon's shoulder. "We should go, sweetie. Say goodbye, then climb into your booster seat."

Perhaps that was the moment that reality set in for her young son. His lower lip quivered. "It doesn't feel like we've been here long enough," he said, his voice tremulous.

"I know, baby. But it's time. We'll have a fun drive with Aunt Maddie. She knows lots of car games."

Her eyes hidden behind a large pair of sunglasses, Maddie turned back to them. Had she been scanning the grounds, hoping to see someone in particular? If so, she kept her disappointment hidden when she spoke cheerfully to her nephew. "Oh, yeah, Si-bot. I know some songs that are going to drive your mom absolutely crazy."

He didn't laugh, but nodded glumly and gazed up at Adam with tear-silvered eyes. "You'll call me?"

Adam ruffled his hair. "Your mom has my number and I have hers. You can call me whenever you want to talk to me, and unless I can't talk just then, I'll always answer."

"Can I do a video call sometimes and show

you things? Like my room and my toys and stuff? And my new room in Seattle?"

"I'll look forward to that," Adam said, and Joanna saw lines of strain around his mouth now. She ached for them both, but what else could they do? As Adam had said, he belonged here. For now, at least. She and Simon did not.

Simon held up his arms and Adam picked him up for a bear hug, burying his face in the boy's neck. Joanna's hands were shaking so hard she couldn't have snapped a picture even had she tried. She thought she heard a snap from Maddie's direction, so maybe the moment had been captured, after all. If so, she thought it might be a while before she'd be able to look at that particular photo. It was all she could do not to dissolve in tears now. She was making no guarantees for later, when she was alone.

Adam loaded the now-sniffling boy into the car, leaving Maddie to make sure he was safely strapped in. Then Adam turned to Joanna. The lines around his mouth were carved even more deeply now. His gray eyes were so dark they looked like charcoal.

"So," he said, his voice as tight as his jaw, "we'll talk."

She nodded. "Of course. I'll send you some of the pictures I took this week."

"Sure. You've got a long trip ahead. Be careful, okay?"

"We will." She had an impulse to hold out her hand for a shake, but that seemed absurd. She kept her arms at her sides, her fingers curled around her phone.

He looked equally conflicted for a moment, then shook his head and reached for her with a mutter. "One last time."

Ignoring her sister and anyone else who might be watching, Adam kissed her. Hard. Thoroughly. Not angrily, but not gently, either. And she returned the kiss with a mix of equally volatile emotions.

He released her as abruptly as he'd embraced her. "'Bye, JoJo," he said with a big step backward.

The most she could manage in return was a whisper. "Take care of yourself, Adam."

"I always have," he muttered.

He tapped lightly on the trunk of the car as he walked past it. And then he was gone.

"Want me to take the first shift driving, Jo?" Maddie offered, her voice compassionate.

"I think that's a good idea."

They moved to separate sides of the vehicle, paused with their hands on the handles for a last look around, then glanced at each other over the top of the car before simultaneously opening the doors and climbing inside. Neither looked back as they drove away.

FROM THE SHELTER of the trees at the side of the parking lot, Adam gripped his neck as he watched the car turn onto the highway and drive out of sight. This was why he hated goodbyes. They were too damned hard.

"So that's it? You're going to let them just drive away?"

He looked around to find Walt standing nearby, dressed in a casual pullover and jeans that made it clear he wasn't working. Adam didn't know why Walt was here, or why he hadn't come forward to say goodbye. Was this merely Walt's way of supporting Adam, or had he felt the need to watch Maddie drive away?

Whatever the reason, Adam's response was cross. "Well, I could force them to stay, but that's called kidnapping. It's sort of against the law."

"Funny. And I was being serious."

"What the hell else am I supposed to do? Chase after them?"

"Is that what you want to do?"

*God, yes.*

Keeping the words to himself, he glared at the man who looked back at him with sympathetic eyes. "Trying to play shrink, Walt? Maybe you should leave that to the professionals."

"Like Joanna."

"Yeah. Like Joanna."

Letting his arm fall to his side, he glanced again at the now empty road. "You're no better yourself or you wouldn't have been lurking back here rather than coming out to see them off. To see Maddie off."

Walt sighed to concede the point. "Maybe you're right."

"So that's it?" The imitation was deliberate. Pointed. "You're just going to let her leave?"

Walt replied with a grimace. "Touché. I guess you aren't the only man scared spitless by a pretty Zielinski sister."

Adam shifted abruptly to walk around his friend. "I've got a lot of catching up to do around here. I think I'll start now."

Walt patted Adam's back a little too heartily. "Looks like we both need to figure out what we really want. And how to go about it without getting ourselves—or anyone we care about—hurt in the process."

"It's a little less complicated for you than for me," Adam muttered. After all, Walt didn't have a son to think about.

He regretted his cranky tone when Walt

said quietly, "I might be older and a little more beat up, but I've got feelings and fears just like you do, my friend. Our circumstances are different, I'll admit, but the risks—and the potential rewards—are more alike than you want to acknowledge."

"Walt, I—"

"—have some work to get to," Walt finished for him, sparing them both the awkward apology. "Go take care of it. I've got some thinking of my own to do."

He turned to walk away without looking back.

DRESSED IN A reasonably conservative, at least for her, blouse and skirt, Maddie looked up from her desk when someone tapped on her closed office door. It was late in the workday on a Friday afternoon almost three weeks after the trip to South Carolina. Most of her associates had already left for the weekend. She had no more appointments scheduled, and she'd thought her secretary had gone already, so she wasn't sure who was interrupting her now. "Come in."

Her frown faded into a speculative smile when an unexpected visitor entered the office, closing the door behind him. Her heart rate increased, and anticipation shivered along her nerve endings. She rose slowly to her feet, cocking one hip into a cheerfully impertinent stance. "Well, hello, Sarge. This is a nice surprise."

Smiling, Walt crossed the room toward her. "I hoped it would be a nice one. And I hope you don't have plans for the weekend."

She felt her lips curve in delight. "If I did, I don't now."

He paused a couple feet away to give her a leisurely once-over. "You look great, Maddie."

"I look like a lawyer," she corrected him, her tone self-mocking as she glanced down at her conventional outfit.

"Yeah, well, it works for you. But then, you'd look good in anything."

She moved closer and walked her fingers up his blue-dotted tie to the neat knot at his collar. "Does that mean you're happy to see me?"

"Oh, yeah," he said huskily, reaching out to pull her against him. "Oh, yeah."

She rose on her tiptoes to greet his hungry kiss.

A long time later, he lifted his head. "Does that mean you're happy to see me, too?" he asked, his voice hoarse.

"Oh, yes. Assuming you're here for reasons that have nothing to do with my sister or your idiot friend."

"Nothing at all," he promised. "Joanna and Adam have to work out their own issues. I plan to spend the next day or so trying to figure out exactly what you see in a divorced, war-damaged lawyer a few years older than you. Doing my best to convince you I don't think you're flighty or irresponsible. And following your advice about finding out where this chemistry between us could lead."

She didn't much like his self-deprecating description, but she figured it wouldn't take her long to convince him she saw a lot more in him. She cupped his face in her hands and brushed a kiss across his mouth. "I'm pretty sure my instincts are right. As I said before, I'm good at that sort of thing."

His crooked smile made her body tingle in response. "I'd imagine you're good at a lot of things."

Wrapping her arms around his neck, she pressed against him. "You have no idea."

She smothered his laugh beneath another eager kiss.

SEVERAL HOURS LATER, Maddie snuggled with Walt in her big bed. Her every inch felt boneless and relaxed. Satisfied. As she'd predicted, Walt used his one hand—not to mention the rest of his very fine body—masterfully.

"Nice apartment," he said, glancing around the colorful room. She hadn't given him time to admire it when she'd ushered him in, straight through the living room and down the hallway to the master bedroom.

"Thanks. I've considered buying, but haven't found a place I liked enough to commit to."

"You should visit me in South Carolina sometime," he said a little too casually. "Got a nice top-floor condo. Ocean view. I bought it just before Christmas. Got a good deal on it because that's not a peak time for home buying."

Amused by the brusque practicality in contrast with his obvious pride of ownership, she smiled and kissed his chin, the only part of his face she could reach at the moment. "You're a funny guy, Walt."

He looked at her with a lifted eyebrow. "You think it's funny that I bought a condo?"

"No. Yes." She ran her fingertips over his firm jaw. "I just really like you."

He shifted to brush her smile with his lips. "I really like you, too. In case you hadn't figured that out."

His smile faded a bit then. "The situation between your sister and my idiot friend is still strained, right? I hope that's not going to be a problem for us. I don't know about Joanna, but Adam's been a bear for the past three weeks."

"Joanna's been so smiley and cheery she could audition for the lead in a kiddie show. And before you misinterpret that, it's roughly the same sign as Adam's grouchiness. She's hurting and confused."

Maddie propped herself on one elbow, the sheet draped over her hips. "As far as you and I are concerned, their problems have no bearing on whatever might develop between us. It's neither your fault nor mine that they're making each other miserable. Why should we do the same? We clicked three weeks ago. So…here we are."

"Here we are." He kissed her lingeringly before asking, "Will she mind?"

"It wouldn't matter if she did. But no, she won't mind. Jo and I lead our own lives. She wants me to be happy. And I want the same for her."

He sighed, twisting a strand of her bright red hair around one finger. "I wish the same for Adam. He's just so damned skittish."

"If anyone can get through that thick head of his, my sister and nephew will manage."

Walt tumbled her back down beside him. "How about we talk about Joanna and Adam later?"

Laughing, she wrapped her arms around his neck. "Much later."

ADAM PAUSED IN his morning run to swipe his forearm over his wet face, his attention caught by the sight of a small group of tourists out for an early horseback ride down the beach. He was taken back to the feel of a child's arms around his waist, the sound of a boy's laughter in his ear as ol' Dez had trudged patiently beneath them. He scowled down at his feet, only then realizing he'd stopped in the very spot where he'd first found Simon. Damn it.

He missed Simon. Missed Joanna. He doubted that he would ever again be satisfied with his formerly commitment-free life now that he'd had a taste of what he was missing. He hadn't been sure about telling Simon he was his father, but that was irrelevant now. The boy knew, and he'd made it clear he wanted his dad to be a part of his future.

After seeing Joanna and Simon drive away, Adam had asked Trevor for a little more time before giving his answer about the change in his job. Trevor had encouraged him to take as much time as he needed to be certain. Adam had wrestled with old doubts and fears during the past three weeks, but he finally had an answer, though he'd yet to share it with his friend and employer.

It was time to stop running. Time for Adam to reach out and grasp what he'd always wanted, but had never expected to find. It was scary as hell to make a lifetime commitment when he'd spent so many years avoiding emotional risks, but this time it was worth his best effort.

He wouldn't be a pop-in, long-distance near stranger known only through phone calls and brief visits. He'd be there for ball games and fishing trips and teacher conferences and whatever else real dads did. In Seattle, if that was where he had to move to be near his son. That was the least his boy deserved.

He still had his doubts, of course. Still worried that he wasn't up to the task. He hated the thought of failing his son. Just remembering the way the kid's lower lip quivered when he was sad made Adam feel gut-punched.

He was equally apprehensive about hurting Joanna. And as much as he hated to admit it, he couldn't help worrying about being hurt by her instead. He'd never allowed any woman into his guarded heart, and the thought of doing so now made him break out in a sweat, though not from running this time.

He drew a deep breath. Regardless of his fears, it was time to make some changes. Time to prove once and for all that he didn't have to be the kind of dad—the kind of man—his own father had been. He only hoped Joanna's faith in him was justified.

JOANNA WAS STAGGERING across her living room with a teetering stack of books when her doorbell rang three weeks and one day after she'd come home from the resort. Simon was sleeping over at a friend's house, and she'd been using the time alone to do some organizing for the move in two weeks. Boxes sat everywhere around her, but the one she'd earmarked for these books was in another room. She looked around for someplace to set the stack quickly, finally tumbling them on the couch to be packed after she saw who was at the door.

Sidestepping a box half filled with framed photos, she wiped her hands on her jeans and made an effort to smooth her hair. She was expecting a delivery today—the vacation photo book she'd ordered. She'd placed the order only a few days after they'd returned, thinking Simon would like to look at the pages during the flight to Seattle. He'd probably be both excited and a little nervous about the approaching changes in his life, so she'd chosen shots that featured him laughing and having fun. She'd tried to include pictures from each day of the week, and as many as possible of the other children he'd met so he'd remember the friends he'd made there. The Explorers Club counselors had sent all the parents snapshots taken during the field trips, so quite a few of those were included, as well.

There were, of course, quite a few photos of Simon and Adam in the album. Simon would love those. He hadn't stopped talking about his dad since they'd gotten back, and he'd been thrilled to have spoken with Adam on the phone a few times since they'd parted. Maddie had sent Joanna the photo she'd snapped of Adam hugging Simon goodbye, but Joanna hadn't included it in the book. Instead, she'd selected the one she'd taken herself of Adam and Simon from behind, walking hand in hand and smiling at each other. The moment Maddie had captured had been too raw, too poignant to fit the lighthearted vacation theme of the book. Joanna would save that for later.

Thinking of how excited Simon would be to see his gift, she opened the door. Only to find Adam Scott standing there, giving her a tentative smile that made her heart skip a few beats. Her hand tightened around the doorknob. "Adam?"

"Hi, JoJo."

"You've cut your hair."

She winced as soon as the words left her mouth. What a stupid thing to say. Wouldn't it make more sense to ask what he was doing here? Or maybe why he hadn't told her he was coming?

He brushed a hand over his hair, which still wasn't as short as when she'd met him, but had been trimmed and tidied in the past couple of weeks. It looked good on him—but then, everything did. "Yeah, it was time. Uh—can I come in?"

"Oh. Of course. I'm sorry, I'm a little—I didn't expect to see you."

"I know." He closed the door behind him, glancing around at the room. "Getting ready for the move, huh?"

"Starting to. I'm trying to throw some stuff away rather than move it." Shaking her head to clear it, she added, "Simon's not here, I'm afraid. He's having one last sleepover with his two best friends here in Alpharetta. They were going for pizza, then a movie."

She'd thought he would be disappointed, but he merely nodded. "That sounds like fun."

She rubbed her hands down her jeans again, feeling grubby from her packing. "I'm sorry you missed him. Had we known you were coming—"

"Actually, I have a confession to make."

She'd been about to invite him to sit, but the hint of sheepishness in his tone made her study him with an arched eyebrow. "What sort of confession?"

"I knew Simon wasn't going to be here this evening."

"How—?" Had he somehow talked to Simon without her knowledge? It wasn't that he needed permission to speak with his son, but Simon didn't have his own phone.

"Your sister told me."

Startled, she asked, "When did you talk to Maddie?"

"I called her to tell her I was coming and to ask if she could watch Simon this evening while you and I talked. She told me about the sleepover. Just as well, I guess. She has company for the weekend. Walt's with her."

Joanna tried to follow. Why hadn't Maddie told her Adam had called? Or that Walt was in town? Why did Adam want to speak with her privately? Had he decided he wanted more active involvement in Simon's life, after all? More input into decision-making? Into living arrangements? She couldn't blame him for that, of course, but—

The only way to know was to ask. She raised her head. "Are you here to talk about Simon?"

His mouth twisted into a half smile as he took a purposeful step toward her. "Joanna, you are a wonderful mother. The best. But not everything is about Simon."

"I don't understand."

He took another step closer. "I came to see you."

"Why?" she whispered.

Placing a hand on either side of her face, he lowered his head. "Because...this."

The kiss rocked her all the way to the soles of her feet. She managed to resist for all of two seconds before she threw her arms around his neck and dove headfirst into the embrace.

# CHAPTER THIRTEEN

ADAM FINALLY LIFTED his head enough to allow them both to breathe. "I've missed you, JoJo."

"I've missed you, too," she confessed, almost unbearably touched by the unexpected admission.

He spoke rather fiercely then. "You said there's a chance we could have more than great sex. Do you still believe that?"

"Absolutely," she answered firmly after taking only a moment to recover from her surprise. "There's been a connection between us from the start, Adam. I've never felt that bond with anyone else."

"Me, either. And no one else has ever scared me quite like you do," he confessed.

Her smile felt shaky. "I'll take that as a compliment."

"You should. It means I've known from the start that what we had was different. Special."

"Potentially life-changing," she said, understanding exactly what he meant.

"Well, yeah."

"And you weren't so sure you wanted your life to change."

"I guess I needed a reason to try," he murmured, brushing his lips against her cheek. "And then you and Simon showed up, and it didn't take me long to realize that I would never find two better reasons. I was just too stubborn—and yeah, too intimidated—to admit it at first."

She stroked his face, savoring his rueful smile. "I'm so glad you're here."

A hint of nervousness returned to his eyes. "I still can't make guarantees," he warned. "We'll give it our best shot, but if it doesn't work out—if you decide this isn't what you want—or if you have any concerns about how Simon will be affected—"

She nestled into him. "All we can do is give it a chance," she murmured. "Whatever happens, both of us will do everything in our power to protect Simon."

"That I *can* promise," he said fervently.

Which only reminded her again of why she was so drawn to him. One of the reasons, anyway, she thought as his mouth closed over hers again.

His hands were on her and she pressed closer even as she murmured, "We need to—"

"Later," he growled, fumbling with the top button of her shirt.

Her hands had slipped beneath his shirt, her palms gliding up his back. She nipped his lower lip. "I don't think—"

"Good." He pushed the shirt off her shoulders. "Don't think."

His shirt went over his head, landing in an open box somewhere. She kissed his chin, his throat, his scars. "This isn't—"

"—going to take long," he said with a rough laugh of apology. "God, I want you, JoJo."

The couch was covered with books. She pushed him down the hallway and he proved how adept he was at walking backward and still kissing her senseless. He almost stumbled over a box in the bedroom. The contents rattled and he muttered a curse, then laughed when she gave another shove and he tumbled onto her bed.

"After this," she said, falling on top of him, "we're going to do a lot more talking."

The smile he shot her could only be described as piratical. "Eventually," he promised.

His arms locked around her, gathering her closer. She had no desire to resist, to make an effort to hang on to caution or common sense, to be sensible and responsible and practical.

The way she always was, always had been—except with Adam.

Her fingers burrowed into his hair, holding him in place. Not that he was trying to pull away. Her tongue welcomed his, and her vulnerable heart responded to the taste and feel of him. How could she have missed him this much when their time together had been so short?

His right hand slid down her back, traced the curve of her bottom. Liquid heat flooded through her, warming her skin, melting any last qualms she might have harbored. She moved against him, and felt a thrill of satisfaction when she drew a deep moan from his throat.

Everything about this man was irresistible—his face, his body, his laugh, the way he moved, the way he looked at her. The way he kissed, the way his hands danced so skillfully over her. She didn't even want to think about any issues lurking outside this cozy bed.

She just wanted to enjoy.

Her clothing proved little impediment. He didn't even fumble with zippers or buttons before they fell away. He gave her no chance to be self-conscious about the changes time and pregnancy had made to her body, but caressed her with an obvious appreciation that made her forget any petty insecurities.

She thought he seemed a little more hesitant when she tugged at his shirt, but she made it equally clear his scars didn't bother her, other than as a reminder of what he'd suffered. The evidence of his pain made her heart hurt, but he gave her no chance to dwell on the sadness. He lowered her into the deep pillows and settled against her, strong and pulsing and thoroughly male.

She ran her hands over his chest, stringing kisses along his jaw, his throat, his collarbone—any part of him she could reach while he explored her with equal enthusiasm. Her pulse raced, her breath escaped raggedly from her throat, her vision glazed as her other senses kicked into overdrive. Every inch of her ached and quivered with a need for release.

Adam drew away only long enough to don protection retrieved from his pants pocket, then returned immediately to her. She welcomed him with a sense of joyous familiarity, a feeling of rightness that, again, she felt only with him.

Maybe this was love. The kind she'd always hoped to find. However she defined them, her feelings for Adam were powerful, exhilarating, and…yeah, scary. And as she surrendered to mindless sensation, she knew that whatever she might call her feelings for him, whatever heartache they might yet bring, they weren't ever going away.

JOANNA LAY TUCKED into Adam's left side, his arm around her, his skin warm and damp beneath her cheek. This was his mostly undamaged side, so she didn't worry about hurting him, but he didn't seem to let his injuries hold him back much anyway.

He brushed her tumbled hair back from her face. "Hi," he said when she looked at him.

She laughed softly. "Hi."

"So, how've you been?"

Though she knew he was teasing, she thought about her answer. How had she been since she'd seen him last? She'd been busy. Deliberately busy. Almost frantically busy, anything to keep her from thinking about Adam. About how much she missed him. How challenging it would be to have him part of her son's life—and in extension, part of hers—without reopening the cracks in her heart.

And here she was in bed with him again, having all but climbed him like a tree at no more than the touch of his hands on her cheeks.

How did he do this to her?

"We've never had any problems with communicating this way," she murmured. "I've never had to ask what you wanted or what you needed from me in bed. Outside the bedroom—well, I don't have a clue."

"You're not going to start calling me a stranger again, I hope."

She flushed at his dubious tone.

He rolled to half pin her to the bed, waiting until she met his eyes before he spoke very evenly and precisely. "You want to know what I want? I want you, JoJo. I have since the first time I laid eyes on you. It was true when I walked away from you the first time, which I did because I thought it would be easier for you than seeing me off to a war zone. It was true when I was in that hospital, letting memories of you ease the pain during therapy sessions."

"Adam—"

He continued as if she hadn't even tried to speak. "I wanted you when you showed up again on that beach, looking as beautiful as the day we met, accompanied by my son, who you'd raised to be such a great kid. And the day I watched you leave without me."

Her heart was beating so fast she had to force her words out. "Then why didn't you say anything?"

"Because, as my friend Walt puts it so succinctly, I'm an idiot."

Her smile was fleeting. The answer was amusing, but didn't really tell her much.

As if sensing she wasn't satisfied, he grew serious again. "There haven't been many people I could depend on in my life. You get used to not expecting anything. To keep from getting hurt and disappointed over and over, you learn to be the one to say goodbye first. You stop asking for anything. You tell yourself you've stopped wishing things were different. That you're alone because you like it. And when someone gets too close, when they start making you want what you're afraid to ask for—you run. But you tell yourself you're moving on because it's best for everyone involved."

It was the most Adam had ever said to her about his past. It was a lot to take in, and yet he'd confirmed so much of what she'd already suspected. She just hadn't been sure he'd been aware of those things. Perhaps he hadn't been before now. Before he'd made himself stop pushing everyone away.

"What are you telling yourself now?" she asked quietly.

"That I've missed you," he said. "Especially after having the chance to spend more time with you."

It wasn't exactly a romantic declaration. She noted that he hadn't used the word *love*. But for Adam, this was major.

Her doorbell rang and she started. She rolled out from beneath him and reached quickly for her clothes, scrambling into them. "I'm expecting a delivery. I totally forgot."

She dashed barefoot to the door without giving him a chance to answer, pushing her hands though her messy hair. A couple of minutes later, she had the package in hand. Seeing Adam leaning in the doorway, mussed and shirtless, she felt her mouth go dry.

"Um, it's a book," she said, eating him up with her eyes.

He grinned, and her knees almost liquefied. After a glance around the book-strewn room, he said, "Looks like you need a couple more of those."

"It's a photo book," she said, shaking her head at him. "Pictures of our vacation at the resort. You're in it."

"I'd like to see it."

"I'll show it to you." She set the package on a table as she walked resolutely toward him. "Later."

His laugh was muffled by the kiss she pulled him into.

"Damn it."

Because Joanna had fallen onto her back, still trembling and gasping for breath as she muttered the curse, Adam laughed. His voice was still gravelly, his breathing still ragged when he asked, "What?"

"We were going to talk."

"We can still talk."

"Not unless you get dressed," she said, rolling over to reach for her own clothes.

He leaned back against the headboard, watching as she gathered garments into her arms. "So the scars don't bother you?"

She spotted her jeans halfway across the room, and had to take a moment to process what he was asking. Clutching her clothing to her chest, she stared at him as the words sank in. "What? No, of course not. Have I given you that impression?"

"No," he admitted. "It's just—well, they weren't there before."

"I have a few marks that weren't there before, too," she said quietly. "Our experiences are part of us, Adam. Some show on the outside, some don't, but the only thing I dislike about your scars is the pain they represent."

He nodded. His expression didn't change, but she thought her answer pleased him. Her throat tight, she carried her clothing into the bathroom.

An hour later, both dressed, they sat on her now-cleared couch, eating delivery pizza from paper plates and looking slowly through the photo book together. Adam seemed to get a kick out of the themed groupings and whimsical embellishments she'd chosen to highlight each day of the vacation. He studied each page at length before moving to the next, as if memorizing Simon's expression.

She knew he'd want to see more photos of Simon's life and she had, of course, captured every stage from birth to the present day in photographs and scrapbooks. She had no doubt Adam would enjoy those—but would they make him sad about how much he'd missed? Probably, though he might not admit it. It made her sad for him, though they were both trying to let the past go and make a fresh start for the future.

The question was, exactly how did Adam see that future? He'd said he wanted her, that he wanted a chance to make something real with her, but did he honestly think they could do that when they lived across the continent from each other?

"This book is still stored in my account at the website," she said when he'd turned the final page. "I could order a copy for you, if you'd like."

He turned his head to look at her. "I sort of thought I'd be able to look at this one occasionally."

"Whenever you like," she answered evenly. At least that was a sign that he planned to visit them in Seattle.

He nodded and set the book aside to reach for another slice of pizza. "Have your parents been told about me?"

"Of course."

"How did they react?"

"They were surprised. And maybe a little suspicious at first that maybe I'd gone back to Wind Shadow specifically to find you, even though I told them that wasn't the case."

He looked offended on her behalf. "They didn't believe you?"

"They did." Eventually.

"So, what did they say after you convinced them?"

She wondered how candid she should be. But then decided she might as well put everything out there. After all, if he was going to be an active part of Simon's life—of hers— he would likely meet them at some point, and her parents weren't the most tactful people.

"They're concerned, I guess. Simon couldn't

stop talking about you, so they hope you'll be a good influence on him. They worry about your effect on me, too. While my career path isn't exactly the one they'd have chosen for me, they don't want you to complicate things for me. Again, as they see it."

"Well, that's an honest answer," he said after a moment.

"You asked," she reminded him.

He nodded, and she watched him swallow before he said, "I suppose I should meet them, though I'm not sure that will set their minds at ease, considering how difficult they sound to impress. Especially when they find out I'm soon to be unemployed."

"Unemployed?" She dropped her half-eaten slice of pizza on her plate and scooted around to face him on the couch. "What do you mean? I can't believe Trevor would have fired you. Did you quit?"

He looked rather surprised by her surprise. "No. At least, not yet. But I can hardly keep my job as his assistant from three thousand miles away in Seattle."

"You're planning to move to Seattle?" she asked blankly.

Losing interest in his own meal, Adam pushed away his plate and wiped his hands on a paper napkin. The easy smile he'd worn for most of the evening vanished. "What the hell do you think we've been talking about since I got here?"

Pressing both hands to her temples, she realized that she hadn't let herself think at all since he'd arrived. Maybe if she had, she wouldn't be so stunned—and so inexplicably anguished—by Adam's announcement.

## *CHAPTER FOURTEEN*

ADAM'S PHONE RANG while Joanna struggled to process his intentions. He took it out of his pocket and tossed it on the table beside the pizza box without even glancing at the screen. He continued to look at her, waiting for her to respond.

Glancing at the phone when it rang for a second time, she bit her lip. She would bet the call had something to do with his work. Even in the few days she'd spent there, well aware that he'd neglected his responsibilities to spend more time with her and Simon, she'd seen how valuable he was to the resort. How much his coworkers respected and depended on him.

"It's obvious you love your job," she said, twisting her fingers in her lap. "And that they feel lucky to have you there."

"I can find another job," he said, though Joanna believed she detected a hint of regret in his voice. "It might be swinging a hammer on a construction site or flipping gourmet burgers for all those highly paid techies I hear are out there, but I'm not picky when it comes to honest work. I'll pay my own way. Would it bother you if I come home with dirt under my nails?"

*Home.* She gulped in response to the word, then scowled when she realized exactly what he was asking. "Don't be insulting, Adam. You should know full well that I don't care about things like that."

He held up an appeasing hand. "I figured you'd see it that way. The point is, yeah, I like my job at Wind Shadow just fine. But I want to be a part of your life. A part of Simon's life. And if that means moving across the whole damned country, then that's what I'll do. The only thing holding me back at the moment is you."

He looked hard at her face as his phone rang yet again. "Maybe I've been reading you all wrong today. Or maybe you didn't understand what I meant. So it's time to spread all our cards on the table, Joanna. What do you want?"

His phone finally fell silent. For seconds that stretched into minutes, the only sound in the room was a clock ticking on the wall as she thought about his question.

Adam didn't rush her into an answer. He

merely sat there, his expression shuttered as he waited, seemingly prepared for her to either welcome him into her future or send him on his way. She had a feeling he was braced for the latter. After all, that was what he was used to, she thought with a pang.

"I want you to have a relationship with Simon," she said slowly, sincerely. "I'll do everything in my power to help you with that. To help make up for the years you missed with him."

"I appreciate that," he said, though he didn't look particularly grateful as he continued to eye her. "But what about *us*, Joanna? What do you want?"

He'd spaced out the words deliberately, all but daring her to prevaricate or procrastinate any longer.

She bit her lip, then released it in resignation. She was well aware of how hard it must have been for Adam to come here. To take an emotional risk when he'd spent most of his life avoiding them. The least she could give him in return was total honesty.

Unable to sit any longer, she stood and took a few steps away from the couch, then turned to bare her emotions to him.

"I don't want a relationship built for the wrong reasons," she said quietly. "You love your son. Of course you do, even though you've only just found him. It's completely natural for you to want to spend more time with him, to get to know him and have him get to know you. I appreciate that you haven't tried to interfere with my plans, even though those are taking him so far away. That you'd be willing to walk away from your job to stay close to him. But I don't want you mixing up your love for Simon with your feelings for me."

Adam was on his feet now. "What the hell are you talking about?"

She held up both hands in an instinctive attempt to hold him off, though he'd made no attempt to move closer. "I know there's attraction between us. I think it's more than obvious I feel it, too. But I know myself too well to think that would be enough for me in the long run. I know you worry about commitments, Adam. I even understand why. I won't ask you to make one to me for Simon's sake. I'll make sure you see him as often as you want, whether you move to Seattle or—" she swallowed before finishing "—or whether we need to figure out other arrangements."

"Joanna." He moved then, taking her hands in a grasp much gentler than his determined expression might have indicated. "You really think this is all about Simon?"

Feeling as though the lump in her throat just might strangle her, she had to swallow hard again. "I think it's all tangled up together," she whispered. "Understandably, of course."

His brief laugh was not exactly amused. "For a fancy psychologist, you really don't know everything I'm thinking."

She sighed. "That's hardly a shocking insight. I almost never know what you're thinking."

"Well, let me tell you, then. I'm not confusing my feelings with you for what I feel for my son. Yeah, I'm crazy about that boy. Have been from the start. Partly because he's mine, but also because he's one great kid. And I want to spend as much time with him as I can, do the things good fathers do with their sons, though God knows I'd have to learn that on the job since my own never taught me. But when I think about a future with him, it's not complete unless you're in it, too."

Both his voice and his face softened when he murmured, "During the past three weeks, I missed you both so much I could hardly think straight. But it was you I saw everywhere I looked. Your face I saw when I closed my eyes."

*This*, she thought dazedly. This was the answer to his question about what she wanted from him. What she needed so desperately from him. But did she really have the courage to let herself believe his seemingly impulsive declaration was real? Lasting?

It might tear her apart if she embraced a future with Adam only to have him walk away again. And after a lifetime of worrying about others, after five years and four months of fiercely protecting her son, she couldn't remember ever being so afraid for herself.

"Adam—"

She wasn't sure what she was going to say, but she was so wrapped up in the intensity of the moment that she jumped half a foot when his phone buzzed again, vibrating furiously on the wooden table, demanding his attention.

"Damn it!" he said explosively. Maybe he'd been almost as startled by the sound. He snatched it up.

"You should answer it," she advised, secretly—or probably not-so-secretly—grateful for the respite. "If they're calling this repeatedly, it could be important."

"It had better be." He lifted the phone to his ear and barked at it, "What?"

Joanna saw his face go suddenly still, maybe even a little pale. The change in his posture made her realize that he was getting very bad news, indeed.

"Where is he now?" she heard him ask, shaken. "Is he going to be okay?"

And then his tone became brusquely efficient. "Yeah. I'm on my way. Call Walt. And tell Phil and Jean to stand by. We're going to need them. I'll meet you at the hospital and we'll take it from there. I'll keep my phone on, so call me whenever anything crops up. Keep me updated, Tamar, will you? Anything you hear."

"Tamar?" she asked when Adam lowered the phone. "Isn't that Trevor's assistant?"

He nodded, his expression stark. "Trev's been in a motorcycle accident. It's bad. He's going into surgery now."

"You have to go." It wasn't a question.

"Yeah. There are a ton of things that have to be seen to at the resort until Trev's back at work."

She noted he'd spoken those last words with a fierce certainty, as if he could will his friend to recover fully. She hoped he was right. She liked Trevor, and she knew how much he meant to Adam.

"I'll help you gather your things," she said, turning toward the bedroom. He'd brought in his overnight bag so he could shower while waiting for the pizza delivery. He'd left it open on the bed.

Adam followed her robotically, stepping into the bathroom to collect the few things he'd left there. She spotted one of his socks halfway across the room and his belt dangling off one side of the nightstand. Her cheeks warmed as she remembered the urgency that had sent both their clothes flying. She moved around the room, making sure she had everything before carrying it to the bag.

She heard his phone ring again, and she looked up anxiously. He came back into the room with the phone at his ear, and she could tell by what he said that the caller was Walt, and that there was nothing new to report.

Juggling the phone and a few toiletries, Adam reached for his duffel bag, cursing when he knocked it off the bed. Clothes and other supplies spilled across the floor. The clumsiness was so unlike him that Joanna knew it was a sign of how worried he was.

"I'll call you from the road, Walt." Adam put away the phone as Joanna bent to stuff his things back into the bag. "Thanks, JoJo. I should pay more attention to what I'm doing."

She watched him stash the rest of his things in the bag and close the zipper. "I hope you'll drive carefully," she fretted. "It's going to be the middle of the night by the time you get to the hospital, and you've already had a long drive today. You're distracted by worry, and you'll want to be on your phone. You can't help Trevor if you're stuck in another hospital somewhere."

"I'll use a headset and keep my hands on the wheel and my eyes on the road. I'll be okay."

She pushed a hand through her hair. "I was in mommy mode again, wasn't I?"

He tried to smile as he leaned over to brush a kiss across her nose. "It's okay. It's nice to have someone care about my safety."

"Of course I care." She threw her arms around him and held him tightly. "Please call me when you get there, no matter what time it is. I hope Trevor is okay."

He returned the embrace. "Yeah, me, too."

She walked him to the door. He kissed her lingeringly, stood for a moment looking at her with hungry eyes, then stepped out of her house. "I'll call you, JoJo."

Her eyes pricked with tears as she closed the door behind him. She wasn't sure exactly why she felt like crying. Maybe in sympathy for the fear he was obviously suffering from. Maybe in release from a day filled with surprises and emotional turmoil. Maybe because she'd miss him. And because she was still afraid to believe…

She put away the leftover pizza, stored the photo book in a safe place and straightened the rumbled sheets on her bed with trembling hands. Her thoughts were still with Adam. She worried about him driving so late and in such an anxious frame of mind. Should she have offered to go with him, to share the driving? Her parents and Maddie would've made sure Simon was well cared for in her absence. She had several things on her calendar for these last two weeks in Georgia, but maybe she shouldn't have worried about those. Then again, she didn't know what she'd have done when they arrived in South Carolina. She suspected Adam would be very busy with his job for the moment.

The job he'd offered to leave for her, she reminded herself, sinking to the side of the bed. For her and Simon.

He hadn't said he loved her. Maybe it was too soon. Maybe he didn't know if he did, in which case her concern about his headfirst dive into such a life-changing relationship was justified. And maybe it was too soon for either of them to be certain. And yet…

And yet she had no doubt. She was so in love with Adam Scott that she was dizzy. For her, the fairy tale was real. She'd fallen in love at first sight, just like in the stories. And then, after putting that early infatuation behind her and moving on with her life, she'd fallen in love all over again while spending time with him and their son. The only thing was, she wasn't sure if her fairy tale would have a happy ending. Maybe she'd guarded her heart behind a prickly hedge, but Adam had barricaded his with solid armor. Was he really ready to take the risk of letting someone in? Could he take his armor down completely?

Staying up wouldn't help her answer any of these questions, so Joanna figured she might as well go to bed. Her bare foot brushed against something soft on the floor. Looking down, she spotted a flat leather pouch sticking out from under the bed. It must have fallen when Adam dropped his duffel. Hoping it didn't hold his driver's license, she bent to pick it up.

A few moments later, she sat on the bed again, unsure of whether her knees would support her if she tried to rise. The tears she'd managed to hold off earlier cascaded down her cheeks as she gently traced the creases in the frayed photo of her own face. This wasn't a new print. This had been packed away in his

few possessions—in his favorite memories—
for six years.

Returning the photo and Simon's drawing
to the pouch, she held it to her chest for a moment before setting it aside and drying her
tears.

ADAM LOOKED AT the stack of contracts, to-do
lists, memos and bills on the desk in front
of him and took a deep breath before diving
under. He was way behind in his work. And
even farther behind in Trevor's work, which
he was doing his best to handle while the boss
was getting back on his feet.

Three days after the wreck, everyone at
Wind Shadow was doing their best to keep the
resort running smoothly. They were successful for the most part. Still, Trevor's absence
was keenly noticed. In his easy, laid-back way,
Trev managed to accomplish more in eight or
ten hours than most people could get done in
twenty-four. Adam was just trying to keep
up his end until Trev returned, which would
be in a couple days if it were up to Trevor,
a good six weeks according to his doctors.
Adam predicted reality would be somewhere
in the middle.

Tamar tapped on the door. "Unless you need
anything else tonight, Adam, I'll head out."

"No. Go get some rest, Tamar. You've put in long hours today."

As loyal and dedicated as everyone else who worked for Trevor Farrell, she merely smiled. "You need some sleep, too. No offense, but you're starting to look like ten miles of bad road."

Chuckling, he rubbed a hand over his face. He likely did look a little rough. But he'd do his job and Trevor's for as long as necessary. At least until he was sure both Trevor and Wind Shadow would get by without him. And then he had a new life of his own to start.

At least, he hoped he did. He'd spoken with Joanna a few times during the past three days, letting her know that Trevor would recover and that Adam would be tied up for a while in the meantime. He'd told her she should go ahead with the move as planned and he'd be out as soon as he was able. Because he'd been so busy and so much in demand here, the conversations with her had been brief. Unsatisfying. It hadn't escaped his notice that she still hadn't given him an answer about whether she actually wanted him to follow her to Seattle.

She wanted him, he reminded himself, scrubbing a hand again over his weary face. She couldn't deny that. As he remembered, much to his tired body's discomfort, she had practically ripped his clothes off that last time. After that—well, after that, neither of them had made any attempt to hold back.

But sex, no matter how good, wasn't the ultimate goal with Joanna. As much as he found it hard to believe himself, he wanted more this time. A lot more. He wanted it all.

Maybe he'd call her tonight. After he'd waded through a few more stacks of paper. "New paperless society, my butt," he muttered, drawing a pile toward him.

Hearing someone in the doorway, he asked without looking up, "Forget something, Tamar?"

"Tamar has gone home. You'll have to settle for me."

He looked up so fast he almost gave himself whiplash. "JoJo?"

Her smile was a little crooked when she came into the room. "I think Maddie's impulsiveness may have finally rubbed off on me."

He walked around the desk to meet her. "Don't get me wrong. I'm happy to see you. I think."

She lifted her eyebrows in question. "You *think* you're happy to see me?"

"Depends on why you're here. What you're here to say," he said bluntly, crossing his arms.

He wanted to kiss her. Wanted to take her in his arms, bury his face in her hair and let her know just how much he'd missed her. Still. But first, he had to know...

"I see." Still smiling a little, she nodded. "First—how is Trevor?"

"Busted up. Sore. Mad at the guy who ran a stoplight and hit his bike. Mad at himself for getting laid up when he has so many irons in the fire here. Mad at the doctors for not giving him a pill that'll magically heal him and let him get back to work. Other than that, he's doing as well as can be expected."

"I'm glad. I know you were worried about him."

"Yeah. I was." The back of his neck felt tight, but he kept his arms crossed. "So, anyway, he's going to be out of commission for a while. He'll be able to make some decisions and stay involved with the big stuff while he recuperates, but the staff will need to pick up the slack while he's gone."

"Specifically, you."

"Not just me. But yeah, I'm taking my share."

"Probably more," she murmured.

He let that go without comment. "Obviously, I can't leave while Trevor's down. Once he's back, I'll have to give adequate notice for him to hire someone to take my job. And for that matter, he'll have to fill the resort manager job he offered me so he can concentrate on his new ventures."

"Resort manager? Wow. Congratulations."

He frowned, wondering what she meant by that. "Thanks, but you know I'm not planning to take the job, right?"

"You would be very good at it. You *are* very good at it."

"But I don't want it."

"Of course you do. This is a great opportunity. You should be proud that Trevor thinks so much of you. With what this place means to him, he would never put anyone in charge who he didn't trust completely."

Adam's right arm fell to his side. His left hand went to the back of his neck, fingers digging hard into the tense muscles. "Okay, fine. I'm getting the message. You think I should stay here rather than moving to Seattle. For my own sake," he added, unable to keep a note of bitterness out of his voice.

"I do," she said, and it ticked him off that she said it with a smile. "I think you should stay. And I think Simon and I should stay here with you. Well, maybe not here. You don't actually have to live on the grounds, right? I know Trevor has a house in town. We should be able to do something like that."

His left arm dropped. His hand hit the corner of the desk hard enough to hurt, which only proved he wasn't dreaming. "I have no idea what you're talking about."

"I'm talking about us, Adam," she said, taking a step closer. Her palm cupped his cheek, soft against his evening-rough skin. "About starting fresh here with our son. Take the job Trevor offered you. I wouldn't be surprised if you end up moving even higher in this resort empire he's planning to build. I'm a licensed psychologist with a moderately impressive resume. I'm not worried about finding work. As for Simon—as long as he's near water and with his parents, he's going to be the happiest kid on earth."

He caught her hand, wondering if she'd lost her mind, or he'd lost his. Maybe both. "You're really offering to walk away from that job in Seattle? The one that will let you do exactly what you've always wanted? For me?"

"Well, you were willing to do the same for me, weren't you?" She raised her other hand, framing his face. "You're happy here, Adam. You're needed here. This is your home."

He was stunned to find his eyes burning. What the hell was that? He cleared his throat. "My home is where you are, JoJo. Where you and Simon are."

She gazed up at him with eyes the color of liquid emerald. "I'm here."

"You are." He couldn't wait any longer to kiss her. He took her mouth with more tenderness than he'd ever felt before, tamping down the passion until later. He pulled his mouth away only an inch to murmur roughly, "No one's ever offered anything like this for me. Ever."

Her arms around his waist, she smiled up at him. "Your life is about to change, pal. I hope you're ready for it."

"I'm ready. I'm scared spitless," he added wryly, "but I'm ready. And I'll give it everything I've got to make sure you never regret taking a chance on me."

He kissed her again, more vigorously this time, then set her away from him.

"Okay, here's the deal," he said, straightening. "You go to Seattle. Get settled in, start that great new job. I'll wrap things up here. It's going to take a few weeks. Couple of months, maybe, and trust me, that's going to feel like a year. We'll talk every day, make plans. I have some contacts, guys I served with. I think a couple of them are out in that area. I'll be making calls, pulling strings, finding a job I'll like as much as this one. You don't have to worry that I'll be making some big sacrifice to come to you. Everything I want will be there."

She was biting her lip again. He smiled and smoothed it with his thumb.

"You're sure?" she asked, clutching his shirt. "Absolutely sure?"

"I've never been surer of anything in my life."

Looking reassured—if somewhat tentatively so—she let out a sigh. "It's going to be hard to be away from you so long. But we'll make sure we do this right. I don't want you to ever have regrets."

"No regrets," he promised. "This is what I want."

Her smile was bright enough to warm him through. "Me, too."

After several more long, celebratory kisses, he drew back far enough to ask, "By the way… where's our son?"

A breathy laugh escaped her. "He's with Maddie."

"He didn't come with you?"

"They're in a suite in Gull's Nest Lodge. Maddie's taking another long weekend. I told her she'd probably get fired, but she just shrugged and said she has a lot of sick leave and vacation time built up. I wouldn't be surprised if she starts looking for work in South

Carolina eventually. She's pretty taken with your buddy Walt."

"Wait—you're saying Simon is here? At the resort?"

She laughed. "As if I could get him to stay behind. He wanted to find you the minute we arrived, but I convinced him to let me talk to you first. Maybe you'd like to walk back with me and tuck him in for the night."

"I'd like that very much," he said, his voice gruff with emotion again.

"I know you're going to be busy, and we won't get in your way. We can entertain ourselves, maybe have meals with you and see you when you get a few extra minutes to breathe. If I'm going through with the move to Seattle, I'll have to go back soon to finish packing, but Simon will enjoy the chance to have a few more days with you here first. He's going to be so excited to hear you'll be joining us in Seattle—unless you'd rather wait and tell him later. You know, in case something changes."

He could tell it was going to take some time before she was convinced he wouldn't change his mind. He could be patient. "We'll tell him now. I won't disappoint him."

She nodded bravely.

"There's just one more thing."

Swiping at the traces of tears on her cheeks with one hand, she asked shakily, "What?"

"I love you, JoJo." The words sounded awkward coming from him. Rusty. He figured he'd get better at saying them with practice.

Joanna seemed to have no complaints. She nestled close and smiled up at him, fresh tears spilling from her eyes. Happy tears, he was relieved to note. "I love you, too, Adam."

Would he get used to hearing the words eventually? Would he ever take them for granted? As he drew her into a kiss that echoed every promise he'd made to her, he knew without doubt that he would never tire of hearing Joanna tell him she loved him.

He hadn't been looking for companionship when he'd come to this resort six years ago. He certainly hadn't expected to find everything he'd ever wished for on a moon-washed beach. Because he'd been too mired in the past to expect a better future, he'd almost thrown it all away. Not once, but several times. He was the luckiest man on earth to have been given yet another chance at the family he'd thought he didn't deserve.

He would never walk away again.

\* \* \* \* \*

*If you enjoyed Joanna and Adam's story,*
*watch for Gina Wilkins's next book in the*
**SOLDIERS AND SINGLE MOMS**
*miniseries, coming from*
*Harlequin Superromance*
*in October 2017!*

# Get 2 Free Books,

## Plus 2 Free Gifts—

### just for trying the Reader Service!

# Get 2 Free Books,
## Plus 2 Free Gifts—
### just for trying the Reader Service!

# Get 2 Free Books,
## <u>Plus</u> 2 Free Gifts—
### just for trying the Reader Service!

# Get 2 Free Books,
## Plus 2 Free Gifts—
### just for trying the Reader Service!